Finding a Light
in a Room
with no Walls

by Matteo Lahm

Publishing Services provided by Paper Raven Books
Printed in the United States of America
First Printing, 2021

ISBN 978-0-578-86129-6

For Giulio

"The most beautiful thing we can experience is the mysterious. It is the source of all true art and science. He to whom the emotion is a stranger, who can no longer pause to wonder and stand wrapped in awe, is as good as dead; his eyes are closed."
-Albert Einstein

Chapter 1

The Precipice

stood wretchedly before the gold leafed
drobe door. The years of wear obscured
. that did not diminish his disapproval. His
as now imprisoned in a layer of flab and his
ind a messy beard.
er! Where are your balls?"

He laughed villainously as he berated himself, his taunts drifting between insults and incoherent mumbling. He sipped his bottle again and neared the mirror bringing his red eyes and gray skin into focus. The liquor burned as it oozed down his throat.

"You're pathetic, and hideous!" He stumbled, wavering back and forth. He reached in his pants and grabbed his cock and balls, cradling them like a corpse.

He wiped his tears and rested his face against the cold glass.

"I wish God existed so I could hate him."

When his words reached a crescendo, he headbutted the mirror, cracking it like a spiderweb. Then he abruptly went to the living room window that overlooked Via dell'Orso and flung it open. The blood on his forehead glistened in the moonlight. He stood like the pope, arms outstretched, preaching from his top floor balcony. His oratory however was anything but Christlike.

"I am a wretched man!" He defiantly proclaimed.

As Marc shouted drunken obscenities, two women approached on the street below.

"Is something wrong sir?"

"I'm fine, and it's none of your fucking business."

"You don't have to be rude." She said.

A young man also stopped. "I heard you all the way up the street! Shut up already, you American pig! Or just jump so we don't have to listen to your bile!"

Marc became enraged and hurled a bottle down at him. When it crashed to the ground, everyone dispersed. "Come back here, God damnit!" He shouted, and then grabbed another bottle and stormed out of the apartment. His feet clapped messily on the marble as he stumbled down the stairs. He burst out of the large wood door, closing it behind him.

He yelled, spinning in circles, looking for his tormentors but as there was no one to confront, a grave realization overcame him, followed by a deluge of expletives. He left his phone, money and keys in the house. He wasn't sure of the time, but knew it was late. He couldn't knock on the door because the neighbors already didn't like him. Even if they did, seeing him in his condition would have made matters worse. His face was bleeding, he was drunk, and he had just committed a crime. He tried to think quickly. What if someone called the cops? He collected and disposed of the recognizable remains of the bottle and hurried away. He needed to clean himself up and get out of sight until morning.

There were drinking fountains all over Rome and he remembered one about two blocks away. He tried to walk as unassumingly as possible, keeping to the side of the street with his head down to conceal his wound. He made it to the fountain with his empty wine bottle in hand. It was intended to be a weapon but nonetheless, it proved itself to be far more valuable for water. He filled the bottle and poured it over his head. It felt like a baptism. He neatened his hair and beard, cleaned the dried blood from his face and hands and drank enough water to quench his thirst. Now he was just a man out late but still drunk enough to be impaired. He focused on walking without stumbling but it was difficult because of the pain in his legs.

He thought the Tiber River was his best bet. There was always a breeze from the current and it was a short walk. He refilled his bottle with water and embarked. To his relief, the sidewalk that lined the river was empty. He found a bench that was dimly lit with some nearby shrubbery. He could even sneak a piss if he was careful.

Just as he felt relief, the adrenaline wore off and was replaced by fatigue. His eyes grew heavy and his thoughts darkened as he dwelled on his shame. The bench was hard, and the humidity made his bones ache.

He cut through the white noise of the Tiber and the rustle

of the trees with a restrained wail. He stood and staggered to the stone wall overlooking the river and wept inconsolably. He was crushed by his self-loathing. He alienated everyone and now had no one else to blame.

He smashed the bottle against the stones. The loud crash made his heart race. He clutched the bottleneck, beheld the jagged glass and then forcefully dragged the shards across his arm.

1:2

Marc first visited Café d'Oro in early April and had since become a regular. The young waiter Giancarlo Graziano asked him why he was in Rome on their first meeting. It was a matter of politeness and an easy conversation starter. Marc looked up from his laptop and with a big mischievous smile said, "Rome is a great place to die."

Giancarlo found the comment foreboding. He remembered it every time he saw him which was why he was unsettled by his visits. He liked Marc but his moods were uneasy. He could be pleasant one day, dry and sarcastic another and at extremes, altogether disagreeable.

Marc also liked Giancarlo and always wanted him to wait on him. One day, Marc handed him a hundred Euros. He told Giancarlo that he would call ahead if he was coming and that his instructions were to reserve the corner table that faced the long view of the piazza. Giancarlo was grateful to have a regular who not only tipped but tipped well. Tipping was not customary in Italy. In the three years he worked at the café, he met many Americans, but none like Marc.

Perhaps by providence or chance, what could be construed as a new friendship was helped along by something they had in common. Giancarlo's father was not only from the Province of Salerno, he was from Sant'Arsenio, the neighboring town of Marc's father's birthplace San Pietro al Tanagro. To Italians, common origins mattered. Salerno might as well have been another planet and though Marc was born in the US, there was cultural familiarity between them. The truth about Italy was that it was unified by Garibaldi in name only. It had since been and will remain twenty small countries begrudgingly living under the same flag. This common connection muddled along the slow dance of their acquaintance and Giancarlo learned more about his strange American friend.

Marc always came to the café accompanied only by his laptop that he pecked away at day after day. Though he was always alone, he had a presence and affected the space around him. As he would type, his facial expressions changed without inhibition. He even talked to himself and laughed out loud on occasion. His appearance was no less striking. He had large dark eyes accompanied by an imposing stare, flanked by a scar on the left side of his upper lip. His slender nose and muscular limbs were more northern European, yet he had an Italian complexion and spoke the language fluently. His height and stature suggested athleticism, but he had gained ten pounds in less than a month, spending his days eating heavy food and drinking a bottle of wine per sitting, sometimes two.

"I've been wanting to ask you something. You told me you are in real estate and you are in Rome on business, but you are constantly writing. Is any of it for pleasure?"

"Why do you ask?"

"I love to read."

"Most of what I do is work related but not all. I have a lot to figure out. And I'm avoiding my therapist."

Giancarlo laughed.

"What's so funny?" Marc asked.

"I have a degree in psychology."

More laughter followed but Marc was not in a chatty mood. In an effort to stop Giancarlo's questions, he ordered him to check on his lunch. Giancarlo went to the kitchen and Marc's eyes turned to the Roman blue sky. They called it Azzurro. Though his mood was growing more cynical day by day, little things like beautiful skies gave him pleasure amidst the carnival atmosphere of Piazza Navona. Marc liked how it was a bustling contrast of history, elegance and kitsch. The great Bernini's Four Rivers sculpture attracted many art lovers, while the local street artists profited from sentimental American senior citizens reminiscing about Audrey Hepburn movies. Amongst the artists were the street performers, the most impressive of whom were the pharos and statues of liberty who stood motionless for hours in the heat. Marc wondered if people tipped them for their talent or out of pity? Piazza Navona was perfectly suited to Marc's desire for a slow pace but with entertaining scenery in his attempt to stay out of his own head.

Giancarlo returned with Marc's favorite dish: Pasta alla Carbonara. As he chewed each bite of fresh pasta with eggs and guanciale, and sipped his Chianti, he was distracted by a brunette with thick black, curly hair sitting two tables away. The resemblance to his wife was so uncanny it bothered him. The simple truth was that a lot more than just her likeness bothered Marc these days. How he came to be in Rome was not all business. It was what began to unfold several months prior, circumstances that had already altered the course of his life.

1:3

One afternoon, Marc surprised Giancarlo with an invitation to dinner. He was puzzled by the offer because Marc always ate alone.

"Do you always invite young male waiters to dinner?" Giancarlo joked.

"Are you scared I'm gay?" Marc played along. "I want to discuss something with you."

When he inquired further, Marc said he would get into the details later. Giancarlo agreed. Marc picked up his laptop and told him to meet him back at the piazza at 8:30.

Marc returned to his apartment on the top floor of a sienna orange four-story building with green shuttered bay windows. It had a large antique wood door that must have weighed several hundred pounds but could be opened with the light touch of a few fingers. The foyer had bone mosaic tile floors with green and red accents. The white marble stairs were so old the footpaths were indented. The walls were antique plaster of Paris and were heavily painted over but showed new cracks because of the humidity. It had a musty smell because of the proximity of the river. Every word echoed up the stairwells. Marc stepped into the brass paneled elevator that was about the size of a closet.

His flat was perfectly private. The floor below was empty, and the apartment conveniently furnished. It had a garish early-twentieth century motif which was not to his taste, but he liked it because it did not remind him of home. The floors were checkerboard green and white marble. The wallpaper had busy green floral patterns. Old-fashioned brass sconces with baroque patterns lit the rooms and the dining room had a traditional seven light chandelier with crystal ornaments. The ceilings were high, the furniture was gaudy, and it had the characteristic messiness of a bachelor pad.

He had a few hours before he had to meet Giancarlo and went to the kitchen to open a fresh bottle of Chianti. He grabbed a wine glass from the dirty pile in the sink and lazily rinsed it out. From the other room, he heard an email notification. When he saw the subject line, he winced. An email or message from his brother Gabe entitled "mom" was like getting mail from the IRS.

Gabe was almost 10 years older than Marc. As a child, his big brother was his hero. Now, he was reduced to what Marc considered a henpecked underachiever working as an associate store manager for a major retail chain.

Marc,

I wrote you weeks ago and you have not answered me. Why? I don't know what you're doing in Italy and why you are MIA, but I want to talk to you. I even called Hannah. She said you hadn't spoken since you left. I asked her why and she said she had to go. She didn't sound good.

Mom's stable but it's getting harder for her to do basic things on her own. I know you don't care, but just in case you might be concerned, I thought I'd tell you.

There is some good news. I may be getting my own store and best of all, Sara made valedictorian!

Would you please get in touch soon? At the very least,

just let me know you're okay.

Gabe

He immediately responded.

Gabe,

Hannah doesn't know anything.
As for mom, did you want to make me think she died or something? Even if something happened, we made a deal and I expect you to stick to it. Part of the arrangement is that you aren't supposed to patch things up between us, so please, no more misleading subject lines. I'm dealing with some things right now.
Regarding your concern, I'm fine. I'm in Italy because I have to be. That's the most I can say. Trust me, if I drop dead, you'll find out.
I'm wiring Sara a gift.
Hope everything works out with your store.

Marc

Marc generously supported his mother despite never seeing or calling her which gave Marc a considerable amount of freedom and power in what loosely resembled a sibling relationship.

Dear Sara,

I knew you'd make valedictorian. I've told you your whole life that you have what it takes to do great things and words cannot express how proud I am of you. As a reward for your hard work, check your bank account. I sent you something. You're going to need it because now the real work begins. College is practice for life and it doesn't prepare you for everything. This should be enough to help you get started.

Love,

Uncle Marc

It was a sizable sum.

1:4

Marc sat on the railing that circled the fountain of the four rivers waiting for Giancarlo. The blue sky had diminished to a cold purple with the North Star steadfast in the dusk sky. The lights on the buildings made the piazza seem lit by starlight. Giancarlo arrived wearing a fitted blue suit with a snug button-down white shirt and black shoes. He looked regal with his hazel eyes, wavy hair and da Vinci-like features.

Marc liked to test people so he played the aloof to see if Giancarlo would spot him first. It was a talent he developed growing up with his mother that served him well in business. He considered it an unintended benefit of her bad influence.

"Marc? I almost didn't recognize you."

"Hello Giancarlo. Thank you for being on time. We have a 9:00pm reservation."

"Where are we going?"

"The restaurant is near the Coliseum."

"That's a bit far. Should we get a cab?"

"I prefer to walk." Marc asserted.

"What made you shave your beard?" Giancarlo asked.

"Because I wanted to. Is it so strange for a man to properly groom himself before dinner?" Marc said sarcastically.

"That never seemed to bother you at the café. Why is tonight different?"

"Do I need a reason?"

Marc was curt and seemed edgy, which made Giancarlo uncomfortable. The truth was he was apprehensive about dinner. He was a little worried about socializing with Marc outside the café. That Marc's ego was on full display didn't help. For a moment, Giancarlo almost envied it. Maybe he would have made more of his life, but then again, this was Italy. They sauntered through the narrow paths as they approached Piazza Venezia: a major traffic intersection and home to what Romans condescendingly called the wedding cake.

As they approached the crosswalk, Marc pointed up. "Do you like that monument?"

It was an infamous neoclassical structure completed by the fascists in 1935 to flatter Mussolini's delusions of recreating the Roman Empire. It was a poorly placed anathematic white box, just like a wedding cake.

"My friends and I used to come here to pick up tourist girls. We would hang around and offer to take their pictures. I guess for that it was okay. Tourists like it, but Romans generally hate it, hence the wedding cake slur. What about you?"

"I guess I must like it because I'm a tourist." Marc said obnoxiously.

"I am sorry."

"I'm only kidding. I think it's a piece of shit, honestly."

Giancarlo chuckled.

As they walked down Via dei Fori Imperiali, Giancarlo interjected with historical small talk. "I've walked this road hundreds of times and can never get over how much lower the street level was two thousand years ago. Have you visited Torre Argentina? It's the temple complex with all the cats near Feltrinelli bookstore."

"I have! Love that store." Mark responded.

"Yes. It's one of my favorite places in the city. Less than a century ago, most of the piazza was covered over. They dug and found a 4th century B.C. temple complex. You never know what's beneath your feet here. Recently I read it was where Julius Caesar was stabbed!"

As they walked, the Coliseum emerged from the obscuring trees.

"I saw the Coliseum when I was a boy. I can never get over how imposing it is." Marc commented.

"It really dominates the forum. Shame it's in such bad condition. Did you know that half the marble in the Vatican was stolen from it?"

"That I actually knew." Marc said.

"Imposing is the right word. It's so iconic, but there are

mixed feelings about it. Many Christians were murdered there."

Marc let out a snicker, "Apparently they didn't kill enough of them."

Giancarlo was startled. That was almost as weird as saying Rome was a great place to die.

"Are you an atheist or do you just have a problem with Christianity?"

"I am, and I do. I hate religion." Marc said snidely.

"Then you came to the wrong city."

As they climbed the stairs towards the restaurant, Giancarlo noticed Marc had a slight limp and was out of breath when they reached the top. They arrived at the host station and were escorted to a table by the window. The entire back wall was glass, and the interior was white with dim lighting. The sight of the Roman forum was glorious. The weathered granite and marble glowed with a yellowish hue. Marc alternated between looking at the view and watching Giancarlo fumble with his menu. He turned pages, obviously not reading them. A sheen of sweat glazed his upper lip.

"Dinner is on me." Marc interjected.

"You don't have to do that. I can take care of myself."

"I insist. Is that alright?" Marc stared intently, making it clear that a refusal would be an insult.

Giancarlo guzzled water to remedy his dry mouth. A few minutes later, the waiter returned with a €600 2005 Brunello.

"Have you ever had Brunello?"

"We serve it at the restaurant but it's out of my price range."

"The Brunello at your café is commercial grade and you don't have a cellar. Some vintages are so small and valuable that they never get beyond collectors and five-star restaurants. This bottle would be at least $1000 in an American restaurant. You're about to have an experience."

Giancarlo watched the waiter swirl the wine in the decanter. Marc inspected the color and the legs. Long streams condensed on the glass as Marc held it to the light.

"Brunello has a very distinct color."

"It looks like blood." Giancarlo commented.

"Very good. Brunello is in the Sangiovese family and its name comes from Latin meaning blood of Jupiter. It dates back to the second century B.C.."

After about ten minutes, Marc poured two small portions and placed one in front of Giancarlo. "Pick up your glass. Swirl it around and then put your napkin over it."

Giancarlo felt like he was in a sommelier lesson.

About ten minutes later, Marc removed the napkin and instructed Giancarlo to do the same. "Smell it first. Breathe in slowly and then exhale through your mouth."

Giancarlo followed and Marc awaited his reaction. His eyes widened.

"What do you smell?" Marc asked.

"I smell cherries and earth."

"What about tobacco?" Mark quizzed.

"Yes! I even smell something herbal."

"Rosemary!" Marc asserted.

"Holy shit, yes! How is that possible?" Giancarlo mused.

"Rosemary bushes are all over Tuscany. It's in the ground. You have a very good nose! Now you can taste it."

Giancarlo brought the glass to his lips and an explosion of flavors erupted in his mouth.

"Swish it around." Marc advised.

"I get really strong sensations on the sides of my tongue and in the back of my mouth. It is really physical."

"That's called 'mouth feel' and the sensation is related to the acidity and tannins. Brunello is a high acid wine. Pretty impressive, huh?"

"I've never had anything like this." Giancarlo said timidly.

"Not many people have."

"It's amazing. Thank you for treating me to this."

"I'm glad you like it."

"Marc, I don't even have enough money in my pocket to pay for half this bottle. What is tonight about?"

As much as Giancarlo was enjoying his wine, Marc could tell he was anxious to know what he had to say.

"Giancarlo! Are you still hung up on the gay sex thing or that I'm some mafia guy?"

Giancarlo smiled but it was the most awkward he had

felt yet.

"I asked you to dinner because I want to offer you a job."

Giancarlo looked like he would pop out of his shirt as a bead of sweat trickled down his cheek. How could he be so petty and immature, he wondered. It was the most obvious reason which made him feel all the more ashamed and stupid.

"Now can you relax? This isn't a big deal. It's a chance for you to make some extra money."

"What makes you think I need extra money?" Giancarlo protested.

"Everybody under 30 needs extra money in Italy."

Giancarlo's first instinct was to be offended by Marc's assumption, but in the end he was right.

"Do you want to know about the job or not?"

"Yes, please." He whispered sheepishly.

"You'd be my personal assistant. I need someone to run errands. I'll start you at 150 Euros per week as a base with extra money when I need you to do extra work."

"That's very generous. Please forgive me for asking, but what would the *extra work* be?"

"I don't know exactly, but I'll tell you when the time comes."

Though the prospect of earning another €600 per month was exciting, Giancarlo still felt hesitant. Then something changed. As he looked at Marc from across the table, he saw him differently for the first time. Beneath the pleasure of the wine, his verbosity and intermittent crankiness, something about him was pained and then he remembered the limp. In that moment, he felt sorry for him and realized that he was a man who might need his help. He accepted the job and they toasted. From there, the conversation became more fluid.

"How did you get started in real-estate?" Giancarlo asked.

"When my father died unexpectedly. I inherited money from a life insurance policy and bought my first property with it."

"I am very sorry about your father."

"Don't be, it was a long time ago."

"How many properties do you have?"

"Many."

Marc's expression darkened, and he looked at Giancarlo intently. The wine had loosened his tongue.

"Money buys many things, but it can't buy what everybody wants the most. Don't envy my money because it can't save me. It's romantic that no matter how rich or poor we are, we all meet the same end. We decay to the same dust and feel the same despair as we look into the abyss. You're too young to know what I mean, but one day you'll understand."

As Giancarlo listened, his suspicions were replaced by genuine intrigue. Marc was an interesting guy and could speak at length about history, philosophy and art—all subjects that interested him. But as Marc kept drinking, Giancarlo realized the "extra work" of his job had already begun. He would need to get him home.

After they departed in a taxi, Marc faded in and out as they drove along. His eyes were clouded looking out the window. He called for Hannah several times. Who was Hannah? Giancarlo wondered. As the cab sped on, he mumbled random curses and then said, "Why me?" The cab finally arrived at Via dell'Orso. Giancarlo struggled to get Marc out of the car. They were alone on the dark street. Giancarlo fumbled with the keys while Marc leaned lazily against the wall. He was clearly anguished. The large wood door opened, and Giancarlo helped him into the foyer.

"Fourth floor," Marc slurred.

They got into the elevator and Giancarlo thought Marc would vomit inside. He tried reassuring him they were almost there, and all Marc could say was vaffanculo.

1:5

Four months earlier, going to Rome not only wasn't planned, it had never even crossed Marc's mind. He laid in bed on the top floor of his 37-story high-rise recovering from a terrible bout of colic. He had the best apartment because he owned the whole building. It approached dusk and the orange sunlight painted the room. The dust particles swirled around in the light, creating geometric designs complementing the modernist décor that shifted with the passing clouds.

His favorite part of the day was sunset. He always left the shades open because that was when he most liked to admire his art collection. He liked acquiring art as much as he liked owning it. Public auctions were glorious to the winner and shameful to the loser. It was where the real titans battled. He particularly liked to swindle people he didn't respect. That was how he obtained his most prized possession: a small, but respectable Picasso oil on canvas.

He convinced the seller by downplaying its value. Her mistake was revealing she needed money. She was a drunk who inherited an estate and didn't even know what she had. That she reminded him of his mother just made matters worse. To add insult to injury, he got her to "throw in" three Picasso etchings. The painting alone was worth more than twice what he paid. He thought it a crime for such a creature to own something so valuable, so scamming her was a moral imperative. Of course, he got an angry phone call accusing him of malfeasance. She was right, however, moral or not, there was nothing illegal about convincing people to sell you something. It wasn't his fault, and he wasn't responsible. That's life.

Regardless, the value of his Picasso wasn't on his mind. He was happy he was in his bed and no longer in the bathroom. The sheets cradled him as he felt himself drift away. His eyes grew heavy as the orange faded to red, purple, and then gray.

He was glad to be alone and found himself feeling that way more often. Luckily, Hannah's career decisions were facilitating more of that. She returned to work as a physical therapist, but not because they needed the money. It was an excuse to not be home.

Marc and Hannah met in college. He remembered cooking her dinner for the first time. He fussed over every detail because boys in their 20s go out of their way to impress women. After 17 years of marriage, though he loved Hannah as much as he was capable, his romantic inclinations waned in middle age and it wasn't just in his marriage. He'd grown bored of success and became afflicted with melancholy.

To ease his nerves, he put on some music and fortunately,

Miles Davis' "Kind of Blue" was next on his playlist. The music was calming but he kept getting distracted by a numb and tingly feeling in his legs. As Miles' horn soothed his ear, and his nerves, his eyes finally started to feel heavy.

He awoke two hours later feeling refreshed. The fatigue seemed to have passed. After eating some rice with lemon and olive oil, he brought the plate to his office which was the room with the nicest view. If he ever felt down, he liked reminding himself that most people could never dream of such a view or such an extensive library. You could find the likes of John Stuart Mill, Michelle Fuco, Machiavelli, Marcus Aurelius, Tacitus, and many others gracing his bookshelves. Unlike most who amassed large libraries that would go mostly unread, Marc had read almost everything in the room.

He shoveled a spoonful of rice in his mouth and called his attorney and best friend from childhood.

"How did you avoid the city?" Asked Paul.

"A lot of shit."

"I'll bet."

"No, I mean it literally. I don't know what I ate, but my ass erupted like Mount Etna. Let me ask you something, do you ever get leg pain, like tingling?"

"Go see an orthopedist. My brother had that. His disks were shot."

That was the last thing he wanted to hear but Paul quickly interjected with some positives.

"You're middle-aged bro, and it is easy to fix. Be thankful you're still in good shape. You've still got your hair, you aren't fat, and your cock still works."

"You and your optimism." Marc dismissed.

Joking aside, the back problems could wait. His immediate concern was a lawsuit involving a staircase that needed to be repaired and a boy who was injured. It was one of his lower-end buildings, so fixing anything was not preferable unless it was absolutely necessary. He never intended to be a slumlord and even went into the business of owning properties with good intentions. He wanted to find good tenants and treat them well but learned very quickly that even if he did, they would not reciprocate. The nicest ones turned out to be the shadiest. After enough people tried to fuck him over, he learned he might as well spend less money if it was inevitable.

He wasn't trying to displace blame, that's just the world and there's nothing he could do about it. He didn't feel he had any responsibility for having to play by the rules of a game he didn't design.

As his conversation with Paul concluded, he guzzled another bottle of water and decided he needed a run on the treadmill. He put on his sneakers and blasted his favorite workout music: Black Sabbath. About ten minutes into his run, he felt the sensation in his legs, and he didn't know if he could keep up. He wasn't out of breath but felt weak. He stumbled and fell forward, smacking his head on the console and was momentarily knocked out. As he regained consciousness, he just laid there. His legs felt weird and his left hand trembled. He touched his head and there was blood. Marc went to the bathroom and saw a gash on his forehead.

After patching himself up, he laid on the couch waiting for Hannah to come. There was only one light on at the far side of the room. He still had ice on his head and by now, a sizable lump. He had always been very fit and healthy. It was a normal run, like any other. He wasn't tired or winded. He just couldn't get his legs to move.

What the hell am I going to tell Hannah? He thought. He needed an excuse for how he fell. Could he just tell her the truth? That wouldn't work. If she found out he was on the treadmill while sick, he would never hear the end of it. If he could run, why couldn't he go to dinner? Maybe it was better if he just milked being sick? It guaranteed they wouldn't fight. He got up from the couch and checked the accident scene. The room was carpeted which posed a problem. There were bloodstains.

"Fuck it! I slept, felt better, got on the treadmill and fell. If she's going to yell at me for that, then whatever."

What to tell Hannah was a distraction from what he was really thinking about: why he fell. He had a tendency for hypochondria and began to research symptoms online. He typed "tingling sensation and numbness in the legs."

That was a mistake. His heart started racing because every explanation was horrid.

After an hour of dismal scenarios, he decided to stop trying to be his own doctor. He laid back, put the ice on his head and tried to calm his mind. It wasn't working so he resorted to a more traditional method: Xanax.

Then he made the mistake of putting on the TV. As he flipped through the channels, he passed by Star Trek reruns from the 60s. That reminded him of his father Antonio, which he would rather avoid under the circumstances. He settled on the news though he hated it. As far as he was concerned, it was just another TV show, signifying everything that was wrong with America: manufactured stories, fake outrage, and blatant indoctrination of the feeble masses—who had no original thoughts as far as he was concerned. People felt what they were told to feel. They thought what they were told to think. The news reminded him of how inept and pathetic everyone really was, and it only exacerbated his contempt. The only humor he found was that people really believed their opinions were actually their own.

His silent condemnation of humanity was interrupted by the sound of the door. Hannah said nothing as she came in with her bag of leftovers that she immediately put away. She had her head down with her hair blocking her view of him. She was obviously still annoyed at him for staying home.

"How was your evening?" He asked her.

She didn't answer. She asked how he was feeling, and he didn't answer either.

"Did you sleep?" She asked.

"I slept for a few hours and then did some work."

The room was dark.

"So, what happened with your sister?"

"Marc, I don't want to get into it now. You not coming tonight was a thing. She gets really hung up on the idea that you hate her."

She wasn't wrong...

"What was her crisis?" He asked.

"Why do you even care?"

"Hannah, when I don't ask, I get accused of not caring

and then I ask, and you accuse me anyway."

Hannah responded, "OK, I'll tell you, but don't act like a jerk because you'll think it's stupid."

He promised he wouldn't, but he knew that was probably a lie.

"The contractor she hired to redo her kitchen is a week behind and she wants to schedule a dinner party with colleagues to help with a promotion. She's worried they'll give it to somebody else, so she needs a plan B."

Silence again. He really tried not showing his disgust, but he couldn't help himself.

"That's all? *That* needed your attention, and *I* didn't?"

"Marc, you promised! I know it's stupid, and I don't need you to tell me that. It's how she reacts, how she feels. You know, feelings? You've heard of them, right? She has anxiety!"

"She and the rest of the neurotic antidepressant junkies. Look at me and how fucking fragile I am," he mocked. "Your sister gets overwhelmed by the smallest things because she's a self-absorbed ass."

"And *you* aren't, Marc? That's rich. Not another word about my sister. In fact, not another word about my family considering yours!"

"You can't say anything about my mother that's worse than what I've already said."

"And you're proud of this?"

He did feel proud and it was something Hannah couldn't grasp, even after 17 years of marriage.

"You can hate your mother all you want. People can't help what they are, but you're too judgmental to know that. So, my sister is nuts. I still worry about her. Lately she's been worse. I think her meds might be losing their affect."

She needs more than meds, he thought, *a lobotomy perhaps*.

"Marc, this is why I didn't want to get into it."

All the while, she had been in the kitchen and he on the couch. So far, his injury wasn't visible, but then she walked into the room, turned on the light, and her brown eyes glared down at him. Though he knew she was furious, all he could focus on was her beauty.

"What happened to your face?"

She inspected his wound and once she realized it wasn't that serious, she exploded. Her voice bounced off the walls like a racquet ball.

"Why do I have to turn on the light to get surprises like this? Why can't you volunteer things like a normal person?" She yelled.

He sat silently and let her go on.

"I can't get a straight answer out of you anymore! What happened, Marc?"

He hesitated and then mumbled, "I fell."

"Obviously you fell! You look like you got into a fight."

"I slept, I got up, I felt dizzy, and I fainted."

"You fainted? Where did you faint?"

He didn't answer again.

"Why is there blood on the treadmill? What were you doing the treadmill?"

He started to sweat.

"Answer me!"

She looked like a lioness. Even as she yelled, he was captivated by her.

"You were too sick to show my family respect and you had the energy to work out? Typical! I've had enough of your bullshit, Marc. You don't talk. You don't tell me how you feel. I have no idea what's going through that head of yours."

Now she was beyond anger and for a second, he hoped she would go straight to indifference, but she didn't. Her eyes welled with tears. She pleaded with him to show her something. He wanted to, but he just couldn't. Then his own anger flared. Why didn't she ask how he felt? Why did it not matter? For that she didn't deserve an explanation. Then her tears turned to outright sobbing.

"Why can't you talk to me?" She asked desperately.

By now she had done to him what only she could do: disarm him. Finally, he saw what he had done.

"I'm sorry." He whispered.

She looked at him, her big, dark eyes wet with sorrow as if she was struggling to see something to reassure her. She was exhausted and it was about a lot more than just that incident, but there was still love between them.

He grabbed her hand and pulled her close to him. Then their attraction overtook their conflict, frustration and mistrust. They ran their hands all over each other as they kissed amidst an array of "I love you's" and "I'm sorry's" that were characteristic of their routine make-up sex. They only reinforced their denial about their relationship. He reached under her dress and felt her warm flesh. He removed her panties, and she removed his pants. He pulled her on top of him on the couch. She put her feet beside him and lowered herself onto him. Her arms got tighter around his neck. Her long hair wrapped around him like a cocoon. She grinded furiously against him as he pushed up inside her. They fucked each other defiantly but affectionately. With each push, they chased something away, as if trying to rebuild something that was broken. They both started to moan louder. She was about to cum and so was he. They squeezed each other even tighter. He could feel his pulse in his cut as his heart raced. Then they rested in silence, tangled and knotted together. Her head was nestled in the pit of his neck. They still hadn't moved, and his cock was still inside her.

1:6

The clatter of dishes and the morning sunlight nudged Marc awake. His eyes cracked open and the room start spinning. He was still partially dressed in his suit from the night before. Why did he hear noise and who was in the apartment? Suddenly he started to remember.

Giancarlo entered the room with a glass and handed it to Marc.

"Drink this. It'll settle your stomach. Are you hungry? I got you a cornetto and the caffè is almost ready. I took some of your cash on the dresser and went to the store."

Without responding, Marc stood up slowly and stumbled to the bathroom which smelled like puke. When he exited, he was lucid enough to notice all the wine bottles and garbage were gone and the kitchen was clean. Giancarlo left his breakfast on the table. He sat down slowly and brought the cup to his lips. The smell of the caffè with the sweetness of the cornetto perfumed the air.

"What happened?" Marc asked reluctantly.

"Who is Hannah?"

Marc's face sank.

"How do you know about Hannah?"

"You called her name several times in the taxi."

"What else did I say?"

"You just called out her name, but you were too drunk for me ask who she is."

With an exasperated, yet resigned sigh, Marc said, "She's my wife."

"You're married?"

"Technically." He gazed out the window with a wry smile.

"What do you mean *technically*?"

He said he would tell him about Hannah another day and changed the subject to the previous evening.

"What's the last thing you remember?" Giancarlo asked.

"We were having tiramisu and grappa at the table, not much after that."

"That sounds about right. You kept demanding more grappa. I tried to tell the waiter to cut you off, but you told me to go fuck myself. You kind of made a scene, then put your head down. It was a challenge to get you out the door. About the only thing you were capable of saying besides Hannah's name, was your address. I finally got you home and to the bathroom. You told me to fuck myself again and then puked your guts out."

"I gathered by the smell of the bathroom."

"When I thought it was safe to move you, I put you to bed. While you slept, I cleaned the kitchen and the bathroom and when I saw you were past the worst of it, I crashed on the couch. This morning I took care of the garbage and went to the supermarket."

Marc sat silently eating his cornetto and drinking his caffè while Giancarlo recounted every grating detail. Marc was clearly embarrassed.

"You've already earned your money this week. Go into the living room. There's a decorated ceramic egg with a handle. The top opens. There's an extra set of keys to the apartment. Did you buy any other food?"

"Yes, I figured you would be staying in, so I got you some prosciutto and bread if you want to make a sandwich. I need to go. I work in a few hours and need to stop home first. Call me if you need anything."

Marc lazily nodded.

Giancarlo went to the living room and found the keys. As he walked to the door Marc handed him €100.

"That's a bonus. Thank you, again, Giancarlo."

"You're welcome, Marc."

The apartment was the cleanest it had been since he moved in. Still feeling woozy, he needed more caffè. On the stove gleamed a classic silver Bialetti pot. It was the old-fashioned type that was common in Italian households. As he unscrewed it over the sink, he saw his father's hands in his own. He placed the top in the base and then tapped the outer bottom piece on the side of the garbage to free the basket of coffee grinds. He blew into the bottom of the funnel and the grinds from the previous pot fell out like a round puck. His father taught him that you never tap the inner funnel because that dents it and disrupts the siphoning process.

As he went through every gesture, he remembered Antonio standing in their kitchen, wearing a short-sleeved, button-down shirt, with a fat polyester tie. He had neatly combed black hair with classic 70's pork chop sideburns. He always made breakfast for Marc because his mother usually slept late. He tried for so many years to forget about his father. Hating him for dying was a habit; but since he'd come to Italy, he saw him everywhere.

1:7

Marc grew tired of the piazza. Rome, for all its grandeur, had failed to seduce him. Giancarlo walked in with Marc's groceries and mail. They hadn't seen each other in a few days, and he hadn't been to the café in two weeks.

"Good morning, Marc. Will you be coming today? The guys have been asking for you."

Marc always said maybe. Giancarlo counted the empty bottles and was concerned Marc was drinking more. Alcohol was always on his shopping list. He'd also started smoking and now the apartment stank of cigarettes. Marc's beard had grown back, and his hair was now so long he needed to wear his red baseball cap to keep it out of his eyes.

"Marc, why don't you get out of the house? It's a nice day; it may do you some good."

"Don't worry about me." He abruptly changed the subject. "I need a witness on this document. Sign it."

After Giancarlo signed the paper, Marc put the paperwork in a large envelope and handed it to him. He told him to ship it UPS second day and bring more cigarettes back. Giancarlo was starting to feel like an enabler and didn't know what to do about it. By doing his shopping, cleaning his apartment and keeping him stocked with booze, he made it easier for Marc to further withdraw.

"Gino is making your favorite today. You should really come."

No answer. Giancarlo grew tired of Marc's quiet abrasiveness. It was starting to make the job less and less appealing. He'd hoped being around him would get easier, but he was wrong. As his state worsened, he thought Marc needed a nurse and a shrink instead of an assistant. He felt like little more than a houseboy and a chaperone.

"Marc, you need a shower!"

"I told you to mind your business."

"You *are* my business and just because you pay me doesn't give you license to treat me disrespectfully."

Marc sat with his legs crossed at the kitchen table and looked away from Giancarlo. He pulled on his cigarette, looking smug and feeling defensive.

"Are you telling me you're quitting? Has my generosity not been enough for you?" He said indignantly.

"Generosity? I told you the night you offered me this job that I don't need the extra money. It's not about that. This is tragic. I want to help you, but not if you don't want to help yourself. I'm worried about you. When is the last time you even got laid?"

Marc looked down at the floor. After Giancarlo left the apartment, he was surprised he wasn't angry. Instead, he felt respect because Giancarlo demonstrated something unexpected: emotional investment.

1:8

It was a beautiful Friday afternoon in June. As Giancarlo zipped around the café, he wondered if Marc would show up. He no longer felt guilty for his participation in Marc's debauchery. It had been days since their last talk at the apartment. Every time he left the kitchen, he hoped to see him at the host station but as the lunch rush raged on, there was no sign of him. He felt disappointment but expected nothing less. Marc was infuriatingly stubborn and after his last outburst, he expected to be fired anyway. He stood in the kitchen eating a sandwich when his colleague sarcastically told him his rich American benefactor was out front. He rushed out to see a clean-shaven, showered, and properly dressed Marc seated at a table.

"Why're you even reading the menu? I already know what you want."

Marc grinned and looked up at him.

"Recently, somebody helped me understand that it was good to try new things, but maybe that can wait."

Giancarlo smiled.

"Any chance I could get a carbonara today?"

"I'll ask the chef."

"Can you bring my favorite Chianti?"

Before obliging, Giancarlo raised an eyebrow and hesitated. "How much have you had to drink today?"

"Nothing. If you don't have plans after work, I am interested in seeing something new. How about you take me to see something later?"

"I have no plans. What do you want to see?"

"Something I wouldn't find unless I was looking for it. It has to be extraordinary."

That was an unusual request, but Giancarlo had just the thing. After Giancarlo's shift concluded, they departed.

"Where are we going?" Marc asked.

"You'll see. I was glad to see you at the restaurant today."

"I thought about what you said, and I respect your conviction. Not many people get away with telling me to go fuck myself and live to tell the tale."

"You are a Mafioso! Am I going to wind up dead and buried in the basement of your building?"

"Oh, believe me, I wanted to kill you." Marc half joked.

"You'd try." Giancarlo countered playfully.

"You challenged me and got away with something even more rare, you changed my mind, and you did it against my will. My money affords me the freedom to be an asshole. After you left, I was marveling at how a fucking kid waiter just kicked my ass."

"Well, I'm more than just a waiter!" Giancarlo contested.

"Don't get cocky! I still might fire you." Said Marc sarcastically.

"Good luck with that. Who else would put up with your shit?"

"Touché." Marc found himself in a peculiar state: calm and trusting. He hadn't felt that in a long time. He walked the streets with his unlikely young friend. Was Giancarlo a friend? He wondered. His father once said a true friend will risk friendship to tell you what you most need to hear when you least want to hear it.

They arrived at the steps of San Luigi dei Francesi. From the outside, it looked rather plain. They entered the dimly lit church and after they took a few steps, Giancarlo stopped them.

"I want you to listen."

Marc heard chatter from the left back corner. The sides of the church were lined with generic renaissance paintings depicting adoring saints experiencing the ecstasy of the holy spirit. No one was looking at them. As they walked, Giancarlo pointed to the crowd that was gathered. They turned the corner to three very famous and very different works from the others in the church. They were much more realistic, dramatic, and moody—the only reason anyone ever visited that church. They gazed upon The Calling of Saint Matthew,

Chapter 1 - The Precipice

The Inspiration of Saint Matthew and The Martyrdom of Saint Matthew by the father of the baroque: Michelangelo Merisi da Caravaggio.

"Caravaggio is to realistic painting what Steve Jobs is to personal computing. I've always wanted to see these." Marc was transfixed.

Strong spotlights lit the three masterpieces and suddenly, the lights went off.

Giancarlo signaled for him to wait again. "Listen," They heard the sound of a coin being dropped into a metal box and the light came back on. Marc looked to the right and saw a coin box on the wall with a sign that said €1.

"They charge money for the light?" Marc whispered in astonishment.

"Yes, and the light is probably always on."

There was a remarkable difference between good and great. Marc studied every detail of the paintings. He'd seen the works in photographs, but this was different. Marc resembled a child seeing rain for the first time. Giancarlo had never seen him express excitement.

"Did this meet your expectations?" Giancarlo asked.

"Not only did it meet them, you surprised me again."

"How much do you know about Caravaggio, Marc?"

"I know his work and his importance. There are several in the Metropolitan in New York, but nothing like these."

"Caravaggio was such a conundrum. His work reflects a man with such insight into the human soul. I think my favorite work by him is Judith Beheading Holofernes. Do you know that one?" Giancarlo asked.

"I do."

"Have you ever studied her facial expression? In her eyes, I see a woman with total conviction in her need to behead her victim. Simultaneously, I see deep regret as if she wishes she did not have to kill him. What kind of a man has that much perception? You would think he must be a man of great compassion, but what we know about him suggests the opposite."

"I remember reading that he was a notoriously unruly character." Marc replied.

"He was a murderer. He supposedly killed the captain of the Knights Templar over a game and then escaped the authorities. The legend goes that he attempted walking up the coast of Italy from Naples to Rome and then died of Malaria."

"That, I didn't know, but I'm not surprised. So, what's the significance?" Marc asked.

"Was Caravaggio inherently an evil man or did his life make him that way? How does a man with the capacity to grasp such humanity also murder people?"

"How does that pertain to me?"

Giancarlo looked exasperated.

"Obviously you aren't a killer and that isn't the point. I've seen you behave awfully and demonstrate genuine kindness. Are you really a ruthless man or did your life make you that way?"

"What's your point?" Marc became confrontational.

"There it is!" Giancarlo fired back. "It's that rage. Caravaggio had it and you have that same spark. Is it part of your nature or did you learn it? Do you see into people? Are you also capable of the same depth?"

Giancarlo's inquiry was starting to hit a little too close to home. Marc felt naked. Was he that obvious he wondered?

"Maybe I'll fire you yet. I knew I should have never hired a psychologist."

Both laughed.

"You know, I'm thinking about getting an advanced degree, but opening a private practice in Italy isn't easy."

"Psychology degrees are a dime a dozen. Maybe you should've picked something more specialized."

"Italia is not America, Marc. Most American students could never pass Italian exams. A tourist in college told me about your nice little multiple-choice tests that any idiot with half a memory can pass. Here, you learn everything in the textbook, and memorize every detail, every title, name, and term. You stand up in front of a committee of three professors you don't know, and they proceed to assassinate you with questions. We have to pass oral exams!"

"Really?"

"Yes, really, and it's ironic considering you still can't

have a career. For all its grandiosity, Italy is still a small town. Talent means nothing. It's all about connections. If you don't have them, you have nothing. I'm weighing my options now. I've considered looking abroad, but I don't know."

"Have you talked to your parents?"

"Yes, but I don't trust their objectivity. My mother doesn't want me to leave and she can't see beyond that."

"You're lucky to have a mother like that, Giancarlo."

They walked along and suddenly Marc remembered that this was what friendship felt like. There he was with someone who only wanted his company, someone who was also willing to deny the money that Marc too often used to manipulate people for the sake of principle. He was so used to being suspect of everyone because they all had their hands out. Could he trust Paul the same way? Paul worked for him but for a lot more money than the meager €150 he was paying Giancarlo. Would he quit to make a point? He wasn't sure. Still, it appeared that Rome did have something to offer him after all: a friend.

1:9

After a series of tests, the tingling in his leg turned out to be a much bigger problem than just a bulging disk. He was diagnosed with Multiple Sclerosis. Marc's life atop his financial empire was crashing right before his eyes and his body was the wrecking ball. At the insistence of his doctor, he reluctantly agreed to counselling. He was referred to an unorthodox therapist who specialized in health issues and patients with evasive personalities. She didn't just listen and wait for people to talk, she engaged, at times forcefully. Her philosophy was that helping people could not always depend upon their willingness to volunteer information. She valued intuition, rejecting the idea that therapists were passive automatons, and had published research that substantiated her methods despite criticism from some colleagues.

Dr. Rossellino knew she was fighting an uphill battle. As his sessions progressed, his behavior highlighted his inability to talk about his feelings. With each passing week, his will waned. He couldn't buy his way out of this. It was something else entirely and he behaved like a wounded animal.

Her office was on top of a three-story office building in Cliffside Park, New Jersey. Like his apartment, it had a nice view of the city. It was a welcoming environment, with lots of plants and amber antique wood furniture. She had an ivy that must have been a decade old. It spread over twenty feet in both directions from its corner perch.

Marc reclined on the couch for this week's session. Dr. Rossellino sat in her red leather chair adorned with brass headed nails. She was a very small, short woman with chin-length, bobbed hair, and thick, round glasses. She often wore a long sweater over her business casual pants suits. Despite her size, she had a strong voice with a distinct North Jersey-Italian American accent.

The session was going slowly, too slowly. Dr. Rossellino had already wondered if Marc should try a male therapist. She suspected he had difficulty opening up to women because of his history with his mother.

"Marc, I can't help you if you don't talk to me. Last week you shared your passion for writing as a boy. Can you talk more about that?"

"I enjoyed writing because I was good at it. I even won contests."

"Did you also enjoy it? Accountants are good at math, but it doesn't mean they sit around and do calculus for fun. Was there another reason?"

"I guess it's because that's where I could express myself." He said.

"Tell me more about that."

"What would you like to know?"

"Why do you just bounce my questions back to me?" She inquired.

He didn't answer.

"Some people in my field just collect a paycheck. They just wait for people to talk and are content charging their patients for silence. Not me. Sitting silently is like going to a restaurant and paying for a meal you don't eat. Why bother at all?"

Chapter 1 - The Precipice

Seeing her comment as a dare, he took the challenge.

"I don't trust people and as you know, I have my mother to thank for that. Truth is, nobody gives a fuck anyway. Everyone is out for themselves. They nod and smile while acting so concerned, but I've watched people be so slick and seem so sincere when I knew they weren't. I remember back in my 20s thinking that the Oscars were so contrived. Why give awards to actors? They're just professional liars. Most of them aren't any good compared to disingenuous assholes I've witnessed over the years. So, to answer your question, I wrote because I could articulate my feelings and thoughts without people breaking my balls or betraying me."

"So, you trust no one?"

"Only fools trust. Sometimes I'm torn between envy and disgust with people's naïveté. Ignorance is bliss. It's a cliché because it's true."

"Do you think people can trust you, Marc?"

"Of course not! But at least I'm honest with myself about it." He scoffed.

"How are you not trustworthy?" She asked.

"The world is simply Darwinian. Relationships, marriages, and even friendships are matters of convenience. Often, family isn't love; it's conflict. It's the world's oldest myth. Cain killed his brother Abel. Romulus killed Remus. Saturn ate his children. Nietzsche said the world is a will to power."

"You really view the world that coldly?" She asked.

"When a young lion vanquishes his older and weaker counterpart, he kills his cubs so his new harem will go into heat just to pass on his genes. A cheetah runs to take down an antelope. If successful, it has time for a few mouthfuls of meat before the lions or hyenas come. They can see the dust cloud and know there might be a free meal. They steal it and sleep with full bellies while the one who did the work starves. There are no savannah cops to arrest the thieves. It just happens. It's simple in the end. Nature has no morality. We created morality and it has no real basis in the world. Is there any moral reason behind why I'm sick?"

"Is your contempt genuine or are you bitter because of

your illness? I'm curious how you can be so judgmental when you see no moral order. If everything is an accident, how is anybody at fault?" She asked.

"It's not judgment. It's the futility of it all. One day entropy will tear apart the universe. The sun will expand and swallow this planet. We fight like ants for dominance and yet we're like puppets on a very tragic and sinister stage. All of this is for nothing and yet we live day to day as if everything we do has divine importance. If the senseless suffering in the world is the work of some supreme being, he's a fucking psychopath. The world *He* supposedly created, is murderous and savage. If you show weakness, people destroy you. You have only one option: beat them down and make them submit before they do it to you. The worst part is we grow to love it. People who are tortured eventually love their tormentors. We desire people who reject us and disregard those who show interest. It's sick."

"You seem to take your insights seriously. Do you think that places you above others? Knowing you aren't trustworthy doesn't absolve you of anything."

Marc dismissed her. "I expected you would counter with some Freudian projection crap, but I don't buy it. There are winners and losers. We can try and console ourselves but it's all bullshit in the end."

"For somebody who says he doesn't like to talk, you sure have a lot to say. You're very good at throwing up defense mechanisms and creating diversions. You give me this manifesto on the depravity of existence as some excuse for willful seclusion. What I hear is something else. Is it possible you wrote your thoughts down because if people knew the real you, you fear they'd hate you or worse, hurt you? Listen to the things you're saying. You show no value for relationships. You're dismissive and condescending about genuine feelings and most of all, you're miserable about it. This monologue is just a bunch of smoke and mirrors to throw me off because you're so afraid of people getting close to you, you'll provoke the worst in them only to justify attacking them in self-defense. You create self-fulfilling prophecies. Now that you're sick, you have another reason to push people away."

Chapter 1 - The Precipice

Dr. Rossellino sensed his fury. Before giving him the chance to regress, she continued.

"Marc, I'm not your judge. The little I know about your mother makes it understandable you have so little trust. You've said a few words about your father's death, and I suspect there's a lot more there. When you spoke of him, it was clear you loved him and you're still not over his loss. And now you're facing a very difficult disease. It's understandable you're angry, and I'm sorry you're hurting. I want you to understand that my singular goal is to help you live your life. As long as you want that too, we both want the same thing."

She paused, awaiting a response, and Marc nodded his head.

"I want you to get back to your writing. Have you ever written about your mother and father?" She asked.

He folded his arms across his chest and tightened his posture. Sensing that meant yes, she asked if he still had those journals and if she could read them. To her regret, he said he threw them out.

"Can you tell me about any happy memories? There must be something."

"When I was 12, my father gave me a telescope for my birthday. We waited until the full moon to use it. We got lucky because it was a clear night. We set it up on our deck and papa showed me how to line up the scope. It was the first time I saw the moon up close. It was beautiful. I couldn't believe how fast it was moving. That was such a wonderful night now that I think about it. It was the first time I ever tasted grappa, too. I kept asking him about it and finally he let me try it, warning me I wouldn't like it. Of course, I spit it out. It tasted like gasoline. He laughed at me as I choked. I had tried being tough and took a big sip. I had no idea he'd die before a year later."

"That's a beautiful memory. Do you still write?"

"I haven't written in a long time. After my father died, my journal kind of took his place. I felt like that was how I could still talk with him. It helped a lot."

"So how long has it been? Five, ten, fifteen years?" She asked.

"It's been about twenty years."

"Are you interested in trying to deal with your past?"

"Of course I am, why do you think I'm here?"

"Then I want you to try something for next week's session. I want you to write something and bring it with you. Is that okay?"

He didn't answer.

"We have to explore this because it might help you clarify your thoughts. You have a very interesting perspective, and I'd like to challenge you on your assertion that things are meaningless. Your father's death and your mother's narcissism matter quite a lot to you. Even your demeanor suggests you care. On the surface, you're a cynic, but I see something else." Doctor Rossellino said earnestly.

"What do you see?" He asked.

"I see a dreamer with a broken heart. You try hard to make me believe you're resigned but I'm not convinced. If you were you would not be so angry. If you're going to come to terms with your illness, we have to try something new."

A week later, he returned for his appointment. Dr. Rossellino noticed he was wearing dark glasses and a baseball hat pulled low on his forehead. He had an envelope in one hand, half concealing it. He sat down and didn't remove his sunglasses. She knew he was scared to give it to her. She proceeded gently, speaking not much louder than a whisper.

"Remember what I told you last week. I'm your doctor. Never fear betrayal in this room."

He slowly removed his sunglasses and put them in his shirt pocket. Then she reached out her hand for the envelope. It was sealed, which she expected. She gently removed it from his hand and before tearing it open, she asked his permission.

"I'm excited to see what you've written. Would you mind reading it out loud?"

"Why would I need to do that? It's only the two of us here. I wrote it and I know what it says. I don't need to hear it."

"Then do you mind if I read it out loud? I think it's important you hear it. You have an easier time writing your thoughts without hearing the words come out of your mouth. Perhaps that might help you imagine saying them eventually?" She looked at him intently. "Do I have your permission?"

Marc agreed.

My parents had a very strange marriage. They were the most unlikely pair and I still can't understand their attraction. Maybe it was just physical in the beginning? Elaine was very beautiful when she was young. My father was also handsome. As for how that led to marriage, Elaine got pregnant. The wedding happened quietly and was curiously seven months before Gabe was born. They used to claim they were really married a year prior and that was just a second wedding to be married in a church. I knew it was bullshit, but people played along because it was the 1960s. There wasn't abortion in those days and as a traditional Italian man, that was what you did under those circumstances.

Beyond why they married, that they stayed together still puzzles me. My father was contemplative, and Elaine was not. The only thing my father and I ever fought about was her and how she liked to dominate him. At the time I was too young to realize that the tail actually wagged the dog, but his submissiveness still angered me. As for her, I particularly hated how she always needed an audience, how she spent money, her drinking and her manipulation. Being home with her when dad was still at work was often a challenge.

I used to do my homework at the dining room table each night. It was my best chance of quiet. She would sit in the den with her phonebook, calling friend after friend to tell them all the same story. On a bad day, I could still hear her two rooms away. The more she talked, the more she drank, and her speech would slur more with each conversation. The later ones were always shorter because her incoherence made people want to get off the phone. Often, I did my best to tune out her nightly tabloid marathons with music or TV.

Her tactlessness was insufferable and her compulsion to blab our business to whoever would listen made it even worse. There was one day that really stays in my memory.

When I was little, I was a bedwetter. I was 8 years old and it should have corrected itself by then, but it continued.

Finding a Light in a Room with no Walls

One day, I was playing in the living room and the Avon lady dropped off an order. They started chitchatting and sure enough, she mentioned my bedwetting, right in front of me. She spoke about me in the third person, as if I wasn't even there! I felt so much resentment. Finally, something snapped. I smashed my Lincoln Logs construction and lunged at her screaming for her to stop. She initially assuaged me and tried to seem concerned because somebody else was watching. Mrs. Mason, the Avon lady, seemed very uncomfortable so my mother tried to maintain appearances. She made up some bullshit story that she was seeking medical attention for my ongoing outbursts and that this just happened sometimes. She had the nerve to blame me!

She walked her to the door and their conversation concluded with the typical formal niceties and my mother handing her a check. The door closed and my mother turned to me. I was terrified. Her lips curled in, her brow tightened, and she walked towards me, picking up speed with every step.

"How. Dare. You. Raise. A. Hand. To. Me?!"

Each syllable corresponded to her steps. I'll never forget it. She walked so hard that it shook the house. I heard the crystal glasses tinkling in the china closet. She loomed over me like a T-Rex, jaws opened, taunting her prey. I shrank beneath the weight of her voice. Finally, I felt a jolt to the side of my head. My ear started to ring. She hit me. All she could keep saying was how I embarrassed her! I couldn't believe it! I embarrassed her? She was there telling a fucking stranger about my bedwetting and I embarrassed her? My fear shifted back to anger and I began to fight back. She grabbed me by both wrists and dragged me up the stairs. She threw me into my room and slammed the door.

I waited for my father to come home. Out of spite, I didn't make a sound. I cried but buried my face in the pillow so she couldn't hear me.

"Maybe I don't like this after all." Marc interrupted.

"Marc, please try to relax. May I continue?"

He agreed again.

I must've waited there for two hours and she never

came in to check on me. Finally, I heard the car pull into the driveway. The door on my dad's Pontiac had a distinctive squeak when it opened. A few minutes later, I heard the door close and they immediately started yelling. I couldn't make out what they were saying, but soon after I heard feet coming up the stairs. The door to my room opened. It was papa.

At first, he questioned my outburst and was very concerned that I hit my mother.

At that moment, all the anguish I had forced into my pillow exploded. I ran to him and hugged him, wailing. He went down on his knees and hugged me tightly. He urgently asked me what happened.

She left out what she said to Mrs. Mason. That put things in a different light. He left the room to confront Elaine, and I hid at the top of the stairs to listen. My mother was a classic gas lighter. She said that Mrs. Mason initiated the discussion and that she brought it up only in response to her.

He insisted she not do that again and she insisted that it was her business what she told her 'friends'. Then I heard the sound of a bottle being opened and scotch being poured into a glass. My mother went to the bottle when anything bad happened. She acted like it never happened the next day, but she got colder towards me after that. Turning on her publicly was viewed as disloyalty. My mother always needed adulation. It was like a drug for her and she was not getting any from me, so I no longer served that purpose. As bad as that day was with my mother, it was the beginning of something good with my father.

By the time she finished reading, Marc was noticeably shaken. She was right that hearing the words would resonate. Though it was painful, it was necessary. Marc didn't initiate conversation afterwards, which she expected.

"This story is a big step and I'm proud of you. Before I say anything else, it's important to note that if you didn't care, you would have never bothered to write it. Now I have a much better understanding of how your inability to open up is related to your childhood."

"So what, I had a shitty childhood. Isn't that just the norm? A hundred and fifty years ago, orphans lived in workhouses if they were lucky enough to even survive infancy. Isn't trauma just a part of life? Can't it be a powerful force for growth? Look at me, I'm a very successful, wealthy man. I didn't wind up on the streets doing drugs after my father died. I turned out fine."

"And that's the problem. While I agree that you used your suffering to grow financially, you didn't grow emotionally. You've reverted right back to a heartbroken teenager since your diagnosis. Your success doesn't mean anything there." Dr. Rossellino paused. "You're right, trauma is a part of life and it's not a problem until it becomes a pathology. That you've known about this diagnosis for over a month and your wife and family still don't know is not a healthy coping mechanism."

1:10

Hannah came in and out of the room several times and neither acknowledged the other as Marc packed his bags.

What am I doing? Just tell her the truth, he said to himself. No, he couldn't be sick or weak for his wife. Even if it meant losing her. The thought of himself in a wheelchair disgusted him. He thought of Hannah looking on hopelessly, her beautiful eyes gazing at an invalid. He feared helplessness even more than death.

He occasionally glanced out the window at the New York skyline and didn't know when he would see it again. He finished packing and exited the bedroom, placing his black suitcases in the hallway. As he walked towards his office at the other end of the apartment, he passed Hannah sitting on the couch and they continued to ignore each other.

He sat at his desk gathering the last of his documents. Paul was taking him to the airport. His office was empty now less the final things he needed until the very end. As a matter of habit, he tried distracting himself with work. As he poured over acquisition clauses, Hannah came down the hall and stood in the door. He could feel her staring at him. Reluctantly, he began to turn his head towards her when she grabbed a lamp from his desk and smashed it. He didn't flinch.

She turned slowly, maintaining eye contact as she spun and walked out of the room. Then he heard their bedroom door close forcefully, followed by the click of the lock.

Marc placed his passport in the breast pocket of his jacket and stood. He looked down at the lamp, a metaphor for the mess he'd made of his marriage. He deliberately stomped on the pieces that were not entirely broken as he left the room. He savored the sound of the crackles and crunches beneath his $700 shoes. *Fuck you,* he thought.

He left his office and saw his bedroom door down the hall as a monolith he would need to surmount to leave. He stopped at the door. It was totally silent. Should he knock, call out her name or tell her the truth? He tried so hard to think it away and was overcome by finally facing the prospect of what he was about to lose. He closed his hand to a fist and raised it to the door. He gestured a knock, but his knuckles couldn't seem to make contact with the wood.

He knew then, what he had done couldn't be undone. He closed his eyes and remembered back to when he and Hannah first met. He was with Paul and saw her sitting there with her bike. It was one of those rare moments when no one else exists. He remembered her gaze and the sheen of her skin in the spring sun so many years ago. He asked her if she wanted to get coffee. When she said no, he got down on his knees, begging her out loud in Shakespearian vernacular. She began to laugh and then accepted. It was a lovely memory, and he couldn't understand why he didn't care. He wanted to, but no matter how hard he tried, it wasn't enough to deter him.

A knock on the apartment door interrupted his reminiscing. It was the porter Hector to help him with his things. He closed the apartment door behind him and never looked back. As he and Hector rode down the elevator, he made small talk and when asked where he was going, he said it was a business trip. Paul was waiting in his car outside. Hector loaded the bags in the trunk and they departed.

"How did it go?" Paul asked hesitantly.

"Day at the fucking beach."

"Did you tell her the truth?" Paul asked.

"No." Marc said indifferently.

Paul was in disbelief. "I don't know why you are doing this. I really don't and as your friend, not as your lawyer, but as your friend, I'm really pissed off that you've given me this secret. Why did you tell *me*? I wish you hadn't!"

Marc tried to make light of it. "I cannot un-tell you. I'm sorry for that but stop whining. I just made you a lot of money. Litigating a divorce with my assets based on infidelity is to your benefit. Let's face it, it's better Hannah remains my beneficiary. I won't be needing it."

His attempt at making light of the situation offended Paul.

"At this moment, you're a complete stranger to me. I can't believe I'm saying this, but this disease isn't even your real problem."

"It's not my *real* problem? It's not real that I might turn into a pile of helpless shit and need somebody to wipe my ass? What the fuck is not real about that, Paul?"

"Your real problems started long before you got sick! People endure tragedies. Remember when my father died of cancer? He didn't lie to my mother and take off on some self-pitying trip. He stayed and we all watched him deteriorate. You aren't the only person who saw his father die! Remember? Do you realize what you just did to your wife? And it isn't even just her. Fuck you for thinking I don't know what you're up to."

Chapter 2

Descent

2:1

"You look good Hannah."

"Paul, you don't have to say that. I don't look good. I don't feel good."

"No, Hannah, really. You're always beautiful."

"And you're always a gentleman. I always wished it would've rubbed off on... on my husband."

The apartment hadn't changed much, but anything connected to Marc was removed.

"My attorney said I shouldn't see you socially because it's a conflict of interest." Hannah said.

"I'm not here as a lawyer."

"I know. We've gone on vacations together." She was pensive, but suddenly yelled. "How the fuck did this happen?"

Paul was very cautious seeing she was so distressed. "I wish I had answers. Has he made any attempt to contact you?"

"No, he must be busy with his new woman. Is she living with him?"

"Hannah..."

"Is she living with him?!"

Hannah's eyes started to tear. "How did I not know? He was so absent the last few months."

"Hannah, Marc was always secretive."

"It got a lot worse." Her voice broke and her grief provoked Paul's honesty. He wanted to tell the truth and feared it would leak from his mouth like a flood.

"As far as I know, he's living alone, and it's not going well."

Hannah interjected. "That's the part about this that makes no sense! The drinking and self-destructive behavior started and now he's fucking some woman in Italy!"

She broke out into a full-blown cry and pulled her knees into her chest. Paul noticed her collarbones and worried she wasn't eating. Her hair seemed to envelop her.

"As Marc's attorney, it's difficult for me to balance my legal obligations and our friendship. If I hear anything that you need to know, I'll try my best to help out."

She continued to cry, and Paul tried to console her.

"Are you keeping busy?" He asked.

"I've tried to work more." She said, sniveling. "Being around people helps. I even have a new client who asked me to dinner. I'm not interested, but it was a nice gesture. He's an ophthalmologist and he even talks."

Paul chuckled gently. "Listen, do whatever you need to do when you're ready."

He was about to say more when her tears returned.

"I know you know more than you can say. You're telling me to move on because things with this other woman are serious. I'm not stupid."

"No Hannah, I don't know anything about that. He hasn't brought it up."

That was one of those true lies that simultaneously couldn't be further from reality.

"Hannah, I'm not telling you to move on because of another woman. I don't know what is going on with him, but I don't like what he's done. I don't think you deserved it." Another half-truth.

He kept asking himself *what kind of a man lies about an affair to cover up an illness?* The more he thought about it, the more disgust he felt. For the past few years, he began to feel more like Marc's attorney and less like his friend anyway. Marc abandoned him too and left him with the burden of his lie.

"He was once loving and kind, even trusting. I'll never forget how he cried when he first told me the story of his father. It took him a year, but I thought I finally saw the real him. It made me love him. I felt special because he showed me sides of himself he didn't show anybody, but as time passed I saw less and less of that person and I think I held on hoping he could come back."

"Funny, I told him the same thing on our way to the airport."

"As hurt as I am, a part of me is happy to move forward... I can't believe I just said that."

"He's an idiot." Paul dismissed.

"You were always a good friend Paul. I never told you

this, but I've thought more than once he doesn't deserve your loyalty."

"I'm starting to agree with you." Paul confessed.

2:2

Enthusiasm can be fickle. As one falls out of its favor, despair grows like mold on damp cheese. It was July and Rome was boiling. Italians did not prefer AC, but Marc's apartment had it and that came with unintended consequences. The windows and exterior shutters remained closed. Day and night were indistinguishable, and Marc meandered through his waking hours with no discernable routine. The air was dank, and the silence rang loudly. His thoughts were non-specific and passed like flashes of disconnected images. He took the last pull from a cigarette and extinguished it in an ashtray that should have been emptied a day prior. His whole body hurt, especially his head and neck. Walking after prolonged sitting was especially painful in his heels. Then the doorbell sounded, and his cellphone rang simultaneously. It was Paul but he didn't answer. Then the phone rang again.

"Hey," was all Paul could bring himself to say. His tone was cold. Then he pressed the doorbell button again.

"Somebody is at my door." Marc grumbled.

"It's me." Paul said sternly.

"What do you mean it's *you*? What are you doing here?"

"Just open the door. It's urgent." Paul said.

Marc hesitated. It wasn't that he didn't want to see Paul, he didn't want Paul to see him.

"Take the elevator to the top floor." Marc hung up the phone.

The buzzer to unlock the door sounded and Paul reluctantly entered the building. When he closed the elevator, it reminded him of a prison cell clanging shut. He arrived at the top floor to find the door to the apartment open a few inches. He entered and saw Marc slouched on the couch clutching a bottle of wine with a cigarette in his mouth.

"Since when do you smoke?"

"Since it's my business. Want a drink?"

Marc raised his bottle to his lips and smiled cynically. Paul shook his head in disapproval as it wasn't even noon yet.

"To what do I owe this grand gesture?" Marc slurred.

Paul reached out and handed Marc an envelope.

"You've been served." Paul remained coldly official.

"Oh, what a pretty manila envelope—and no bow? I would have thought my soon-to-be ex-wife would have had a little more taste."

"I didn't come here to listen to this."

"And why did you come? To serve me my divorce papers? You could've hired a service for that. You look great by the way."

Paul could not tell if he was sincere but regardless, he did look great in stark contrast to Marc.

"Thank you for the compliment."

"What did you want to talk about, *friend*?"

"Do you really need me to fucking answer that?" Paul spat out.

Marc's cruelty became unrestrained. "You came to check on me? How sweet. Are you sure that's the only reason? I can't help but wonder that you might be enjoying this. Look at you. For once, you are clearly superior to me. Congratulations for emerging from my shadow."

"I would really like to punch you in the face, but I shouldn't hit a cripple."

Suddenly, the bottle in Marc's hand flew across the room towards Paul's head. He ducked and it exploded against the wall. Then he saw Marc coming towards him. Paul pivoted and Marc lost his balance. He fell to the ground on a piece of broken glass. His cheek started to bleed.

"On the floor and bloodied, and I didn't even have to hit you." Paul breathed heavily from his adrenaline.

Marc made no attempt to get up.

"You son of a bitch. I did come to check on you! That's what friends do, but now I realize I made a mistake. I don't have any friend here. Also, I'm no longer your attorney. At least my conscience is now clean."

Marc got his answer. Paul would quit on principle. As he looked up at him from the floor, his cut was in plain view and now his fear of abandonment made him even more aggressive. "I hope seeing me at my worst becomes a treasured memory."

"If you really believe that, you're as crazy as your mother."

"Fuck you!" Mark screamed.

With that, Paul kicked Marc in the stomach.

Marc groaned in pain as Paul slammed the door behind him. After the pain passed, he peeled himself off the floor, sat back in his chair and removed the documents from the envelope. Pride pushed away his regret. What surprised him most was not the divorce or that Paul came unannounced, it was that he didn't care thirty years of friendship just ended.

Several hours later, Giancarlo, filled with dread, rode up the elevator. Marc's altercation with Paul was no longer indicative of unusual behavior. Though Marc increased his stipend to €200 per week, it no longer mattered. He didn't want to be his maid, his nurse or worse yet, his punching bag. He got out of the elevator and heard loud music coming from the apartment. Though he had the key, he thought it best to knock. He thumped loudly. "It's Giancarlo."

"Come in!" Marc yelled.

Marc was raging around the living room playing air guitar in his underwear to Led Zeppelin's the Immigrant song. He saw Giancarlo but didn't bother to stop. He even slipped in a good morning in between his air guitar power chords. Marc continued uninterrupted until the song ended. It was like watching a freak show.

"Led Zeppelin is fucking awesome, aren't they?" Marc was almost out of breath.

"Yes, they are." Giancarlo responded mechanically.

Marc was manic. Giancarlo wanted to have a serious talk with him, but after seeing the Wembley stadium encore performance, he decided it wasn't the best time. Then he noticed the scab on Marc's face and some swelling.

"Please put some caffè on the stove. We need to discuss something."

The couch was covered in paper and Giancarlo saw the words "Attorneys at Law" in the header. Giancarlo wanted to ask about his face and the mail but decided otherwise so he went to the kitchen as requested.

"Hannah filed for divorce." Marc yelled exuberantly. He lit a cigarette and placed it in the ashtray that still needed emptying. The butts started to burn, making the room smell of smoldering cotton.

"So, what do you need to talk about?"

"I want to teach you my business, Giancarlo."

"I don't know the first thing about real-estate. I don't-"

Marc cut him off mid-sentence. "You'll learn. You're smart and it's a great way to make a living. How would you feel about quitting the restaurant?"

Giancarlo was speechless.

"Right now, you're making €1800 per month between the café and me, which is very good money. You could make so much more!"

Giancarlo was at a loss for words but summoned his courage to speak honestly.

"Why is your face bleeding?"

"Never mind that." He had no intention of sharing his altercation with Paul, but Giancarlo persisted.

"I cannot accept that answer. It's completely relevant because of why I came here today. This is the most generous and exciting offer I've ever had. Under any other circumstances, I would be crazy not to accept it. It is a chance for me to have a real job with real opportunity."

"So, what's the problem?" Marc asked.

"You. I have a permanent contract at the restaurant. Those are hard to get. Yes, it's not a prestigious job, but it's stable. That is something you cannot give me."

"Stop being dramatic." Marc said dismissively as he threw his hat from the couch.

"I'm not being dramatic! Look at you. Look at this dungeon. I walk in and you're spazzing out to music while your divorce papers are spread out like old newspaper, and you obviously fell or got into a fight with somebody! How could I possibly give up a permanent job to work for you?"

Marc tried to interrupt but Giancarlo continued. "Put yourself in my shoes. You are a huge risk. This is not about the job or the offer; it's about you!"

Marc reached for his pack of cigarettes and pulled out

the last one. He lit it and fell back into the couch. He tried to seem like he was ignoring Giancarlo by staring off into space. He expected Marc to be angry, but he wasn't. Then out of nowhere, Marc made a confession.

"I have a debilitating disease. Considering your fear about finding me dead, maybe this wasn't the most opportune time to tell you, but you don't need to worry just yet. I have MS. It's going to take a long time to kill me, too long. It's like a crucifixion, prolonged pain and delayed death. That is what this feels like."

"I knew something serious was wrong with you, I could tell the night you offered me the job. Is that why your wife divorcing you? How can she divorce you while you're sick?"

"She doesn't know." Marc said testily.

"What do you mean 'she doesn't know'?"

"My binge drinking started after my diagnosis. It had been months of tests. She thought it was just depression and I kept playing along while I was trying to figure out how to say it. One day, I was on my balcony. I really wanted to jump but I didn't have the courage. She came home to find me in a lawn chair and told me she couldn't go on like this anymore. I could see the tears in her eyes. I had this overwhelming intuition that she was going to tell me that she wanted a divorce and before she had the chance to say it, I blurted out that I didn't love her anymore and told her I was having an affair. I didn't even plan it. It just came out."

"Instead of telling her you were sick, you said *that*?"

Marc sat in silence.

"Marc, I never told you about my older brother. He died of a heroin overdose. They found him in the bushes with a needle still in his arm. He was only 26. I was 19."

"Giancarlo, I'm very sorry. My father died of a heart attack while my mother was passed out drunk."

"I am really sorry about your father."

The exchange of tragic losses was the best chance of salvaging the conversation. Both men had seen tragedy, but as much as Giancarlo wanted to feel compassion, it was difficult. He could understand everything but not that Marc lied to his wife. Considering that he and his parents grew closer after his brother's death, he ventured into an even more precarious subject.

"You never speak about your mother. Is she still alive?"

"Yes, she is." Marc said with resignation.

"It must have been hard for your mother to lose your father. How is she handling your diagnosis?"

"I haven't spoken to my mother in almost a decade."

"Marc, that's terrible!"

"You don't know Elaine."

"Marc, I quit."

The words exited Giancarlo's mouth without hesitation or premeditation. It was as easy as taking a piss. Marc on the other hand was furious.

"You sanctimonious son of a bitch. Who are you to judge me? And to think of how generous I've been!"

Giancarlo's body tightened to withstand the force of Marc's voice.

"I've been generous with you! Being around you is generous." Giancarlo protested.

"My relationship with my family is none of your business!" Marc screamed at the top of his lungs.

"You've made it my business! Just like your illness is now my business! At least now I know the truth. That's what all this has been about from the beginning."

"What the fuck do you know? You aren't sick!"

"Look at what you've achieved, and you appreciate none of it! Someone with your resources could have started a foundation, financed research, but not you."

Marc slowly rose from the couch. The veins in his neck bulged and the muscles in his forehead twitched. He began to move slowly like a cat stalking its prey.

"Let me tell you something. Family is an accident of birth. Some people, like you, are lucky to have loving parents. I had a loving father and he was taken from me. It wasn't anybody's fault, it just fucking happened. Your brother dying just happened."

By now Marc was talking at the air. He wasn't even addressing Giancarlo anymore. It was as though Giancarlo was witnessing a monologue from behind a pane of glass.

"People pray to Gods that never answer because they don't exist! I had to watch that woman piss all her money away. She acted like a bitch and felt better because there was always Jesus's forgiveness. She would have had nothing if my father wasn't smart enough to make sure she never got her hands on the money he left me. One by one, strange men walked in and out of her life."

He turned his gaze to Giancarlo, who was ready to run out the door if things got out of hand.

"Don't pass judgment on me for that either! I never abandoned her. I escaped her. I don't have to love her—or fucking explain it to you!"

Marc tripped on the leg of the coffee table and fell to the floor again. He screamed in frustration.

"I'm glad I'm not your son and even gladder you're not my father."

"Forget I ever said it!"

"You act like you're the only person who has ever suffered!"

As Giancarlo spoke, Marc kept saying "shut up" but Giancarlo would not waver.

"You have your pain and it's so important. I'm not saying what's happened to you isn't tragic. It is terribly tragic but what you have made of it is even more tragic and you have nobody to blame but yourself!"

Marc banged his fist on the floor. "Enough! Enough…"

"Marc, there you are on the floor and I feel sorry for you."

Giancarlo left. Marc laid staring up at the ceiling for a second time. Two fights with two friends on the same day resulting in both walking out on him was quite a feat. Then a thought more abhorrent than death entered his mind. He couldn't un-think it. He heard it over and over like a broken record. *I am like my mother.*

2:3

Giancarlo had not visited in weeks. With no one to run his errands, Marc had to run his own. That was his only contact with the outside world. He had stopped going to the café and abandoned any resemblance of personal hygiene.

Strangers whispered about him in the supermarket. He smelled. A week prior, a police officer approached him as he tried unlocking his door. He produced the keys and the proper documentation, but his appearance was so suspicious he was mistaken for a burglar.

Now his only outlet was ranting in his journal. There was no one left to listen as he festered through the Roman summer.

I have so much muscle pain. If only my shrink could see me now. How could I have actually convinced myself that I would find inspiration here? After all, it's Rome. I'm surrounded by art and history and I could give less than half a fuck about any of it. If this can't inspire me, I don't know what can. I wanted to feel the memory of my father here. I wanted it to find me, but it hasn't.

Before I left, Dr. Rossellino encouraged me to keep writing. She said it would help me continue to understand myself. In one respect, she was right. She was just wrong in her assumption that I would like the person I rediscovered. She thought too highly of me. Instead of finding my better self, I have nothing but self-loathing and contempt. When I found out I was sick, my instinct was to hide, but there isn't enough wine to distract me entirely. I keep drinking to deaden my senses but it never fully works. My stomach burns and I wake up gasping for air. It is never enough to forget.

I was always so disciplined. I squirreled away my money compulsively. I exercised and ate diligently under the delusion of immortality. How much pleasure did I miss and for what? I find it absurd. How many buildings could I buy? How much art could I possess? How much is enough? My thirst for conquest has teased me like that last line of cocaine. You hope it will fulfill you, but it just leaves you wanting. That is so indicative of life. We are like the blind groping about in the dark, trying to find the light in a room with no walls. We are lost and condemned to never be satisfied. Therefore, the only solution is indifference. Stop expecting completion and looking for absolution. For that,

I'm grateful there is no God. When one truly contemplates the sheer savagery of existence and the incomprehensible violence of life, it's comforting to know that some supreme being did not create it. I would be even more terrified if this was actually by design.

Despite my zeal to reach the nirvana of disregard, weakness nags me when I think of Hannah. She is my only real regret. Maybe that represents the last piece of my humanity? I think I would have to apologize to her, but not for lying. I would apologize for not leaving her sooner. She deserved better. She would have made a good mother, but I didn't want children. My mother did a good job of making me detest childhood. No, now that I think of it, I would have to apologize to Hannah for hating my mother more than I loved her.

2:4

"You wrote about your father." Dr. Rossellino said.

"No, I wrote about Darth Vader."

Marc taped the envelope shut so she took out a large, antique bronze letter opener from her desk drawer. She glanced at him and said, "I have a light saber." He actually laughed. She artfully dragged the blade through the paper and watched him closely.

She removed the pages from the envelope and returned to her chair.

"Is it really necessary that you read this out loud?"

"More than ever," she said.

Papa and I were watching TV together. He had been having rough days at the lab. My father was a chemist and worked for a pharmaceutical company. Cutbacks had caused staff reductions and he said he was doing the work of two people. On this particular evening, we'd been watching The Tonight Show. My mother was in her room and Gabe wasn't home. I noticed my father wasn't laughing at the jokes. That struck me as strange. He had a great laugh, but he seemed so distracted. Punch lines flew past him and he just sat there like a stone, looking concerned. I asked him if he was okay.

He said he was fine.

When I pressed, he said he was tired, and we kept watching the show. At a random commercial break, he turned it off. When I asked him why, he didn't answer and diverted to asking me about school. I told him I was working on a project about weather and cloud formation. He loved it. It made him happy that I really liked school.

I kept noticing that he was licking his lips a lot. His skin looked clammy and his eyes were glassy. He said he was thirsty. As he got up, I offered to go for him, but he waved me off and went to the kitchen. A few moments later, I heard a loud crash. I sprang from the couch. Papa yelled out loud. He was on the floor holding his left arm. He upended the table, and the floor was covered in sugar and broken glass. His body jolted in pain as I held him.

He grabbed onto my shirt and looked me in the eye. It was a gaze like nothing I had ever seen before or since. He kept yelling, "oh God, OH GOD. Marc. MARC!" The last time he said my name was like someone impaled him. He let out a groan and then he fell limp. I was alone with him with nobody to help me. I called for my mother over and over. Nothing.

I shook his face and again, no response. I continued to yell for my mother, still nothing but I knew I had to act. Instead of getting my mother, I called 911. I grabbed him tightly and pleaded with him to wake up. That my mother didn't awaken from my screams in every way defines our relationship. A few minutes later I could hear sirens in the distance grow louder. I heard them stop and saw the lights flashing through the front windows. I ran to open the door. My dad still laid unconscious. The medics descended on him and the older gentleman checked his pulse. He told the other man to power up "the jump starter." He began CPR. The other medic set up the machine and they tore open papa's dress shirt. He jolted my father. His body contorted and I screamed. Every second was an hour. I never felt such anticipation. With every jolt, my father's body bounced off the kitchen floor. Eventually, the medic stopped and checked his pulse.

"It's been 14 minutes. He's gone."

I cried, pleading with my dead father, telling him he couldn't die. The medic tried to console me, but I pushed him away. I ran upstairs to my mother's room and opened the door. Her TV was blaring as usual. I turned on the light and screamed right in her ear. "Wake up!" She opened her eyes and was disoriented. I just kept yelling that papa was dead.

At first, she shook her head in disbelief and then I grabbed her by her nightgown and shook her. At that moment, I had no desire to hug her. The thought of her embrace never crossed my mind. All I felt was rage. Papa was dead. I pulled her out of bed, and she stumbled out of the room.

Moments later, she screamed. I collapsed and laid in the fetal position on their bedroom floor. It was the most alone I had ever felt. I decided then and there that I was never going to feel like that again.

Everything changed that day. I chose to deal with his passing by hating him for leaving me. I viewed his heart attack as abandonment. Now I obviously see it differently. No man wants to die in front of his kid, but when you are 13, that's very hard to understand. I remember how my brother cried hysterically when he came home. He and my mother mourned together but I didn't join them. Even at the wake, I kept mostly to myself sitting in the corner with old photo albums. I didn't shed one tear during the wake, the funeral or the burial because I was too angry at something my mother said. She said God needed dad more than us. That was the first time I ever wanted to hurt her. God needed dad more than me? Considering God has the pick of everybody who has ever died, I would consider that a little selfish. I would've given anything to have just ten minutes with him if God could spare him, but I doubt that will happen. I would sell my soul—if I had one—for it. Maybe papa could've helped me not feel so afraid of what my disease might do to me? I need my father more than God ever could have.

"You never told me he died in front of you."

Marc didn't acknowledge her comment. "I almost deleted the last paragraph." He laid on the couch with his head facing the back cushions.

"I am glad you didn't. I actually think the ending is the most important."

"Why?" He grunted.

"The end is about now. It's about what you feel about your life now and that is more important than anything. The present is what is happening, and it's only in the present that we can hope to affect the future."

"I don't have much of a future, do I?" He dismissed.

"Maybe not in the long term, but this is a very slow disease and you still don't know if it will be totally debilitating. There are different types of MS. You still have time and life if you choose to make the most of them. You said you were afraid. Don't you think that it would be easier for you to face that fear if you allowed the people close to you to help you bear it? Have you told your wife yet?" she asked.

He didn't respond.

"Have you still not told anybody in your family?"

"I can't be sick to them. If I admit it, then it's real."

"Marc, it's real whether you say it or not!" She asserted.

"No! It's not real because they don't know about it. Until they do, I'm still me to them, independent and strong me. When they know I'm sick, I'll be sick Marc and that will change everything."

"I have an idea for next week. Can you write a fantasy of how you would tell Hannah?"

Before she even got to the end of her sentence, he sat there shaking his head.

"Please try," she asked.

"I don't know…."

2:5

"Dad, who were you speaking Italian with on the phone?"

Gabe rested his balding head in his hands and his stomach pressed the buttons of his shirt as he slumped in the chair.

"His name is Giancarlo and he works for your uncle. Something's happened." Gabe said wearily.

"How did he reach you?"

"He got my number from your uncle's files. He said he was trying to reach him for days and eventually went to his apartment. He said Marc's cell phone was still on the table and saw all the missed calls. I need to go tonight. How am I going to pay for this and what the hell am I going to tell your mother?"

"My graduation gift." Sara said,

"No, you can't."

"Yes, I can *and* I'm going with you." She insisted.

"Your mother will never agree to that."

"I'll handle her."

The same went for Gabe. His protests were futile. Sara was petite but made up for it with spunk and wit. She didn't stand taller than 5⊠3⊠ but her size had little to do with her forcefulness. Not only did she easily sway her father, Gabe came around to the idea that Sara would be an asset. Marc's affection for her would be a big help and Gabe conceded that he couldn't do this alone.

They quickly gathered their things. Within half an hour, Sara procured two direct flights from JFK. It was after 5:00 and their flight was at 9:50. There was no time to lose. Soon after, the taxi pulled into the driveway of their split-level home in Ridgefield, NJ. They hurried out the door. As they drove away, Gabe stared nervously at his cell phone.

"We have to call mom now."

Without a second thought, Sara took out her phone and called her mother herself. Gabe froze in anticipation. Not only would this plan sound crazy, Linda was not a fan of Marc.

"Mom, I need you to listen to me… There's an emergency and Dad needs me. Somebody who works for Uncle Marc called. He's missing in Rome. We're on our way to JFK airport."

After a terse exchange, Gabe was able to make out the words "put your father on the phone!"

"Mom, promise me you won't yell."

Sara looked at her father and instead of seeing a grown man, she saw a scared boy. Gabe reluctantly took the phone and brought it to his ear slowly, but his anxiety was unfounded.

Sara had done her job well. As her parents conversed, she felt accomplished as she quietly stared out the window on I-95 as they approached the George Washington Bridge. She was pleased when the conversation ended with "I love you too."

"I don't know why I didn't just think to have you tell her in the first place?"

Sara smiled. Though the problem of telling Linda was behind them, there was still the issue of Marc. Gabe scratched his salt and pepper curly haired head aggressively and quietly groaned with anxiety. It was the kind of noise people make when they would rather eat glass than do what awaits them.

"I have to admit, I'm glad you insisted on coming. Your uncle is... my brother is... difficult."

Sara giggled.

"No, I really mean it. There's so much you don't know."

"I know enough." Sara liked her uncle but knew he gave her father a lot of stress. She didn't like that he never came to see her grandmother, but she felt conflicted because he was always so good to her.

"Dad, why do you and Uncle Marc have such a weird relationship?"

Gabe never explained his past with Marc but knew the eight-hour flight made straight talk inevitable. When Sara asked what he did, Gabe said it was what he didn't do. He felt as though he abandoned his brother after their father died.

"I should've been around more. There are things about your grandmother you don't know, things Marc had to deal with alone. If you knew the whole story, you would know why he doesn't speak to her."

"What happened with Grandma and Uncle Marc?"

"Your grandmother's relationship with me as a child was normal but not Marc's. They were estranged. When Marc rebelled, she took it as a moral offence. Your grandmother equates love with obedience."

"So that's why you take his abuse?"

"Yes," said Gabe regretfully.

"Dad, you can't punish yourself for what happened over thirty years ago."

"I don't punish myself. He does, because he reminds me

of my bad decisions when it suits him."

Sara didn't know what he meant by that. From her perspective, her father was always responsible and dependable, but some men change when they become fathers. They deliberately don't tell their children things about their pasts, as if that would save them from their shortcomings.

"Dad, what do you mean by bad decisions?"

"I avoided my responsibility as a brother and a son. I also blew a small fortune."

Sara listened intently and for the first time, she saw him as a man beyond herself and his role as her father. Gabe adequately provided for his family and because there was always a lot of love and laughter, it never occurred to Sara that they didn't have a lot of money. That was the irony between Gabe and Marc. They had an abundance of what the other lacked. Gabe struggled but had a loving family. Marc had a lot of money but was alone.

"Your uncle was smart with the money we got after grandpa died. It's why he's so rich today. I spent what I didn't lose. Like your grandmother, I also enjoyed gambling."

"You were a gambler dad?" She tried not to sound disappointed. He'd never shared any of this with her and she didn't want him to suspect that she judged him.

"I did a lot of things you don't know about, but I guess you need to find out sooner or later."

Gabe became noticeably sad. Sara urged him not to worry.

"I haven't told you everything about the conversation with Giancarlo. He said that a lot of bad things have happened."

Sara and Gabe talked all the way to the airport. The car finally pulled up to the curb and now Sara understood the urgency.

"You ready? C'mon, let's do this." Sara charged.

Gabe still hesitated so Sara reached across the car and tugged him out the door. They walked briskly but Gabe was still noticeably distracted. As they walked, Sara asked about her grandmother. Gabe chuckled darkly. "That's a whole other conversation."

2:6

It was after 4pm. He was late. Dr. Rossellino fidgeted with a pen cap at her desk. Finally, Marc came through the door and apologized. She could smell the alcohol across the room.

"I told you not to come here under the influence and on top of that, you're late."

"I said I was sorry." He grumbled.

"Please let's try not to make this a habit."

In his usual fashion, Marc handed her an envelope. The memoirs were getting longer, which the doctor saw as a good sign. She held the letter, weighing it in her hands.

"Would you like to try to read this yourself?"

She always asked and he always said no.

"Maybe next week. As you've already noticed, I've had a few drinks. Perhaps when I'm sober."

She couldn't tell if he was mocking her.

After spending my Friday getting the electricity turned back on and working at my job all weekend, I got home Sunday to find Carl's car in the driveway. He and my mother had another one of their gallivants to Atlantic City. That was enough to ruin my day. I entered the house and could hear them talking loudly in the kitchen. I did my best to be discrete and headed up to my room without being noticed. I closed the door and laid down. As I drifted off to sleep, I heard a loud and obnoxious knock. It was Elaine. I told her I was busy, but she insisted. She said she got me a gift.

When the door opened, she complained about me calling her by her first name, but I didn't care because I couldn't get past her appearance. I found her repulsive. She needed a shower; her makeup was messy, and she was obviously hungover. Her attempt to seem 30 instead of 48 was humiliating.

She handed me a small pleather pouch. I unzipped it to find small bottles of toiletries, a comb and a lint brush for clothes. Not only was it a useless gift for a 17-year-old, she had already given me the same gift three months earlier. To make matters worse, she didn't even buy it. It was a freebie from Avon.

She actually asked me if I liked it. I didn't and I liked cleaning up her messes even less. I was yelling so loud that my voice trembled. Elaine resorted to her usual denial and tried blaming the electric company. She said she called to make the arrangement and that 'somebody' granted her an extension. Meanwhile I spoke with them. They never mentioned that.

She called me ungrateful and cruel because 'I' upset 'her'. Me! Then I called her a whore. That made her cry. I slammed the door on her face and could still hear her whimpering. Then I heard heavy feet stomping up the stairs. Before I knew it, my door was kicked in. It was Carl. I sprung out of bed only to find myself blindsided. Carl liked jewelry and wore heavy rings. That's how I got my scar. I was knocked back into my bookcase which fell on me. He then pulled me up by my shirt and continued to hit me. Before he knew it, my right knee was on his balls. I started kicking him uncontrollably. He screamed for me to stop and instead of my mother protecting me, she came to protect him!

Then things really got ugly. I chased her through the house, and she locked herself in the bathroom. I think that was the first time she was really afraid of me. I finally came to my senses and realized what was happening. I trembled from all the adrenaline and somehow my reason kicked in. I walked to the kitchen and called the police. When my mother heard me on the phone, she came out of the bathroom screaming for me to hang up.

The police arrived. Carl was arrested for assault and battery of a minor, but instead of arresting him formally, Carl went to the hospital. Elaine cried the whole time. She didn't talk about me chasing her for the same reason I didn't tell them: keeping up appearances.

After they left, her tears turned to rage. She screamed at me hysterically that Carl would never come back. As if I gave a shit? In typical fashion, I lied at school and work about the injury to my face. I said that I fell skateboarding. I just didn't want to have to talk about it.

This was the first time she had been able to get through one of his accounts without him interrupting her.

"Marc, this is your time. Is there anything else you'd like to share about that experience?"

"I really thought about killing her. Does that surprise you?"

"Do you want me to be surprised? I think you do because you like getting reactions from people."

Mark scowled.

"If you must know, I'm not shocked at all and it's not because you said you wanted to kill her, because I don't even believe it. I find it interesting you're so critical of your mother."

"You mean Elaine!" Marc growled.

"I mean your mother, Marc. You're so judgmental of her drinking and you come to my office late, smelling of alcohol. That's really interesting to me." She said.

Marc was silent.

"Oh, now you have nothing to say? I would like to explore you lying for her. You were taught to cover up. Is it possible that your inability to be honest about your pain and suffering, your illness and your sense of loss, is because you are covering up like you always have? As a result of your distrust for your mother figure, and sense of abandonment from a father figure, is it any wonder you still haven't told your wife that you're sick? Isn't your inability to share your illness just another defense mechanism? I don't how I can get you to understand that you can't run from this. It's going to follow you no matter how far you run because it is inside you."

2:7

Giancarlo, Gabe and Sara rushed through the crowded streets towards the police station that flanked Via del Corso. Giancarlo spoke with the desk clerk about the officer they needed to see. A young policeman in his mid-20s greeted them. Giancarlo presented Gabe and explained that they were looking for the homeless man found by the river a week ago. Gabe was confused by the description and that the officer knew to whom he referred.

"*Why* would you describe my brother as homeless?!"

Giancarlo apologized profusely and tried to calm him down. Sara was more suspicious than ever. Despite his attempts, it did not seem to pacify Gabe. "Enough of this evasive bullshit!"

Giancarlo fired back. "I promise you will find out. We have to go to the hospital."

"Why can't you tell us now?!" Sara interjected.

"The hospital is a ten-minute walk, but we have to stop at Marc's apartment. It's on the way. I'm asking you to trust me that it's better you don't come in yet. You'll see it soon enough."

Gabe and Sara reluctantly agreed. They sped through the neighborhood and in a few minutes arrived at Via dell' Orso. Giancarlo went up to the apartment and returned with Marc's phone, wallet and passport and handed them to Gabe.

When they arrived at the hospital, they were told to wait. A tall man dressed in a dark suit with a dark red tie met them.

"Gabe may be the brother of the man who was brought here." Giancarlo explained.

"Hello. My name is Doctor Martorelli and I'm the director of the hospital."

"Hello Doctor, thank you for your time." Gabe said earnestly.

"A man was brought here this week. He had no identification, so we didn't know who to contact."

"Why are you speaking about him in the past tense?" Gabe asked.

The doctor insisted he calm down and instructed them to follow. They got in an elevator and Gabe looked on at the doctor's hand to see if they were going up or down. He prayed for up because the morgue was always in the basement. The Doctor pushed the button for the sixth floor and Gabe let out a sigh of relief, but he was still very nervous.

"Doctor please, why can't you tell us anything yet?" He pleaded.

They exited the dreary elevator that smelled of bleach

and laundry into a long gray hallway.

"Until you identify him and prove that he's your brother, I'm legally not permitted to tell you anything."

"But Doctor, is this man alive?"

"Please follow me."

They gave up and followed the doctor through a maze of hallways until they reached a nurses' desk. Dr. Martorelli was soon greeted by another doctor named Dr. Tullo. She led them around the corner to a room with a closed door but stopped to warn them about what they were about to see.

The young doctor opened the door to see a man with a feeding tube and his left arm bandaged. Gabe began to cry.

Doctor Martorelli asked, "Is this man your brother?"

Gabe's tears gave way to sobbing and he was able to squeak what barely resembled a yes. Dr. Martorelli asked for identification. Gabe handed him his and Marc's passports.

"Thank you for clarifying the matter. Sir I need you to calm down so I can explain what happened."

Sara hugged her father. Giancarlo got him some water. He drank a few sips and handed it back, seeming to catch his breath. He looked like a large, late middle-aged doll as he sat blubbering. His full cheeks were drenched and his thinning hair disheveled. Sara just kept telling him to try to relax. She on the contrary was stoic and firm. She peered at the doctor and asked quietly but forcefully, "What happened to my uncle?"

"He is in a coma. He arrived in the emergency room eight days ago. He was found by the police along the Tiber river. His left arm was bleeding badly, and he was already unconscious. They treated the wound but because of blood loss, he went into cardiac arrest and had to be revived with a defibrillator."

Sara and Gabe listened in disbelief.

"He will wake up, but we don't know when or what to expect. He lost a lot of blood so we can't know how long his recovery will take. I am so sorry."

Gabe began sobbing again and finally Sara broke down. Seeing that Gabe and Sara were not up to it, Giancarlo interjected with some questions.

"I'm sorry, but could you explain the wounds on his arm?"

"That's where this gets complicated. While nothing was found near him, the location of the wound suggests it might have been self-inflicted. If and when he wakes up and we learn that this was an attempted suicide, we'd have to keep him here. Italian law says we cannot release a person who is a danger to himself without further evaluation and treatment."

Sara turned to Giancarlo and asked if there was anything he could tell the doctor about Marc's situation that might help in his treatment. Her eye contact sent a clear message of expectation. Giancarlo saw that she and her uncle had similarities. When Sara got angry, she made no attempt to hide it.

"He's a very heavy drinker and I think he suffers from depression. There's something else. He has MS."

Giancarlo finally volunteered the big secret and despite Marc's condition, that was the last thing they expected to hear. Giancarlo promised full disclosure about Marc's time in Rome. He started to speak but Gabe stopped him and asked if he and Sara could give him a minute alone in the room.

Sara and Giancarlo exited into the hallway. The hospital bustled around them as they waited. Giancarlo was surprised by the silence between them. He expected Sara to interrogate him, but she didn't.

"I'm so sorry this has happened."

"Thank you, Giancarlo. It's so sad to see my uncle like this and I can't even imagine how it is for my father."

"I wish I could say the same."

Sara didn't know what to make of that. She waited to see if he would say more but he didn't.

Gabe closed the door and walked to Marc's bedside. He looked even older than Gabe though he was nine years younger. None of it made sense.

"I know you can't hear me, but if you could, I want you to know that I wish I knew you better." Gabe's anguish intensified.

"I'm here and so is Sara. We're going to stay here until you wake up, and you will wake up! I can't change the past, and

I hope that when you awaken, you will give me the chance to make up for things. And how do you have MS? And how did we not know?" Gabe was now yelling. Sara heard him and tried going back to the room. He told her to stay out. He wiped his nose and continued speaking with a broken voice.

"Obviously you didn't tell us because you didn't want anyone to know. Out of respect, I won't tell anyone back home. It'll be our secret. You know, Giancarlo is your friend. We wouldn't be here without him. I hope you remember that when you wake up."

Gabe leaned over Marc and kissed his forehead. He went into the bathroom, splashed some water on his face, collected himself and exited the room. Sara and Giancarlo were still there on opposite sides of the hall. He looked at Giancarlo with gratitude. "Thank you for calling me. I'm sorry I was suspicious."

Giancarlo interrupted, "Please, don't give it another thought."

"No, I mean it. I understand why you wanted to wait."

"I have no reason to keep anything from you any longer. I just needed to verify that Marc was not able to tell you himself. He would've held it against me." Giancarlo said.

"You have come to know my brother well in a short time."

Sara interjected. "I'm sorry too."

He smiled quietly at her.

Marc's apartment was the easiest place to start. As they walked, Gabe went right into the questions. Sara walked behind her father and Giancarlo. Her mind was tired, not just from the journey, but also because she had been listening to Italian all day. Though her skills were better than decent after a semester in Florence, it was still a strain to follow every detail. As they walked, she drifted in and out of the conversation. Her eyes danced along the beauty of the Roman streets and the people. She was overcome by the smells floating out of the restaurants. Still, those were distractions from the haunting memory of her uncle with a feeding tube. How could this have happened? What would possess him to lie or try to kill himself? At least Marc was alive, she thought.

That part was resolved, but now there was the gravity of his coma and his disease.

They arrived at the door and entered the elevator. Giancarlo was nervous and knew this would be especially disturbing for Gabe.

"You should know that one of the reasons I quit my job was that I worried I'd find him dead. I opened the windows earlier to air it out."

He placed the key in the door and opened it slowly. Gabe and Sara walked in first. If the smell wasn't bad enough, the sheer volume of wine and liquor bottles, the sink full of dirty dishes, empty cigarette packs and the broken glass that littered the floor was that of a man unknown to them. Giancarlo continued to tell them everything that had transpired. When they went into the bedroom, they saw the broken mirror and the shards on the floor stained in blood.

2:8

My aunt and uncle were celebrating their 35th wedding anniversary. I had been avoiding family functions more and more, but this was for my Aunty Dorothy. She was an intermediary between my mother and me and she was the one person on that side of the family I liked. I was sad when she died.

I still had to force myself to go because I knew exactly what to expect. Elaine would act predictably embarrassing. Gabe and I would be forced to act like brothers. Now that I think about it, that was the one good thing about family gatherings. He and I always stuck together because we were much more like each other than either of us were like them.

Aside from that, the day would be at best annoying, and at worst excruciating. It mostly depended on how much Elaine drank. Everything worked against me that day. I was already in a bad mood before we arrived. When we finally got to the VFW, Hannah grabbed my hand and shook it lightly, telling me that it would be okay. She knew how much these gatherings bothered me, and she cared. Perhaps I never appreciated it enough.

Chapter 2 - Descent

I hadn't seen Elaine in months. Since we were late, I knew she would already be there and announce me when we walked in. The worst part was why. I was by far the most successful person in the family and she liked taking credit for it. It bothered me a lot more in my 20s but by my 30s I just played along because it was easier.

We walked up the stairs and I felt like I was being led to death row. We walked down the hall lined with dark wood panels, sashes and medals hanging on the wall, most of which commemorated the dead. For a moment, I felt like one of them. As we approached, the chatter got louder. I could already make out Elaine's voice in the crowd. We walked in the door and Elaine didn't miss a step. Thankfully, Sara greeted us first. She was about 12. That broke the initial tension, but it didn't last long. Elaine lit up and asked loudly enough for the whole room to hear for me to come and kiss her. Of course, when I reluctantly did, she didn't say anything nice. She could only focus on the gray hairs in my beard. With Elaine, everything was calculated towards getting attention, her own aggrandizement and exerting power. She would taunt me with passive aggressive jabs to belittle me especially when she had an audience. I was a prop she tried to parade around: a show dog. I put up with it because I had given up. It was no longer worth battling with her.

I remember she was wearing a bright red blouse with a corsage which I found vulgar. She wore red and flowers to someone else's celebration and I knew why. She loved being the mother of the richest member of the family. She knew most of them envied me and she liked that it made them also envy her. Sure, I probably came across like a snob so I can't blame them entirely. I always felt they were beneath me and perhaps I was too obvious. Still, most of them never showed it even if I acted like a dick, I could never tell who was nice to me because they genuinely wanted to be or, if they had their hands out. That is one of the biggest drawbacks of wealth; everybody has an agenda.

My cousin Don was one who never pulled punches. He was notorious for saying things like "must have taken a bath in the market last week" and he would act almost happy if I did lose money. It didn't bother me though. Don was one of the weightlifter types when we were young, but by then he was just an average fat fuck with a wife who was as mean as she was ugly. He was an idiot when we were kids and the steroids he took as a teenager made him dumber than he already was. I never thought more of him than a troll. He was older than me so when we were growing up, he used to beat the shit out of me. For that, I rather enjoyed his jealousy. It was quiet revenge for all his taunts. Even then it felt so weird to be ogled by the family because before I was successful, I was the odd kid who was made fun of by my cousins because I was nerdy and ethnic.

I made my rounds, trying as hard as I could to ignore Elaine's boisterousness. I sat with Gabe and his family at a table and hoped to be a wallflower, but I knew it would be hard. The volume of her speech got progressively louder. She did what she always did, monopolize the conversation.

As I listened, the food started losing its taste. Then she shouted over the room. "Tough love, right boys? I raised you right." I can still hear her Bayonne NJ accent and her tone in my head. Gabe and I attempted to smile our way through it but that was also futile.

Then I heard it. She brought up my bedwetting again. I could feel my hands tighten and my teeth clench. Then she actually boasted about ridiculing me for it. She spoke about it as if she had some master plan for scorning me to make me stop. Then, she finally crossed a line she should've never crossed. She bad-mouthed my father. She said that my father was too easy on me and that it was his fault I had such a difficult childhood. I couldn't take anymore. I grabbed Hannah by the hand, and we left. I never saw her again.

Marc sat smugly on the couch as the Doctor concluded reading. His eyes were squinted as he looked at the window where the raindrops were smattering the glass.

The doctor remained quiet for several minutes.

"Did this really happen?"

"Of course it did." Marc insisted.

The silence returned. Her piercing eyes poured over him from behind red rimmed glasses.

"Are you saying that you don't believe me?"

"To be honest Marc, I'm not insinuating anything. I'm confused because something seems very out of place. I have trouble ascertaining what was different about this particular day? Your mother has a rap sheet that rivals Al Capone. Why was this time different?"

"I'm not really sure. I guess it was just my breaking point with her and her bullshit."

"So, you're telling me this was just a random day where you finally had enough and that led to you completely severing the relationship? I will ask you again Marc, did anything else happen?"

"No... I don't know." He grew agitated and began fidgeting. His leg started to shake.

"Which is it? I can't help you if you don't tell me the truth. Don't you remember when I told you that you are safe here?"

Marc's face transformed. He gave the faintest suggestion of a nod, but his expression was hard and mean. Then his eyes locked with hers which made her heart flutter.

"You're a smart woman. So, tell me, where do you get off telling me I'm safe? I'm no safer from you than you are from me."

His tone was especially sinister, and he sat forward in the chair. He was obviously confrontational.

"Marc, you're not saying you want to hurt me?" Her breathing quickened.

"No. I'm not saying that. But for a moment you weren't sure. That, my good doctor, is the illusion of safety and I fucking envy you for it. You know what it is to trust. I don't. That feeling you just had defined my entire childhood."

"Perhaps you've had enough for today." Her voice was trembling.

"What if I haven't?" He said contemptuously.

"How dare you intimidate me? Your condescension is insulting! You are just covering up because you can't bear the truth. Now stop bullshitting me and tell me what happened!"

"Most of what happened in the dining room was true. What wasn't true was that we just left. I got up from the table and asked to speak with her in private. We went to a meeting room and I confronted her. I pleaded with her not to talk about these things publicly. She started calling me bedwetter again and when I demanded she stop, she berated me for trying to buy out her mortgage. I was doing it for her benefit, but she saw it as me trying to take away her autonomy. Then she said what really made me stop talking to her. She said she wished I was never born."

2:9

Giancarlo, Gabe and Sara were exhausted from a grueling afternoon. Contrary to the delight of the other tourists, they were sweaty and dirty from cleaning Marc's apartment. When they arrived back at the hotel, Gabe thanked Giancarlo again for all his help. As he was about to walk away, Sara surprised him and asked if he wanted to go for a drink. They agreed to meet back in front of the hotel in an hour.

Giancarlo arrived first, clean shaven and well-dressed. Sara met him outside a few minutes later.

"I *really* needed a shower!" Sara said.

She asked if he didn't mind speaking English, assuring him his English was better than her Italian.

"I haven't spoken this much Italian in over a year, and I was never very good in the first place. It's like exercising."

"It's quite alright. I always welcome opportunities to practice my English."

"But your English is so good!"

"It only sounds good. Some of the accents are so difficult and my vocabulary is lacking. I get to speak with customers at the restaurant but all we talk about is food and history. I can talk about that a lot, but I rarely get to have more involved conversations so please correct my mistakes." He said bashfully.

"Please, you're fine." She insisted.

"So you and my uncle speak Italian mostly?"

"His Italian is much better than my English."

"My dad speaks really well also."

"So you want a bar?" He asked.

"I prefer beer, but I know you Italians love wine."

"Don't be so pretentious." Giancarlo joked. "Not only do Romans drink beer, we rather like it. There are Irish pubs all over town. Actually, there's a very good German beer hall and they brew their own. They have great food too."

"A beer hall and German food in Rome? This trip has been so weird already, why not stick with the unusual?"

"I'm not use to being asked so many questions. In psychology, the psychologist does that. That's what I studied. What about you?" Giancarlo asked.

"I studied economics and finance. I was always good at math."

"Maybe you'll be as successful as your uncle? I've never seen a man spend money like him."

"My uncle is loaded."

"He made a very generous offer to me. He wanted to teach me real estate. It was hard to turn down."

"Why did you?"

Giancarlo looked at her dumbfounded. "We both saw the same thing at the hospital and the apartment, right?"

"I guess you have a point."

"I had two reasons for saying no. I have an indeterminate contract at the restaurant. It means I can't be fired. There are guys who have been there for 25 years."

"How can you live on a waiter's salary in Rome?"

"My house has been in my family for generations. It has no debt, and I will inherit it. I don't need more than what it costs to maintain it. I know being a waiter isn't the best job, but contracts are hard to find. I would be crazy to give that up."

"You'll inherit the whole house? You're an only child?"

Giancarlo became quiet. "Being around your uncle really started to have a bad effect on me. Watching him self-destruct was personal. Remember what I said outside Marc's hospital room about knowing how your father felt?"

"So, you're an only child now but weren't always?"

Giancarlo somberly shook his head.

"My brother Roberto died of a heroin overdose. His body was found in Villa Borghese. It's one of the most beautiful parks in Rome and I never go there."

"I'm so sorry Giancarlo."

They walked along silently for a few moments. "It was a moral decision. I felt like I was an accomplice. I knew I was enabling him and since I never stood up to my brother, I knew I had to stand up to him. The only thing I could do was quit because I was not going to feel guilty twice."

"You're very insightful. Do you plan to further your studies?" Sara inquired.

Giancarlo laughed disdainfully.

"What's so funny?"

"This is Italy."

Sara wasn't quite sure what he meant.

"Let me paint you a picture. To the outsider, Italy is perfect, like a gift wrapped in gold. Then you unwrap it only to find many more layers each less interesting than the previous. When you finally get to the actual box, you see it's terribly ordinary. Then you open it, and you know the truth, because you find death. That's what it's like for us. To tourists, everything seems ideal but to Italians, it's a backwards corrupt country. There's no social mobility, way too much bureaucracy and economic stagnation. You don't get a job unless you know someone, and competency matters little or not at all."

"Is it seriously that bad?"

"We live in denial, but the fact is, a good job pays 900 Euros a month and unless you have a family who owns a house like mine, that's about enough to rent a room with other twenty somethings far outside the center of the city with enough money left over to feed yourself."

"That's terrible. Looking around, that seems so far away. I would have never known that." Sara reflected.

"Of course you wouldn't. It takes time to understand and we're so good at covering it up publicly that you could never tell unless an insider explained it. That's the metaphor of the layers of wrapping paper. So many in my generation are leaving or have already left. One of my friends is considering moving to Germany. I've thought about leaving too but I'd never move there."

"What's wrong with Germany?" Sara asked.

"Germany traded their guns for a money printer. After two world wars, they finally conquered Europe without a shot being fired. They control the Euro and that's how they control us. When we had the Lira, we used to manipulate currency valuation to offset debt and interest rates but with the Euro, that's impossible, and it's crippling our economy. I don't want to seem mean-spirited because I don't hold the German people responsible for this, but their government controls us."

"Now that you mention it, I remember reading about this when I was in school. I had a professor who said the EU was doomed because the Euro is ultimately flawed. How can you have one currency with universal value for over 20 countries with different GDP, tax codes and costs of living?" Sara added.

"Exactly!"

"What you just said makes me understand what all that means to everyday people."

"How is it that we know this, and our government officials don't? That scares me. Either we continue to elect incompetent people or there's a darker game at play." Giancarlo reflected.

Sara grabbed his hand. She only intended to do it momentarily but once she did, she didn't let go, not only because she didn't want to, but also because Giancarlo held on tight. He was different than the average twenty-something back home. She never had a lot of luck with men. She was too smart most of the time and viewed most college-age guys as children living an extended adolescence. The good ones were mostly in relationships and she wasn't interested in being somebody's affair. That narrowed the choices considerably, which led to her not dating very much despite her beauty.

"This is the most original conversation I have ever had with a guy."

Giancarlo laughed. He remarked how Italy was a country full of cultured and well-educated young men with nothing to do but work in tourism.

Chapter 3

Awakenings

3:1

Electronics beeped like techno music. The light hurt his eyes when he tried opening them. He felt a plastic mask cover his mouth and was agitated because he couldn't swallow with a tube in his throat. Two nurses came bursting through the door and stood over him. They pulled his hands away from his face, but he resisted. Then he felt a pinprick in his arm and drifted back to sleep.

Three hours later, he opened his eyes. The mask and tubes were gone. His mouth was pasty, and his throat throbbed. Then a whisper slowly grew louder. "Hello? Hello?!"

"What is your name?"

"Marc Diodato." He croaked.

"How old are you?"

"45."

"Where are you from?"

"New Jersey."

"Do you know where you are?"

Marc's eyes squinted.

"I'm in a hospital."

"Do you know where?" She asked.

"I'm in Rome."

His words were labored. He asked for a glass of water. It was hard to talk.

"Do you remember what happened?"

He said he didn't, but he was lying. He remembered everything well enough to know he couldn't admit what happened by the river. Though he was groggy, he was quick enough to turn the tables and play dumb.

"How long have I been here and what happened to me?"

Dr. Tullo looked down at him suspiciously. "You were brought into the hospital two weeks ago."

"Is that why my arm is bandaged?" He asked.

"About your arm, are you sure you don't remember anything? You had a very significant wound and the doctors who treated you were all but sure it was self-inflicted. You do understand what that means?"

He maintained his story and even said that he had faint

memories of a struggle, but he didn't remember any details. Dr. Tullo stood stoically with her clipboard, scribbling down notes. She didn't like having to treat him coldly, but she had to ascertain whether Marc tried to kill himself. Luckily there were no witnesses and the weapon wound up in the Tiber.

"When the police found you, you were bleeding and unconscious. Luckily you were only a few blocks from this hospital, because your heart stopped in the ambulance. You were dead"

That was real, he thought to himself. His breathing quickened.

"Mr. Diodato, you have been in a coma."

Marc was despondent.

"There's one more thing, your brother and niece are here. They were the ones who identified you. A young man…"

"Giancarlo." He interjected.

"Yes, he brought them here."

Marc raised his hands to cover his face in shame. He pressed so hard his fingertips whitened.

"Mr. Diodato?" Dr Tullo repeated.

At first Marc didn't answer but as she turned to leave, he asked her not to tell his family yet. When she asked why, he desperately said he was not ready to see them. She nodded her head and left. Not only did he remember everything up to the moment he lost consciousness, he also remembered everything *after*.

Marc had a near-death experience. He saw his father Antonio. They embraced. It was the reconciliation of a lifetime. Though he was consumed by sublimity, his joy was corrupted by terror. Marc didn't believe in life after death and he was sure he was right, until he wasn't. As he labored at the mercy of possibility, balancing on a tight rope between rationality and hope, he felt like an elastic band in the hands of a manic chimpanzee. Then he remembered Antonio's words.

"I'm proud of you my son, for what you've done, and what you have yet to do. You are not finished. Your brother will be there for you. Forgive your mother. You don't have much time."

3:2

Sara waited on the other side of the Four Rivers fountain for almost half an hour. She and Giancarlo had their first fight. They had spent every day together since her arrival in Rome, but as with every new romance, passion eventually stumbles, and Giancarlo had reservations. He said they shouldn't spend too much time together, and they did. He said they shouldn't have a physical relationship, and they did. Then he said it was okay as long as they didn't have sex, and then they had sex. Finally, he said they couldn't fall in love and that was when he realized things had gone too far. Sara could have anyone, he thought. How could she possibly stay happy with a waiter from Rome? Furthermore, how could she stay at all? He knew she would eventually leave and he would be left alone, with only his broken heart.

Sara, on the other hand, wasn't thinking about tomorrow or the next week. She was calculated in other matters, but not with her romantic attachment to Giancarlo. This was a new experience. He wasn't chasing her; she was chasing him. She just couldn't convince him of her feelings. His insecurity bested him, and he reasoned that stopping their relationship before it got out of hand was in everybody's best interests.

In their last meeting, they stood atop the Spanish Steps. Sara pleaded with him to enjoy their time together as long as they could. That was the wrong thing to say. As far as he was concerned, she all but admitted it was just a fling. She tried to explain herself, but he refused to listen.

As she peered around the Bernini sculpture, she saw him exit the restaurant. He didn't see her coming at first and suddenly her ice blue eyes were like missiles headed straight for him. He stopped and before he had the chance to speak, all he heard was "shut up and listen. My father left this morning because my grandmother is in the hospital."

Before he could offer condolences, he was told to shut up again. "I'm staying in Rome for a while without a set departure date."

Giancarlo had trouble hiding his happiness. It did, after all, nullify his argument. The edges of his lips curved up to give the faint impression of a smile. She rested her hand on his heart.

"I insisted to my father that one of us needs to stay here until my uncle wakes up. He accused me of using that as an excuse."

"An excuse for what?"

"To stay with you."

"Is it?" Giancarlo asked hesitantly.

"Yes, but that's not the whole reason, so don't get ahead of yourself."

Though Marc was not her father, there was a shared trait that was undeniable. They had deep disdain for presumption, especially involving their intentions.

"I'm sorry I asked that. Please tell me the rest." He asked.

"Assuming my uncle *does* wake up, somebody is going to need to look after him. I want to help him and, I have my own reasons for staying in Rome aside from you. I just finished school, I don't have a job and I have money saved. I'll never have the chance to do something like this ever again. All that, *and you*, are why I am staying."

Since she was not leaving, there was no more argument. In the end, he was in love with her.

"Don't you have anything to say?!" She asked.

He reached out for her and pulled her close to him. She wrapped her arms around his waist, and they embraced in the piazza as if they were alone. He rested his head on top of hers, inhaling her scent, which felt like home. They remained locked for several minutes and it was Sara who broke the silence. She looked intently into his eyes, holding his sleeves tightly.

"I'm not just some stupid girl with a crush. I know exactly what I'm doing, and I'm responsible for my choices. It's my business who I choose to love, and you will not question my judgment or intentions about you again. You understand?"

There was nothing left to contest. He looked down at her and answered her question with a simple nod.

"What are you grinning about?" She laughed.

"Well, since your father isn't here, that means you're alone in this big city and don't really know anybody else but me." He said warmly.

"And?"

"Let's go to the beach in Ostia. I've wanted to take you there."

"What makes you think I have nothing else to do?"

"Well, do you?" He challenged.

"No." She said smiling.

He grabbed her hand and led her away.

"Can we stop at my house on the way to the metro? I need to clean up. My mother will be happy to see you."

He was overcome by the guiltless enjoyment and pleasure of her company. It was almost novel because he'd done nothing but resist his affections. He put his arm around her and for once he didn't have to ask himself if it was okay. Sara looked up at him and noticed there was something different. He was warmer and more spontaneous.

At Giancarlo's house, Sara and his mother had caffé and some pastries while Giancarlo changed. Sara thought it was amazing he wasn't fat. Every time she visited, his mother had an arsenal of sweets.

Giancarlo returned to the kitchen wearing a pair of slim fitting salmon shorts and a tight-fitting white shirt with sandals. The water still clung to his curls. Without saying a word, his mother handed him the saucer with the demitasse cup on it with the sugar already added. She then tried to convince him to eat a pastry, which he obliged after she begged forcefully. They chatted for a few minutes and then departed.

It was a glorious September afternoon, and the couple made their way to the metro at Piazza di Spagna.

"Your mother loves to fuss over you. I can tell it bothers you, but you let her do it anyway. That's sweet."

"I've never liked too much attention. I used to hide at my own birthday parties."

Sara burst out laughing.

"What's so funny?"

"I'm not laughing at you. It's endearing."

"She's been so sad since my brother died and all that loss gets put on me. Sometimes it's suffocating but I try so hard to not let it bother me. It makes her happy. That's one of the biggest reasons I'm still in Rome. Since he died, I don't have the heart to leave my parents."

Sara squeezed his hand. They moved along through the streets and went underground towards the subway platform. The train came and in typical mid-day fashion, the subway was packed like cattle in boxcars. Worse yet, Romans didn't have the courtesy of New Yorkers who allowed people to exit before boarding. It was a shove fest on and off the train and it was impossible to not be touching somebody in any given direction.

"I keep telling you to put your bag in front of you!" He insisted. "Metro thieves have turned pickpocketing into an art form. They can and will get you and I, for one, don't feel like changing our plans with a trip to the US embassy because you lost your documents!"

Knowing he was right, Sara moved her purse to her abdomen.

The train arrived in Termini where they had to change to the blue line. That train wasn't much better but after a few stops, the congestion finally thinned. They arrived in Ostiense and caught the train to Ostia. This train was above ground and provided a good view of the urban sprawl that spiraled out from Rome's center.

"I've grown very fond of the graffiti here. It's not like graffiti in America. It's political and some of it's very beautiful." Sara said.

"Graffiti is an ancient tradition here. Some people complain about it but most of us accept it as part of our history."

"Is it uniquely Roman?" She asked.

"It's common in the major cities. Milan and Naples have a lot, but not so much in the smaller cities."

"During my stay in Florence, I never saw anything like this."

Giancarlo chuckled.

"Florence is beautiful, but it isn't Rome. It attracts millions of tourists. Without them, it would be a ghost town. Florence is much smaller than Rome and it's not much of a contemporary city. It really is a living museum. Rome, on the other hand is a beast. It's alive and its violent past still lurks in the shadows."

"I find Romans to be very polite people, but I guess I see what you mean. I still can't get use to all the communist and Nazi graffiti. If you draw a swastika in America, it'll be on the nightly news followed by a police investigation."

"I need to take you to a soccer game at Olympic stadium. Then you will see how polite and we really are." He said jokingly. "There aren't enough cops to investigate all the swastikas. Italy has a fascist past that we try to ignore but there are open fascists and communists in our government."

"I've definitely realized that American political division is kind of a scam. We have this binary left/right and liberal/conservative thing, but we're not nearly as varied as the politics here. Conservatives thought Obama was a communist, which I thought was funny, because Goldman Sachs got him elected! Here you have a communist party that has seats in the parliament. Money has so much control over our politics that something like that could never happen. The Democrats wouldn't even let Bernie Sanders, a 'democratic socialist', win the nomination. Communists will never have any legitimacy. Now liberals are all worked up that Donald Trump is a fascist. They compare him to Hitler."

"Donald Trump is no fascist. In the 70s and 80s, the fascists and communists conducted bombing campaigns all over the country. My parents always talked about it. It was a scary time. My mother had a friend who was killed."

"Well, there's definitely a wider swing of the political spectrum here." Sara said.

"Not that it does any good. Italia changes governments like a mother changes diapers of a newborn."

"You're so witty."

Giancarlo smiled and thanked her. "So how about we start off with something historical and then head to the beach later?"

"That sounds good." She said.

"I want to take you to Ostia Antica first. It's a few kilometers from the coast, and it has gorgeous ruins.

Everybody always talks about Pompeii, but I think Ostia is every bit as beautiful and better preserved." Giancarlo grinned. "So what about my wittiness?"

"It's refreshing." Sara noted.

"Is it really that uncommon for American guys?" He asked.

"Yes!" Sara exclaimed. "You may have interacted with Americans through work and tourism but they're the ones who travel. That's the exception, not the rule. We have this weird tradition that goes back to the 50s. I remember debating it in school. Smart kids are portrayed as weak and boring. The ones who skip school and don't care much for culture, are the cool kids. Being sexy means being rebellious and stupid. We depict the smart kids as ugly, unattractive rejects who couldn't get laid in a brothel with a fist full of fifty-dollar bills. Today, things are even worse because men are portrayed as inept feminized idiots. Commercials show guys as fools who can't do anything on their own. People copy this stuff, and between that and all the self-obsession with social media, the US is full of man-children. I find them to be exhaustingly boring and anything but sexy. Sure, I like a man to be sensitive, but I also like a man who is tough when he needs to be."

Giancarlo laughed through her whole thought. "That's too funny because I said something similar to your uncle once!"

"Because it's true!" Sara exclaimed.

"Considering that Italy has been a colony of the US since the 40s, don't be surprised if that happens here soon." Giancarlo was regretful but they laughed. "But in all seriousness, I've observed the same thing in our culture. We have our own version of it here and it's no less insufferable. So many of us have mothers who pamper us well into adulthood. It makes Italian men arrogant, yet inept and lazy. We live at home until we're 40 and still think we're God's gift to women. If my mother wasn't suffering, believe me, I wouldn't tolerate her doing so much for me." Giancarlo said.

"It's worse in the states. For all your problems, Italians seem to have a more sober understanding of day-to-day life.

I guess what I'm trying to say is that I don't feel the pressure to pretend everything is great here. Growing up with my generation was so difficult because there was this expectation that you had to be positive all the time. Any negative emotions are treated like mental illness. I love talking about politics and history and when I try it with people back home, especially guys, they look at me like I'm crazy! I don't have to pretend with you."

"We have to get off here." Giancarlo said.

"What's this place called again?" Sara asked.

"It's called Ostia Antica." He said.

"Tell me more."

"Ostia is believed to be Rome's first colony. Supposedly it was founded in the 7th century BC. The oldest ruins date back to the 4th century BC. Most of what we'll see was built during the imperial period. Julius Caesar modernized it first and it continued to be fortified under Augustus, Tiberius and Claudius. By the 3rd century, over a hundred thousand people lived here."

"Why was this town so important?" Sara asked.

"All the grain and trade came through here. The Romans actually dug the harbor. Imagine that without construction equipment."

"Why not build it closer to the coast?" Sara asked.

Giancarlo grinned, "Because a town on the coast is a sitting duck for attack and vulnerable to tidal waves. It had to be protected so they built it about a kilometer from the sea."

"Tidal waves?!"

"There are many legends about sea monsters causing huge catastrophes that were tied to actual events. This whole region is seismically active. One of the largest eruptions of the past ten thousand years in the northern hemisphere happened at Santorini. It's believed to have caused a tidal wave a thousand feet high. It brought the Minoan civilization to an end and was probably the inspiration for the Atlantis myth. There's another instance where a large piece of Mount Etna in Sicily supposedly cracked off and slid into the sea. That was another catastrophic event. So aside from military risks, there were also natural ones to consider. That's why they bothered to expand the harbor and build the capital inland on the river."

"How do you remember all this information?" She asked.

"I'm interested in it." He said it as though it were a foregone conclusion. "I must admit, I have really enjoyed excellent conversations with your uncle. I really hope he will be okay."

They entered the antique city under the arch of the fortified walls. Sara marveled. They walked along Roman roads laid with paver stones that were still functional. The town was full of multilevel brick structures, temples and statues.

"This reminds me of the grid system in New York."

"Of course, it does. What most people don't know is that western civilization is basically post-Roman. It's common for historians to credit the Greeks and there's no denying their contribution and influence, however, when you understand the extent of how far Romans took Greek culture on their own, you realize they are even more important."

"I was always under the impression that the Romans were like cultural synthesizers and built their civilization on improving the ideas of others."

"That's a small detail. After the empire fell, the recipe for concrete was lost for a thousand years. Look at the Pantheon. Are you aware that almost the entire building is made of cement? It was built in the second century by Hadrian and it's still the largest free-standing concrete dome in the world. It has lasted without even so much as a crack for 1800 years and our bridges crumble in a decade. Whether it's engineering marvels, construction techniques, city planning, legal systems, courts of law, governing bodies or even our worldview and languages, the Romans have their fingerprints all over virtually every aspect of our civilization. Did you know that London, Paris, Cologne, and Barcelona are all Roman cities with exactly the same city planning? They're all centered on a land extension bordering the curvature of a river. Remember when I told you that at its height, this 'town' had a hundred thousand people? Rome had over a million!"

Sara interrupted Giancarlo's historical PhD dissertation

by impulsively grabbing his face and kissing him aggressively. Their lips parted and they gazed into each other's eyes. She said, "If we were alone, I'd fuck your brains out right here."

The couple broke into vigorous laughter, the kind that makes your side hurt. Wayward tourists passed curiously but they cackled without regard for their audience.

"I guess I can get a little carried away with my monologues." He admitted.

"Carried away? I fucking love it. Now let me ask you something. If they were so important, why are these stone ruins all that remains? For all their might and innovation, Rome fell." She said.

"Yes, it did, and it makes you wonder what will happen to us?"

Giancarlo's expression changed. He still smiled but there was a cynicism to it. He gazed around at the skeletal remains of what was once a bustling town.

"I remember reading Cicero when I was in school. Your uncle is a big fan also. It made such a huge impression on me not only because of his wisdom. I couldn't get over how much he could have been talking about our world today. I remember swapping out names in my head as I read, and it was exactly the same problems we have now. Had I not known that he lived in the first century BC, I could have believed he was someone alive today."

"I would like to read that some time. Are there any quotes you remember?"

"I have a few favorites. One of his funniest is 'children no longer obey their parents, and everyone is writing a book!'"

"That's hysterical. Describes the social media generation perfectly."

"And he said that over two thousand years ago."

The two walked along and it was as though the conversation would never end. They arrived at the remains of the public bathhouses. He thought she would find the mosaics very interesting. Then Sara's face changed from wonder to discomfort.

"More swastikas?! Are you fucking with me?" She protested.

"Sara, that symbol is a lot older than Nazi Germany. The swastika is said to be over twelve thousand years old. Prior to the 1930s, it was a symbol of good luck, which was why it was very popular in Roman design."

"I told you, I'm still not used to seeing them." Once she got past the initial shock, she poured over the remains of the floor in wonder, gasping at the depictions of Gods and Goddesses, sea mammals and horses, and intricate patterns of design that must have taken so long to create. There must have been millions of tiles. She imagined people enjoying the evening in the baths, making conversation, and sipping wine by the light of torches.

"I love these floors because you get a glimpse of how ornate these buildings really were." He said.

Sara remarked, "It's a shame that the exterior marble of all these temples is gone."

"Not only should you imagine these buildings faced in marble, don't imagine them white. That's a glaring misconception in modern depictions. I remember when I saw Gladiator, and though I loved the CGI renderings, I was annoyed by all the white marble. I remember telling your uncle that everything was painted. Even the sculptures were painted in flesh tone." Giancarlo insisted.

"Is that really true?"

"Without question. If you take micro samples of these statues, you will see the residues of flesh tone paint. Rome was a very colorful civilization not only in its architecture but with its people. America is not the first multi-cultural civilization. That's another thing the Romans did first and they arguably did it better." He said.

They spent almost two hours walking around Ostia and their last stop was the remains of the great theatre. They climbed to the top and sat on one of the bleacher stone slabs.

"This held three thousand people. It was originally built by Agrippa in the reign of Augustus." Giancarlo said.

"It's so beautiful. I can't believe how much is still here." Sara noted.

"I have a book I'll show you that has artist depictions of what Rome actually looked like. It's safe to say the modernity of it will shock you. Now there's nothing here but a few bricks, rubble and dust. Most people in Rome even a hundred years ago had no idea that so much history laid buried beneath their feet."

"If mighty Rome could fall, imagine how fragile we are?" Sara proposed. "Think about my uncle. He was kind of untouchable. His wife was like a model. Aunt Hannah was gorgeous, she still is. I wanted to be her when I was growing up." She sat there with a faraway gaze and became sad. "Look at them now. They're divorced. My uncle is in a coma. Maybe decay is inevitable?"

"I think about that a lot. People have this illusion of permanence. It's kind of weird when you think about it. Nothing stays the same. Everything is in a state of flux, yet we try so hard to achieve permanence. How do we not realize that it's a losing battle?" Giancarlo said.

"That's one of the reasons I decided to stay. I want to seize every opportunity I have, while I have it. No one knows when our time is up, when everything changes."

She reached out and placed her hands on Giancarlo's face, pulling it close to hers. She gently kissed his lips and his face whispering "my beautiful man" over and over.

Giancarlo stopped her and asked, "Yours?"

Sara whispered in his ear, "Yes, *mine*."

She kissed him again as they were bathed by the Mediterranean sun. Evening was approaching, and the angle of the light was starting to produce more dramatic shadows that accentuated the architecture. They could hear jets taking off nearby from Fiumicino airport, the sound of birds and the buzzing of wasps.

They made their way back to the train to head for the beach. Shortly after, they exited the antique train station. Sara immediately remarked that modern Ostia looked similar to parts of the Jersey Shore. They hadn't yet eaten, and Giancarlo suggested they go to a good seafood restaurant. Ostia was known for seafood and most was caught locally. They went to a place Giancarlo knew and feasted on oysters, shrimp and crab. They had pasta dishes with clams and mussels and finally whole branzino al sale, a Roman classic.

The wine flowed in their glasses like the conversation rolled off their tongues. They finished with a caffè and dessert.

It was a perfect meal for their already perfect day. Dusk was approaching so they left the restaurant and made their way to the outdoor bar in time to watch the sunset. Ostia was a great place for sunsets as it was on the west coast of the Italian peninsula. The sun set on the water. They sat there on the black volcanic sand beach and the waitress brought them two beers. There were many people enjoying their pit fires and the beautiful evening air. Sara sipped her beer and chuckled at the idea.

"This is illegal in New Jersey. You can't make a fire and drink beer at the beach." Sara said.

"People in your country love to talk about how free you are and how the rest of the world envies you for it. From what you and your uncle have told me, I'm starting to think you've been scammed."

"My uncle always said that in politics, truth is irrelevant. What people believe is true is all that matters. Pretty cynical, huh?"

Giancarlo took a big swig from his beer and said, "Your uncle is a pretty cynical guy."

"My uncle, despite all his flaws, is a tragedy—especially now that he's sick. How much do you know about him?" Sara asked.

"Not that much, I guess. He doesn't share much."

"You had to have made an impression because you knew he's sick. None of us knew." She said.

A warm wind was blowing from the southwest and Sara shook her head to get hair off her face. The sun was starting to turn orange as it neared the horizon on the sea. They both watched the sky illuminate and the warm bands of orange spill onto the water.

"What did you mean by tragedy?" He asked.

"My uncle had a hard life."

"I knew about your grandfather. He shared that with me. He refers to his mother as 'Elaine'. All I knew was that he hasn't seen or spoken with her in years."

"Did he ever talk about my dad?" Sara inquired.

Giancarlo didn't want to get into that. Marc had spoken of his brother and it wasn't always flattering.

"I really like your father… and based on how Marc described him, he was not what I expected. Do you know anything about what happened between them?"

"I know it has to do with what happened after my grandfather died. I don't know how he's going to take the news that my father had to leave because of my grandmother?"

"He has to wake up first. You know, I'm such an ass! I haven't asked you about that once today. Has your dad called with any news?"

"She's fine, it was just a scare and I suspect one of her stunts for attention."

"That really sucks."

"I'm fine. She is who she is and my uncle's disdain for her is not all one-sided. Beyond that, I don't mind that you didn't ask because I don't want to think or talk about it. My family is going through a lot with my uncle. Today has been the most beautiful of beautiful days. That's all I want to think about right now."

A tear fell from Sara's eye as Giancarlo looked at her with adoring concern. He reached to wipe it from her face. At his touch, she grabbed his hand and pulled herself towards him and sat between his legs. She pulled his arms around her like a blanket and nestled there as he caressed her arms to warm them as the evening breeze blew harder. Sara leaned her head back to kiss him on the cheek.

"Will you stay with me at the house tonight?" She asked.

"I was hoping you would ask."

Neither came out and said it, but it was different, and they both knew it as they gazed at one another. They were in sublime agreement and marveled at how they were together under the most unlikely of circumstances. What were the odds of meeting Marc, their fathers coming from neighboring towns and everything that happened to eventually bring Sara to Rome? After all that and thousands of miles, they rested in each other's arms as the sun said goodnight. It felt like fate. Regardless of chance or destiny, it was so good, one of those rare moments where you feel safe and totally absorbed in someone. Giancarlo was going home to Marc's apartment with her. There was nothing more to do than to enjoy the dusk fading into the night, the sweet smell of her skin and the angelic sound of her voice. For the moment, life was truly grand.

"Remember when you asked me about my favorite quote by Cicero? I have another one and it's my favorite. He said, 'gratitude is not only the greatest of virtues, but the parent of all others.'"

"That is so true." Sara whispered. "Why is it your favorite?"

"At this moment, I'm most grateful for you."

3:3

Did Marc really see his father or was it just a delusion? He woke up often during the night waffling between preoccupation and sleep. It was slowly driving him mad and the first glimmer of salvation didn't come from the prospect of an afterlife.

He was in a new reality. He even wondered if he had somehow experienced a quantum fluctuation and that in his coma, his consciousness migrated to an alternate reality. He felt like himself and at the same time, he was a stranger in his own skin. He remembered Marc Diodato as though he remembered being someone else in a previous life, but now his feelings, thoughts, priorities and goals were all in flux. He no longer felt bitter, which was good, but it was replaced with anguish. He didn't know how to process it and even when he felt happiness, he still felt naked because his nihilism no longer had supreme authority. All he could do was lie in bed, minute after minute, going over the same questions. Even his experience of time felt different. He stared at Gabe's number for an hour but could not bring himself to call.

Marc put the phone down on the bed and sobbed. His eyesight was blurred and as he looked up over the pillow that covered his face, he saw that someone was standing at the foot of his bed. He blinked quickly and his heart raced as the likeness began to take shape.

"Hello Sara." He didn't even get past her name and his voice cracked. The tears started again.

"How long have you been awake?!" She was overjoyed but confused.

"Three days." He said ashamedly.

"Why didn't anyone call us?"

"I asked them not to?"

Seeing him in his state made her understand it was better not to pry. There must be a good reason.

"I know I don't look it, but I'm really, really happy you're here." His sobbing intensified. Sara approached him slowly and cautiously placed her hand on his shoulder. As soon as he felt her touch, his sobbing increased.

"What is it?"

"Where's your father? I need to see him."

"Dad had to go home and I decided to stay." That was all she could say for now. "I've been staying at your apartment."

"You've seen my apartment?" Marc gasped.

"Yes, I saw it. Dad, Giancarlo and I cleaned it. You don't have to be embarrassed."

"But I wasn't ready."

Sara recounted Giancarlo's phone call, the flight and everything that had happened so far. This only deepened his shame.

"I treated Giancarlo terribly and he still tried to save me."

"He did and I want you to know something. He actually made dad and I angry because he led us around and wouldn't tell us anything until he could verify that you couldn't tell us yourself."

"He knows me well."

"You should know, he admires you."

"Somehow I get the impression that you admire him too." Marc studied her face. She glowed. "Are you and he…?"

"Yes, and I need you to listen because I think I'm falling in love with him. I don't want you to…."

Marc cut her off mid-phrase. She expected disapproval. To her surprise he said, "Nothing would make me happier."

"I'm really glad to hear you say that because I have something important to tell you. I've decided to stay in

Rome, and it's not only because I'm in love with him. I'm also staying to take care of you. I'm already taking steps to teach English so I can make a little money, but your graduation gift was more than generous. Between that and my savings, I'm good for a while. So, I'm here, and you're not getting rid of me."

"I don't know Sara."

"Uncle Marc, it's not up for discussion and while I respect your opinion, you have no say in mine."

It was the first time he smiled since he woke up. "If you're going to stay, it's good you don't take any shit from anybody, especially me."

"I can take care of myself."

"What happened to your father?"

"Dad had to fly back to the States a few days ago."

"Why?"

"Grandma had an accident, but it turned out okay."

"Are you sure she's okay?" Marc began to tremble as he remembered his father's words. He gripped his pillow in disbelief. How could this be a coincidence?

"What is it, Uncle Marc?"

"Nothing."

Sara took out her phone and pulled an international calling card from her purse. Marc stopped her.

"Sara please, I said I need to talk to your father, but I didn't mean now!"

She saw the terror in his eyes.

She called her father and briefly said that Marc woke up. She didn't even say she was at the hospital.

3:4

Dear Doctor Rossellino,

I hope you've been well, and I wish I were contacting you with good news. I'm not doing well, and as you predicted, Italy has been disastrous. Worse yet, you and I had agreed that I would stay in touch and I disappeared. I'm aware that I broke a commitment, but I really need to speak with you. Something has happened and you're the only person I can

93

talk to about it.

I was pronounced dead and I had a near-death experience. I saw my father and I'm freaking out. I don't feel like me anymore.

I hope we can schedule a video session.

Despite how grave all this sounds, there has also been some good. I made a friend here who ended up saving my life. I have so much to tell you. I imagine that a FaceTime session isn't very orthodox, but it's the best I can do. I'm not coming back to America any time soon and I need my doctor.

I expect to be out within a few days and then we can set a date and time. Lastly, I want you to know that you were right. I'm going on meds for bi-polar disorder. Please get back to me as soon as possible.

Thank you.

Sincerely,
Marc Diodato

3:5

The taxi pulled up to the green door on Via dell'Orso. Marc had been awake for a week and he still hadn't seen nor spoken to anyone besides Sara. He remained despondent and withdrawn with a faint expression of anguish that never seemed to leave his face entirely.

The apartment on the other hand looked very different, not only because it was clean. Sara liked flowers which perfumed the air and added color. The windows were all open and the sun shone brightly. Marc walked through the apartment, eventually arriving at the mirror he smashed with his head. All the broken glass had been removed from the wardrobe.

Sara studied him carefully. For the first time she really noticed how her uncle had aged. The last she had seen him was the previous year, and by his appearance, it may as well have been five years. He had more gray hair and his skin had thickened. It made her sad.

"I wish you could've known your grandfather. He was subtle and patient, just like you."

"You're going to find out that sometimes I'm not so subtle."

"Believe me, your grandfather had the patience of a saint."

"I'm not sure I am patient either Uncle Marc."

"That's because you have your mother and grandmother in there."

"Uncle Marc, when you describe grandpa, it sounds like my dad. I wish you knew that."

"You're right. He is like him. My whole life I always thought I was more like your grandfather but recently I realized that he's a lot more like him than I could ever hope to be. I may have gotten some of his intellectual qualities, but your father has his warmth and character. I lack both. He's a good man and how little I've noticed really bothers me."

Sara was interrupted by the coffeepot. As he watched Sara prepare the caffè, he visualized someone else in the room. Suddenly, he had an urge to see Giancarlo and Sara together. The thought made him happy and better still, he didn't feel the urge to resist it because it was for their sake, not his.

"Tell Giancarlo to come over."

"But I thought you didn't…?"

"Never mind what I said about not wanting to see people. It was dramatic and stupid. I've had too much time alone and would be far better off in both your company."

They drank their caffè and Marc suggested a walk to the supermarket. He put on some presentable clothes and the two departed. When they exited to the street, Sara grabbed his arm and he felt so fortunate. *The most beautiful girl here is with me.*

Sara kept asking about her grandfather. As Marc thought more about him, he was beginning to feel like Ebenezer Scrooge after his visit from Jacob Marley, trying to dismiss his near-death experience as the result of sour food or a burst of cold air, but it was futile. Then he remembered one of his favorite stories about his dad, one that he had heard from his uncle when he was a boy.

"I've got a good one. Have you ever heard the lunch story?"

"No, I don't think I have." She said.

"Great, I haven't told this one in years! Your grandfather had an internship in high school with a chemical company. Some of the other boys tried to push him around because he was younger. One day, his lunch was missing. He asked around and no one knew. The next day, the same thing happened. On the third day, it was stolen again but about an hour later, they were back in the lab and all of a sudden, one of the boys ran to the bathroom. Your grandfather signaled for a few of the other boys to follow him if they wanted a good laugh. When they got to the bathroom, they heard the boy groaning on the toilet. Your grandfather supposedly said something to the effect of 'terrible case of diarrhea huh?' and 'it's a shame you don't have any toilet paper.' The boy demanded the toilet paper and your grandfather told him that he could have it but on two conditions. He had to admit to stealing his lunch and agree to buy him lunch for the next month."

"How the hell did grandpa know all this and how did he get him to agree?"

"Easy. He had the toilet paper because he knew somebody was going to get diarrhea, he just needed to wait and see who it was. He also found out this guy had stolen from other boys on the team which earned him some loyalty."

"But how did he know?!"

"The sneaky bastard spiked the food with a laxative and waited to see who ran to the bathroom."

Sara stopped dead in her tracks and began to laugh uncontrollably.

"Is that not the best fucking story ever?" Marc asked.

"I have to admit, I know I said dad is like grandpa, but I cannot see my father doing that."

"Me neither. Me on the other hand, I could definitely do something like that."

"That I believe! Really nice to hear these old stories."

Marc was just as happy to tell them. Still feeling like he was seeing ghosts, he pivoted to a very unexpected topic. He asked Sara if she believed in God. Sara was surprised by the question and Marc even more by her answer.

"I don't know what I believe?" She wondered.

"If you had to say one way or the other, would you believe or not?"

"OK, one way or the other? I would say I do but, in the end, I am agnostic."

"Agnostic or Atheist?" Marc asked.

"Agnostic, I do know the difference." She asserted.

"And what about life after death?" He asked,

"Maybe, even probably, but I don't know."

"But you think it is possible?"

That she said yes intrigued Marc, but their philosophical discussion was cut short by something far more profound. They arrived at the supermarket.

"I don't know if I can go back to American supermarkets after getting used to this." Sara joked.

"I remember when I was nine, your grandfather took me to the markets down in San Pietro. I can still smell the butcher shop and the endless rows of dried sausage hanging from the cciling. My father bought a three-inch thick steak with sausages and cooked everything on the outdoor fireplace with natural wood charcoal. I can still remember the taste and the smell."

"Oh my God. That sounds unreal." Sara said ravenously.

"Believe me, it was, and it wasn't just the meat. They had fish, poultry and cheese markets that were all separate stores. The pasta was made fresh at another small store. None of the stores were corporate and the food was local. Unfortunately, that Italy is dying."

They wandered around the store and filled their cart with the night's menu. They stopped at the deli counter and were faced by an entire wall of different types of prosciuttos, salami and other lunchmeats. The scent of salted pork and succulent fat was consuming.

Sara turned to Marc. "Regarding your question before about God? When I eat prosciutto, I really think I do believe in him."

"Ahh, the truth!" Marc cackled loudly.

Their number was called, and the laughter continued. After the man finished cutting the prosciutto, Sara asked with a sweet smile, "One slice please?" The man affectionately grinned at her and peeled away a transparently thin slice from the plastic sheet and handed it to her. She thanked him and turned to Marc. She tore it in half, made the sign of the cross, and said, "Body of Christ." Marc followed with "Amen."

As they shopped, Marc recalled how funny she was even as a child. He remembered when she was about six years old at Christmas. She wanted a doll but got the blonde one instead of the brunette. She said she was going to write Santa another letter and then decided she would write Mrs. Clause because if it were addressed to her, Santa would read it. Then when Linda explained that Santa has millions of children to bring toys to and mistakes happen, Sara was worried Christmas was too much work for an old man.

As Marc recounted the story, Sara listened and shook her head in amusement. Then she reminded Marc how not everything was bad and that there were good times too.

They finished their grocery shopping and as they waited to check out, Marc realized they bought way too much food for three people and told Sara to ask Giancarlo to invite his parents. He was enjoying the spontaneity of the evening, but Sara was no less surprised by it. Marc went from not wanting to see anybody to planning a dinner party. He paid for the groceries and they left the store. Moments later, Giancarlo texted back and confirmed his parents would attend.

Marc was having what normal people called a nice day and for once, he made no attempt to ruin it. Also, he was in a good mood because despite his humbuggery, Marc liked spending money on people. They stopped at his favorite wine boutique on the way and got something special. It was a night where no expense was to be spared. At first Sara questioned whether or not he should have alcohol but Marc assured her that he was not an alcoholic. He drank with an intention that he no longer had. She was skeptical but understood.

Though he hadn't seen Sara and Giancarlo together

yet, he knew things between them were serious and it was as though tonight was an old-fashioned Italian ritual of the parents of the couple meeting to officially recognize their relationship. Then he thought he should share this with Dr. Rossellino. She'd be pleased that he was not only enjoying himself but that he was doing it for others.

They arrived back at the apartment and expected Giancarlo in less than an hour. They no sooner put the bags down and Marc asked Sara to call her father. They hadn't spoken yet, but this seemed as good a time as any. Sara took out her phone and as soon as he saw she placed the call, Marc grabbed the phone out of her hands.

"Hi honey, how are you? Any news on your uncle?"

"I'm okay Gabe."

Gabe was delighted by the surprise and even more delighted when Marc insisted on buying he and Linda tickets to return because he wanted to plan a family reunion in their father's hometown. He was even more surprised when Marc asked about "mom." Gabe could not remember the last time he had called her that.

They concluded their call and Marc heard a male voice coming from the kitchen. He opened his door and stood in the doorway watching them do food prep with their backs turned.

"Maybe we should open a restaurant?" Marc blurted out.

Giancarlo turned around quickly and smiled. He rinsed his hands and the two embraced without saying a word. Sara looked on happily. It was a very special moment that Sara exploited to poke fun.

"Why don't you two get a room?"

The two men laughed loudly and then Marc took the joke a step further. "That's an interesting idea. Come with me."

The two walked back to Marc's room and he closed the door.

"I told you when we first went to dinner that I wouldn't suck your cock." Giancarlo joked.

Marc laughed loudly. "You should be so lucky."

"It's good to see you, Marc."

"You too, Giancarlo. Thank you for being a good friend. Without you, I might be locked up in some state hospital right now."

When Giancarlo asked about what happened the night of his suicide, Marc declined to elaborate but promised he would eventually explain. He wanted to talk about Sara and set the record straight about their relationship.

"I want you to know I have been very respectful and honorable with her."

"Would you relax, please? I know and I approve."

Giancarlo was very relieved. "I'm very happy you feel that way."

"I do; but as a matter of formality, know that if you hurt her, you die."

Giancarlo smiled warmly. "Well, I won't, but even if I did, you'd have to catch me old man."

Marc scoffed. "No, *I* won't. I'm rich and I'll just hire somebody faster than you."

"In all seriousness, I've been waiting to tell you something. It's about my brother. I've lived with so much guilt that I didn't do enough for him. I've had this feeling that through you, I could redeem myself and to see you like this really means something to me."

Marc smiled back at him. "I want to tell you something in all seriousness too. I can't think of a more deserving guy to be with my niece. I'm sorry for what I put you through. I also want to assure you of something. I don't want to die anymore. Now, let's go make dinner. I'm fucking hungry."

"We've reported for duty, madam general." Giancarlo said sarcastically. Then he joined Sara at the counter and the two gazed at each other adoringly as Marc looked on.

"You can kiss each other in front of me—I know you want to."

"How dare you be so presumptuous!" Sara joked.

Kidding aside, he was right. They did want to kiss one another, and it delighted him. It was the first time he felt light. He gave the kids instructions, and they did most of the work in preparing the meal all the while Marc was fanaticizing about how his life might have turned out if he had children.

Suddenly he realized that this was his new reality and that pleased him even more. Sara was a wondrous addition to his life in Rome and Giancarlo was back. As he watched, he found he couldn't stop smiling, which made him smile even more.

Chapter 4
Family

4:1

The chest pains that lured Gabe back from Italy were nothing more than indigestion. Elaine was back home with her TV blaring. She sat at attention in her wheelchair, awaiting her favorite televangelist, wearing her born-again Christian merit badge proudly on her sleeve. Because she'd accepted Christ as her lord and savior, she could always depend on his forgiveness, which justified past and future indiscretions. Her kitchen table was her altar, complete with her bible, cordless phone, the TV remote and a stack of mail order catalogs that were mostly for show. Gabe took away her bank card long ago.

Her mobility problems started in her 60s but by her 70s, her laziness accelerated her decline. She was physiologically already in her 80s. Aside from getting herself on and off the toilet, microwaving water for tea and preparing basic meals, she had no remaining independence. She could be alone during the day but needed help bathing and getting in and out of bed. Though Marc was absent, his money wasn't and without it, her lifestyle wasn't possible. She had not a penny to her name beyond her social security, but as far as she was concerned, it was still her house and her decisions, which she affirmed to whomever would listen. Marc used to say a monster that ate her money lived in Elaine's purse.

As for her Gabe, he was either a champion or a loser on any given day. Today he was the loser because there was a problem at the store and he was two hours late. His wife Linda was convinced there were parallel realities where the two Gabes interchanged through a porthole in Elaine's kitchen. One Gabe was wonderful, obedient, dutiful and loved his mother. His double was conniving and ruthless, intent on stealing her house and putting her in an institution.

In her contempt, she didn't bother to notice the sweaty sheen on his forehead as he walked in the door; she was too busy feeling neglected and disregarded.

"Good thing I wasn't holding my breath." She grumbled.

Ignoring her sarcasm, he said hello and asked how she was feeling. She continued watching TV and never asked

Gabe how he was. All that mattered was his tardiness. Gabe stood invisibly at the counter going through the mail.

"Mrs. Walsh's son is taking her to Florida. I just adore her."

She yelled because her hearing aids were not in and this must have been the sixth time she mentioned it. She had a penchant for repeating herself and it was only because she liked hearing herself talk. Gabe's relationship with Elaine as an adult was very different from his youth. As children, Gabe was the chosen son and Marc the black sheep. Marc was not only unplanned; he was a mishap of faulty birth control. Gabe was athletic and popular. Marc was moody, introverted and rebellious.

Since Elaine made everything about herself, Marc's withdrawal from her and his relationship with Antonio were indicative of betrayal. But things had changed. Now Marc was her wealthy and genetically superior son to whom she imparted the noblest values of work and industriousness. She enjoyed bragging about him and telling amalgamated stories—combining fantasy with little tidbits she heard from Gabe to have new material. Most of the people she spoke with regularly only knew her for a few years. She conveniently left out that Marc and she no longer spoke.

She met Mrs. Walsh in sub-acute rehab after a hip replacement. They were roommates and, in all likelihood, Elaine regarded Mrs. Walsh much more fondly than she regarded her. She was one of many people who wandered in and out of Elaine's life. When she wore people out, she found new ones. Most of her longer relations were either dead or no longer speaking to her; that made inventing stories easy.

In typical Elaine fashion, the subject changed like the wind and she was back to all things televangelist.

"I love him so much." Her voice cracked as she beheld her savior looking so magnanimous in his megachurch studio. "He has a foundation for children in Africa. They're so helpless and can't do anything for themselves. Have you ever seen his house? It's so beautiful."

Gabe overlooked her overt racism as she rambled from one subject to the next. During the commercial break, she went on about a movie she saw for the third time that week. Then she got around to her usual complaints about her sister.

"Your aunt Colleen called me three times today! She keeps going on and on about the neighbor across the street parking in front of her house. She could give coffee nerves!"

Of course, Aunt Colleen was the only one of her generation who was living and the only family member who still spoke to her. Elaine had burnt many bridges. She borrowed money she didn't pay back and was notoriously two-faced. But to Gabe, she was just an old lady now. At this point, what did it matter? Keeping the peace was the most important thing. Even when she got nasty, Gabe blew it off. Elaine never admitted she was wrong and challenging her was futile.

When her evening nurse arrived, Gabe kissed his mother good night. She never looked up from the TV when he left.

4:2

"I like you better without the beard." Dr. Rossellino commented.

"Thank you. Before we get into anything, I want to apologize again."

Marc was fidgety and twitchy. She heard his fingers nervously tapping the desk.

"I've been basically losing my mind over seeing my father."

"Your email alluded to this. Do you know why, specifically?"

"I accused people with faith of mental illness. Now, *me* of all people, the antichrist of atheists has a near-death experience. You can't even make this shit up. This is why I've been so desperate to speak with you. How the fuck can I know if this was even real?!"

"I'm not sure what I can do to help you with this, Marc."

"Do you think it could've been real?" He retorted.

"As your doctor, it's not appropriate for me to offer opinions on entirely subjective experiences."

"Forget that. As a woman, as a human being, do you

think this is possible?!"

"As a woman? Okay, the truth is that I don't know."

Marc's head slumped. He grunted in frustration and then laughed dismissively.

"What's funny?"

"When I asked Sara if she thought God existed, she said the same thing! I can't find anybody I respect to offer an opinion." He lamented.

"Marc, nobody can answer this except you, but I might have some advice if it helps?"

Marc eagerly listened.

"Only you know what you've experienced. I've worked with you long enough to know that you will not be satisfied until you work this out."

"Not even death is an escape! Most people get all warm and fuzzy about forever, but it terrifies me. I feel like I'm having a panic attack."

Marc's desperate laughter continued.

"Before analyzing the experience, can you give me some details?"

"I could smell him when we hugged."

At the utterance of those words, Marc finally broke down and sobbed loudly. Dr. Rossellino let him cry and resumed with her questions when it began to subside.

"That must've been beautiful. What was it exactly that made you cry?"

"I loved it. There are no words."

"Many people would give anything for an experience like that. You should think about that. My advice to you is to focus on how you feel instead of what you think. Perhaps that'll help."

"But I have always tried to ignore my feelings because I've never trusted them."

"That is exactly why I am suggesting it; can we backtrack a moment? As much as I'm interested in your experience, I want to know how you died in the first place."

"This is the hard part and I want you to know before I say another word that I don't want to die, and I'm not suicidal. Do I have your word that you trust me?"

"I trust you as much as I can, Marc. If I suspect you may be a danger to yourself, I have to act accordingly. You understand what that means?"

"Yes, and I guess I'll have to take my chances." Marc continued. "Killing myself was probably my intention all along even if I didn't want to admit it. My drinking got worse and one night, standing on the banks of the Tiber river, I dragged a broken bottle across my arm." He broke eye contact with her and started crying again. "When I realized what I might've really done, I panicked and that actually surprised me. I started to walk towards Castle Sant'Angelo and screamed for help. I tried flagging down a car but nobody stopped. Finally, I lost my balance and wacked my head against a stone wall."

"Why would fear of death be a surprise, Marc?"

"Because I thought I knew I wanted to die."

"Marc, this is the first time you ever openly expressed an emotion other than anger with me. It means you're reconnecting with yourself. Do you remember anything else?"

"My father hadn't aged. He was as plain as you are now. I can't remember the last time I felt so happy. After our encounter, it was a blur. I saw pieces of my life. Then I remember seeing my body and all the medics around. I watched them use a defibrillator to revive me. Suddenly I was taking in a huge breath and I opened my eyes. From there I remember nothing until I woke up in the hospital to learn that I'd been in a coma for two weeks. I've not been the same since."

He banged his fist on the desk and then turned his face away from the camera.

"At least I'm not feeling sorry for myself about my ex-wife and ex-best friend."

"Your ex-wife?" She interrupted.

"We're divorced and Paul is no longer my lawyer. He came to Italy to check on me. We got into a terrible argument and I threw a bottle at his head. As for Hannah, I'm not allowed to contact her. It was part of the divorce. Maybe we pay for our sins in this life? I guess some things are so bad you can't expect forgiveness."

"Actions have consequences and people aren't obligated to forgive us. We take that risk when we treat people with impunity." She commented.

That stung to hear. Marc also brought her up-to-date on Gabe, Sara and Giancarlo, which she regarded as positive.

"You're very fortunate, don't forget that." She responded.

"I know."

"Marc, despite everything that's happened. I'm so relieved by your progress. Whatever happened to you, some good is coming of it because you've never been so forthcoming. I urge you to focus on that. You've spoken without solicitation or provocation in this session—more than in all the others combined. I'm not reading your life to you; you're telling me yourself."

4:3

Life on Via Dell'Orso started to resemble something delightfully ordinary; Marc worked in the morning and spent his afternoons out. He was finally enjoying the city.

On the domestic front, Sara was teaching English, which afforded her the time to accompany Marc around town. Giancarlo basically lived at the apartment and life had settled into something almost harmonious. It was October. The weather was more like September in New York without the humidity. It would be the rain season soon, but for now, the days were warm with cool nights.

One afternoon, Marc and Sara were exploring a little-known museum beneath Piazza Navona. He had eaten there for months but never bothered to notice that the oblong shape of the piazza had an explanation. It was built on top of the stadium of Emperor Domitian, completed in 86 AD. It was part of the Forum and could seat 80–100k people!

Sara and Marc wandered about the massive stone portico that was the old entrance. There was a trove of artifacts and models of the old structure, but Sara seemed distracted. She wasn't her usual self. After hushing his inquiries, Marc insisted they return to the apartment.

It was late afternoon and Marc left his room for some water to find Giancarlo sitting at the table.

"Something's wrong with Sara and I'm worried." Marc said.

"I'll go check on her."

Giancarlo rushed to the room and opened the door to find Sara curled up on the bed with her back to the door. He closed the door. It was dark.

"I'm pregnant, Giancarlo."

"Are you sure?"

"I bought several tests. I'm pregnant." She whispered. "What do I tell my parents?"

"Your uncle is going to freak."

Sara began to weep. Giancarlo tried to console her, but she rejected his affection.

"Aren't you the slightest bit excited about this?" He asked tentatively.

"Excited? My parents are going to lose their shit. I'm only 22. I was supposed to be vacationing and helping my uncle. Getting pregnant wasn't part of the plan!"

"Will you marry me?"

"What?"

"That wasn't the answer I was hoping for." He said sadly.

"Giancarlo. I just graduated top of my class. I want a family, but I was hoping to start a career first." She said desperately.

"Sara, I want to marry you." He insisted.

Marc overheard raised voices. He got up from his desk and approached their room. Amid the back and forth, Sara and Giancarlo heard a knock on the door.

"Can I come in?" Marc asked.

"Come in." She said reluctantly.

Marc saw that Sara had been crying. Neither said a word.

"Are you pregnant?"

Sara and Giancarlo tried to be stoic.

"You are, aren't you?" He asked forcefully.

"Marc?" Giancarlo nervously interjected.

"I wasn't asking you."

Sara began to cry. His gaze turned to Giancarlo.

"I want to marry her!" Giancarlo said passionately.

Marc's eyes changed from anger to shock. Sara finally screamed.

"Both of you get out!"

Marc led the way, and both went into the living room. Giancarlo sat down staring off into the distance. Marc went to the kitchen and returned with two glasses and a bottle of grappa.

"Just drink it." Marc said plainly.

"Are you...?" Giancarlo blurted but before he could even finish his sentence, Marc responded with an assertive, "No, I'm not angry."

Giancarlo let out a sigh of relief.

"Honestly, I'm surprised you're not."

"You love my niece?" Marc asked. He was leaning back in his armchair, head slightly cocked to the side like a military officer conducting an interrogation.

"Please don't look at me that way." Giancarlo murmured.

"Then answer my question."

Giancarlo's large hazel eyes made contact. He was almost in tears.

"I love her more than you could know."

"I know you do and that's why I'm not angry."

"Then why make such an issue of the question?" Giancarlo retorted.

"I wanted to hear you say it. How did you feel when you found out she was pregnant?"

"Honestly? I was happy."

"If you were happy, then why are you crying?"

"I'm a waiter in Italy, and now she has to choose between her career and motherhood. I'm fucked because there's no scenario where this ends well. She will suffer and the thought of it kills me."

"Were you serious when you asked her to marry you?"

"Of course! It just flew out of my mouth, but as soon as I said it, I knew I meant it. But at the same time, I'm terrified. What could I possibly have to offer her? Love doesn't pay the bills. I'm not stupid, Marc. When the lovers finally kiss in the movies, six months later, they're fighting about money and throwing dirty underwear at each other."

"Doesn't even take that long." Marc said in jest.

The two started to laugh.

"Is money your only concern?" Marc asked.

"No, it's her career. She's brilliant and she's going to have to stop her life at 22 to be a mother? As much as I want her to be the mother of my child, that really bothers me."

"What if her career didn't have to be compromised and you had the chance to earn a lot more money?"

"I can't think clearly enough to process hypotheticals right now…"

Marc interrupted again. "Just answer the question."

Giancarlo looked up. "It would be great."

"Okay then. Go get her." Marc insisted.

"Bad idea."

"Go ask your fiancée to come out here."

Giancarlo didn't expect to hear Marc call her that. He got up reluctantly and walked slowly back to their bedroom, but they didn't come out. Marc heard raised voices again. He went to the bedroom and entered, this time without knocking. Sara was sitting on the edge of the bed holding a pillow and Giancarlo stood with his back to the dresser.

"Giancarlo, would you mind giving us a minute?"

Giancarlo left and closed the door.

"Uncle Marc, I don't want to talk about this now!" Sara began to sob again.

"Sara, do you love him?"

"What difference does that make now? My mother is going to lose her shit and daddy is going to be so disappointed." Her tears worsened.

"I've never been terribly affectionate. I've even been accused of being cold and I don't handle emotions well. What I'm trying to say is that it's hard for me to know what to do in moments like these."

Sara didn't respond.

"Can I sit down?"

She nodded.

"The other day I was in my room and I heard you and Giancarlo laughing so hard together I thought you would faint. I stopped what I was doing and just listened. I couldn't stop smiling. Then a second later, I was filled with remorse because I felt the sting of never having my own children. For a few moments, I enjoyed the fantasy of being your dad."

Sara's head turned and she slowly leaned into Marc's shoulder. He put his arm around her and they sat quietly. Then she unexpectedly said, "Yes." She lifted her head to look at him.

"Your question, if I love him. The answer is yes."

"Please come out. I need to speak with both of you."

"Can I have a little more time?"

"Actually no. We need to talk now." Marc's tenderness grew stern like any father who wanted obedience. He stood up and opened the door, gesturing her to move.

Giancarlo's eyes followed her through the room, watching her every move. She sat on the couch but left about a foot of space between her and Giancarlo.

"I have a solution." Marc said.

"Of course you do." Giancarlo dismissed.

"I heard you ask her to marry you. I'll ask one more time if you were serious."

"I was!"

Turning to Sara, Marc said, "So what's your answer?"

"It's not that simple. It's not just a matter of what I want. There's a lot to consider and I have to…."

Marc cut her off. "I get it. I'm saying take away the consequences, worries about money and career, and just answer based on how you feel about him. What would be your answer?"

Sara stared back at him and then turned her gaze to Giancarlo. Her body softened. She placed her hand on his knee and said unwaveringly. "My answer would be yes."

"Then we will figure this out as a family. Let's start with a toast."

"Pick up your water, Sara."

She smiled and the three raised their glasses.

Marc said, "To family."

He and Giancarlo clinked their glasses, but Sara withdrew hers.

"What's the matter?" Marc asked.

"It's not the right toast." She protested.

"What is then?" Asked Giancarlo.

"To *our* family."

4:4

A day had passed and Marc was still elated. For the first time, his experience of seeing his father didn't anguish him. He sat there, staring off into space with a faint grin across his lips. His hands dropped to his side and he began to laugh. It started with a soft chuckle that deepened into his belly. Not wanting to be heard, he got up to close the door. When he sat back down, he covered his mouth to mute himself but couldn't.

Sara overheard him and was concerned. It was an odd kind of laughter, maybe even manic. She knocked and his laughter grew even louder still. When she entered, she saw tears in his eyes, but he looked joyful.

He got up from his chair, grabbed her, and started waltzing her about the room. He hummed melodies, prancing like a giddy schoolboy. Sara was led around like a mannequin in amazement. Marc had the smile of the Cheshire Cat.

"What is all this about?" She demanded.

Marc's laughter hastened as she waited for an explanation. He caught his breath and as his heaving diminished, he gazed at her earnestly.

"Do you remember when I asked you if you believed in God and life after death?"

"Yes, and now that you bring it up, I need to ask you a very serious question. I've been wanting to ask you this for so long but haven't had the courage. I know it might be impulsive, but now feels like the right time."

"Ask me whatever you want." He said.

"Did you see anything when you were dead? I've read about near-death experiences but don't know anyone who has had one … or do I?"

"I didn't realize I was so obvious."

Sara sat down on the bed and pulled her hair back into

a ponytail.

"When I saw you the first time at the hospital, you were terrified. I'd never seen you like that."

Marc told Sara everything about seeing Antonio. She listened in awe.

"When you saw me in the hospital, I was being torn apart. I drove myself crazy trying to understand it, but just now, your pregnancy was the final piece of this puzzle."

"What puzzle?"

"There are different levels of truth. Some truth is objective. It can be observed, measured and quantified. You and I can both watch the sun come up. We both see it. Put us in separate rooms and we'll still describe the same event. We could set our watches and prove that it happened at a certain time. Better yet, we could even film it. That truth gets to be called fact, but what about truths that can't be independently observed? How can I prove my joy about your child to you? I can say it and you can see behavior that substantiates it, but you can't feel my joy any more than I can feel yours. It can't be recorded or displayed. Does that make my joy any less true? Your only choice is to believe me or not, and if you do, it will be an act of faith. I was laughing because I've realized that faith and trust are almost the same thing! It is not just about God; it is about people, it's about life. I had no trust because I had no faith."

She always admired her uncle but never thought him profound until now.

"As for faith, I had another epiphany. Believers and non-believers are the same. I either believe in God or I don't. They are equal statements differentiated only by a positive or negative verb. Both assert something that can't be known and to accept the incomprehensible as truth is an act of faith. The skeptic falls short of a decision and understands he or she has the option to believe, or not. I was remembering our conversation the day I came home. I reflected on what you said, and you helped me understand that belief and knowledge are mutually exclusive."

Unable to remain silent, Sara interjected, "How do you mean? Are you saying there's no bridge between scientific fact and faith?"

"That's exactly what I'm saying. You might find this funny, but if God miraculously decided to manifest and finally put all the contentious bullshit to rest, proving to the whole world that he exists, it wouldn't be belief anymore. It would be knowledge. I don't need to believe in facts just like we don't need to believe in the sunrise because it's information. I don't need to believe what I can know, and I cannot know what I can only believe."

Sara sighed. "You're lucky I can't drink or smoke pot. We would be here all night. What does this have to do with grandpa?"

"There's no way to know if the experience was real. I can only choose to accept it or not. On that basis, either decision is no more plausible or probable than the other. It was so real, and to accept it, I need to make that leap of faith, because I can't prove it, not even to myself. Now I understand that the choice is not factual, it's aesthetic. Dismissing it makes me sad and depressed. Believing it makes me happy. I've craved some kind of absolution with your grandfather and somehow, now I have it. That's why I said what I did about dying. It made all this possible, and the idea that grandpa sees all of this makes me even happier."

Sara saw Marc as a new man. "Before I say anything else, you're blowing my mind."

"I'm blowing *my* mind!" He laughed harder. "The doctor was right, I solved it, but the part I can't get over was that I solved it by realizing I couldn't solve it!"

"Uncle Marc, you're fucking crazy and I adore you for it."

"I can't wait to tell your father, but it has to be face to face when we're in San Pietro al Tanagro."

"We're going? Is it planned?" Sara asked.

"I have been talking with our cousin Paolina."

"I cannot wait to go!" Sara said. Then she remembered her own ordeal.

"Telling your father about grandpa will be an easy conversation compared to the one about you. We have to discuss how and when we're going to tell your parents."

Sara put her hands to her face and slumped onto the bed.

"It can't be a phone call and we can't just ask him to come over. He's already asking me how long I intend to stay and now I'm getting married and having a child. If I try to tell him this over the phone, he'll freak. And if that's not bad enough, my mother? Ugh. What the fuck am I going to do?"

Marc chuckled.

"I'm glad *you* think this is funny! Seriously, what am I going to do?"

"You're wrong. There is a way and I need you to trust me. I've resolved centuries of theological dissonance, so I think I can handle your parents."

4:5

Sara was happy to be back in Florence playing tour guide for Giancarlo and Marc. She was continually reminded of how she remembered Florence being bigger when she was in college. After living in Rome, she now considered it Disneyland for cultured adults, a comparison Giancarlo found amusing.

By evening, they came by a small restaurant outside the center of the city called Il Gato Nero, the black cat. They arrived there haphazardly as Marc had grown tired and wanted to sit. It had good reviews, but the restaurant was eccentric with only a handwritten menu on photocopied paper. Giancarlo was skeptical of the musty smell, but they decided to stay nonetheless. The tables were long picnic-bench style with wooden chairs. The walls were covered in guest photographs that dated back decades. Despite the odd first impression, there was consensus about the extraordinary quality of the food. While enjoying their pasta, a man in a bloody apron, wearing a blue bandanna, wandered around the dining room. "Check out Hannibal Lecter." Marc said.

When he asked for Parmesan cheese, the man refused on the grounds that it was an offense to the meal because you were not supposed to put grated cheese on Bolognese sauce. He was the chef, Giuseppe, who Marc dubbed the pasta Nazi.

They then shared a Bistecca Fiorentina. When Giuseppe

returned, Marc made a point to tell him it was the most flavorful steak he'd ever had. They started talking and eventually Giuseppe sat with them. He enjoyed speaking with tourists about their experience in his restaurant. He eventually ended up comping a bottle of wine for the table. Every time a bottle was opened, Sara asked to smell it. Her face would contort in agony wishing she could have just a sip. Giancarlo joked that after the baby was born, he was going to buy her a kilo of prosciutto and a gallon of the best Brunello.

It was late in the evening and most of the other guests had left, yet their time with Giuseppe showed no sign of slowing down.

"You're missing a glass." Giuseppe said to Sara.

"I can't have alcohol now." She said regretfully.

"Are you sick?"

"No, I'm pregnant." She was still unaccustomed to saying it freely.

"That is wonderful news! Who is the father?"

Marc and Giancarlo chuckled. Giancarlo took a sip of his wine; with a look of pride and awkward gratitude, he said, "I am."

"Let's have a toast—but wait!"

He called over the only remaining waiter working and asked for a special drink for Sara. He also asked him to bring another bottle. A few minutes later the waiter came back with an orange-colored drink in a champagne glass and an old looking bottle.

"This is blood orange juice and sparkling water with a sugar cube." Giuseppe said.

Sara smiled widely. "I love blood orange juice!"

The waiter brought fresh wine glasses to the table and opened the bottle. It was a '97 Chianti. He poured it into a decanter, swirled the wine around and poured a drop in Giuseppe's glass to taste. Giuseppe did the usual smelling, swirling his glass, holding it to the light. He then drew his head back, taking all the wine in his mouth. He squelched it around like mouthwash, opening his lips slightly, pulling air in to continue to oxygenate it. With his eyes closed, he swallowed, and his face slowly transformed into a warm smile.

"Is it ready to drink so soon?" Giancarlo asked.

"It's ready now!"

"How long have you had this wine?"

"Since it was bottled. I have a lot of wine downstairs that has been there for years and the longer it stays, the more it costs."

"I'm expecting this to wow me." Marc commented. "I'm more often disappointed by older wines. If it sat on a shelf and exceeds eight years, it's usually over the hill. I've returned expensive bottles."

"Once the wine is exposed to room temperature for any period of time, it goes through changes that cannot be undone. Temperature is so important and to have what is in our glasses right now, the wine has to remain at about 13 degrees." Giuseppe explained.

"Wouldn't it freeze?" Sara asked naively.

"That's Celsius, my dear," Giancarlo said.

"I still feel like an idiot here with the measuring system."

"55–58 Fahrenheit." Marc added.

"What you're about to drink has gone through the proper aging process. Aged wines are pricey because it gets expensive to provide the proper conditions. So, are you married?" Giuseppe suddenly asked.

Sara and Giancarlo laughed and discretely said they hadn't set a date yet.

"The news keeps getting better and better. There's nothing more beautiful than young love. We have a lot to toast to." They raised their glasses again. "It has been my pleasure to have you as my guests. I meet people from all over the world. It's one of my favorite things about having my restaurant, but I do not often get a pregnant, soon to be newlywed, especially one as beautiful as you—and who speaks such good Italian."

Sara blushed. He turned to Giancarlo, "You are a lucky bastard and if you screw this up, I will find you and feed you to the wild boars that will be in next year's tomato sauce."

"I will bring him to you, ready to be butchered and you can pay me by the pound." Marc joked.

They all laughed. "I told you once that you'd have to

catch me first, old man." Giancarlo said playfully.

"And I said I wouldn't have to." He made the money gesture with his fingers.

The volume of the laughter increased as their glasses raised again. "To new friends." Giancarlo said. "And family," Sara added.

A woman with dark eyes, wavy blond hair and a slender figure walked through the door and unexpectedly sat at their table. She turned to Giuseppe. "Are you getting drunk with the guests again?"

"These are special guests! This is Marc and his niece Sara from America and Giancarlo from Roma."

Giancarlo cut him off. "I'm only half Roman. My father is from Salerno."

"You look Salernitano. This is my sister Giovanna."

Everyone exchanged greetings and the waiter brought over a glass and placed it in front of her. Giovanna asked for the bottle.

"You opened this tonight? You all must have made quite an impression." She raised her eyebrows.

"Sister, we have much to celebrate. These two beautiful kids are in love and expecting a child." Giuseppe said jovially. The wine was starting to bind his tongue.

"That's lovely news!" She turned to Sara. "You're such a beautiful girl. Your father must be very proud of you. She looks just like you." Giovanna looked at Marc.

"She is my niece, actually. I wish she was my daughter." Marc admitted.

"That's very sweet," Giovanna said. "It's nice to see so much love in a family. Families find too many reasons to fight about nonsense. Who is your father?"

Marc interjected. "My brother. He's in America. Sara is my Godchild."

Giovanna turned to Sara, "Your father must be so happy."

An uncomfortable silence followed.

"My brother doesn't know yet."

"Are you afraid he'll disapprove?" She asked.

"I just graduated college with honors and I came to Italy to help my uncle with... some things and met Giancarlo who was already working for him. It just kind of happened. Thankfully Uncle Marc is helping us work things out."

Giovanna turned to Marc, "How good of you."

"Don't say that yet; I'm trying to devise a way to tell my brother that he will accept without getting killed."

"Easier said than done." Sara was half joking and half serious.

"He might get hysterical, but he would not be the first father to hear this news. Is he really going to deprive himself of his grandchild? He will be fine in the end." Giovanna dismissed.

"I surely hope your optimism wins the day." Marc replied.

"So, are you here on vacation?"

"No, I'm a real-estate developer and this trip is partially business. I've been here for a few months and have no plans to leave."

"We are all working together, actually." Sara interjected.

"How lovely." Giovanna remarked.

"I never had children of my own, so I'm teaching the kids my business. It is nice to share with them because I won't live forever. As for my brother, he and my sister-in-law will be back in a few weeks for a family reunion. We plan to tell them then. We want to show them that the kids are doing well and building careers. That should soften the blow. Contrary to your expectations of a good outcome, Giovanna, I still don't expect my brother to handle this well."

"I love an old-fashioned man, you lovely boy." Giovanna said to Giancarlo.

"Are you married?" She asked Marc.

There was another uncomfortable silence. "I was."

"Welcome to the moral majority. I was married too."

"I'm divorced." Marc said. "You?"

"Yes. I'm better off now. He had a secret life."

As she spoke of him, Giuseppe's facial expression darkened. "That bastard. If I see him, one of us will leave in a police car and the other a hearse."

"Easy with your blood pressure." She said nonchalantly. "Giuseppe hates him. Me, I don't give a fuck. Leaving him was a good thing. It's just hard to date; most people after 35 who aren't married are single for a reason. Have you dated much?"

"No. Not at all, actually."

"Not to ruin it for you, but everybody is crazy. You'll see. This is why porn for women is a fast-growing industry!"

The whole table burst out laughing except Giuseppe, who turned red. The conversation continued and the restaurant had long since closed. They sat there as if it was Giuseppe's kitchen at home. Not only did they finish the wine, they also finished half a bottle of grappa and two rounds of dessert.

It was approaching midnight and Sara noted they should be headed out.

"Headed where?" Giuseppe asked.

"Back to Rome. I'm sober and I can drive." She said confidently.

"I forbid you to drive at this hour. My brother and I own a bed and breakfast and we have a vacancy for a family. You will stay there tonight."

"That's so kind, but we don't want to be an inconvenience." Marc said.

"That's ridiculous! I insist."

"You are very kind." Sara said. She looked at the table and it was full of dirty glasses and plates. The staff had already gone home. "Since I'm the only one who is sober, let me clean up before we go?"

Giovanna smiled at her. "You kind girl. Come, we will do it together. First, these men look like need some caffein."

Giovanna and Sara made caffe´ and while the men drank, they cleaned up.

"Your niece is lovely." Giovanna said to Marc as she and Sara brought the glasses away from the table. Marc smiled at her.

"Thank you for putting us up tonight." Marc said to Giuseppe.

They finally left the restaurant. They drove through the city and arrived at a square on the northern side of town.

"It's that one." Giovanna pointed. Giuseppe and Giancarlo had already arrived. The building had three floors. It was cut stone with large bay windows.

"Do you live here?" Mark asked.

"No, this was our family home growing up. Now my brother and I live on a property outside of town. We have a farm."

Giuseppe interjected. "Our eggs, milk, some cheese, vegetables, olives, olive oil, and table wine come from there."

"That's amazing." Sara exclaimed. "Can we go see it?"

"But of course." Giovanna said kindly. "Tomorrow."

She and Giuseppe led them into the building to the apartment on the first floor. There were three rooms and a kitchen. Giovanna helped them get settled by providing them with fresh pillowcases and turning on the heat because it was chilly. The house was old and quaint, perfect for a family who wanted to vacation in Florence. It had high wood plank ceilings with plastered walls and ceramic tile floors. The rooms were spacious with large beds. Giovanna handed them the key.

"I will take my leave of you." She said.

"We'll see you tomorrow?" Marc asked.

"Of course you will. I'll be here in the morning around 11. There's a great bakery on the opposite side of the square. We can go there for breakfast."

"I'm very happy to have met you." Marc said timidly.

"It was nice to meet you as well."

They exchanged the customary two kisses and then Marc grabbed her by the hand and kissed it. Sara came bouncing through the room and kissed Giovanna and Giuseppe good night followed by Giancarlo. They exited and in less than a second, Sara turned her big eyes towards Marc with unrestrained vigor. "You like her!"

4:6

Gabe had nine missed calls and four voicemails in 20 minutes.

First message: "This is your mother. I'm not going to stay in that damn nursing home while you go off to Italy! I know what you're doing. You're trying to put me away and take my house! I am *not* going."

Second message: "You are conniving and ruthless. I'm calling my lawyer!"

As he listened, he was both amused and worried because her lawyer died three years ago.

Third message: "You answer this phone, you ungrateful son of a bitch!"

Fourth message: "I wish I was dead! That's what you want anyway. You see me as a burden and want me out of your way. Why don't you just kill me and get it over with."

Gabe sat in his office with the door closed. He was draped on the chair like a dirty apron. He had two hours before his shift was over. That didn't seem like a long time, but she could do a lot of damage in two hours. At least now she couldn't get drunk anymore and her pain meds were under lock and key. Two years earlier, she went through a month's supply of pain pills in a week. She was found on the floor mumbling about losing five thousand dollars at the craps table and shouting that the dealer had stolen her money.

Managing her care was becoming a full-time job which could've been ended by putting her in a nursing home. Gabe continued to resist that idea. He knew his mother could be cruel, but he made excuses for her. Her father had been an abusive man and she grew up in a toxic environment. While he believed his mother was just crazy and couldn't help herself, her need for attention and anger issues were worsening, and today he couldn't indulge her tirade.

He blocked Elaine's number for the rest of his shift. It was a risk he had to take which made the next two hours crawl along. He felt like a 5th grader enduring 30 minutes of detention. It was hard to focus but he did his best. Finally, 5pm came and he slipped out of the office as fast as he could. No sooner was he out the door and he tried calling. There was no answer. It was a 20-minute drive to the house and of course it was rush hour in northern New Jersey. twenty minutes would likely be forty. He never beeped his horn or lost his temper despite the anxiety gurgling in his belly.

He zipped around corners of side streets lined with swamp maples and white oak trees and pulled up to the house. Elaine's precious red door signified danger that was verified when he entered the house. Her wheelchair was empty, and she was laying on the floor in front of the old record player in the living room.

"Damned shoes got caught on the rug and I fell! I'm fine. Just can't get up myself. I called you so many times!"

"Mom, what the hell were you doing up in the first place? You know you're not supposed to get up with nobody here." Gabe said.

"You will not tell me what to do. I raised you!"

"One day you're going to make a mistake and it's going to get you killed."

"I don't give a damn if I die. What is my life worth anyway?"

"Oh yeah? Then why were you so hysterical when you called me from Italy? You seemed pretty scared about dying then."

She looked away through the glasses that sat crookedly on her nose. Elaine notoriously passed over anything that was inconvenient or inconsistent with her version of the truth. Gabe sat her up and grabbed under her arms.

"Okay, one, two, threeeee!"

Gabe heaved and up they stood. Elaine held her walker as Gabe quickly pulled the wheelchair beneath her to sit down.

"Are you sure you're not hurt?" He asked somberly.

"I'm fine," she snapped.

"I don't know how much more of this I can take, mom."

Elaine remained defiant.

"You're terrified of a nursing home and yet you seem to keep doing everything to end up in one."

"That's what you want!"

"Mom, Marc and I are the only reason you're not in one already! You'd have been in a nursing home a long time ago. I don't know how to get you to understand that you need to stop these outbursts. You think falling will keep me from going back to Italy? The arrangements for your stay at Twin Pines are made. You'll be there while Linda and I are gone. That's it!"

Elaine continued to look away.

"Mom? MOM? Look at me!"

Elaine's eyes slowly turned towards Gabe.

"I know we're not supposed to talk about him, but Marc is sick, and I have to go. I need to give some of my attention to him. My daughter is there with him!"

"Bring me the cordless phone. I have to call your aunt. You know how she gets."

Gabe despaired.

"Get me the phone!"

"Mom, no."

Elaine started sobbing, which only made Gabe feel worse. That was her usual get out of jail free card whenever there was a discussion she couldn't handle. Her tears were self-pitying, but Gabe was too soft-hearted to resist her charade even if he knew it was just a manipulation tactic. In the end, Elaine got what she wanted. Her son was at her house, giving her attention and trying to console her.

"Mom, the aid will be here soon. Let's have tea together."

He wheeled Elaine back over to the table and then filled the kettle with water. No sooner than putting the kettle on the stove, he heard the numbers on the phone start to dial.

"Hi Colleen... No, I'm fine. I was asleep. I asked the aid to put me in bed before she left at lunch. Forgot to bring the phone…"

Elaine said nothing about falling. She didn't even say that Gabe was there. She just invented an excuse to not tell her sister she fell. Gabe leaned against the counter listening to Elaine pontificate. Was it a delusion? Maybe in the past she would've waited to call her sister, but Elaine was becoming more unhinged. The water boiled and he turned off the stove. He dropped a tea bag into a cup and filled it with water. She acted as if he wasn't there. He put his mug back in the cupboard and left.

He arrived home to find Linda at the computer working on bills. Dinner was in the oven. He walked into the den, having already opened a beer, and sat on the couch. Linda's iMac and Ikea desk seemed out of place with the old paneling. Linda typed away and said nothing, not even a hello. Gabe reclined in the deep beige couch wearing his tie that he loosened hours earlier.

"She's getting worse."

"I know," Gabe whispered.

"I never thought I'd find myself agreeing with your brother, but I'm starting to think he's right. I spoke with Sara today." Linda said.

"How is she?"

"Did you know she's working for Marc?" She asked.

"Yes, and I think it's a good idea." Gabe said.

"How can you be so sure?"

"I had all the same reservations as you at first, but we've talked more since he woke up than in the last two years combined. When I speak to Sara, the way she talks about him almost makes me jealous."

Linda finally stopped working and turned to him.

"Do you really think people can change like that?"

"Linda, he insisted we come see them. I don't know what it's all about, but I've never seen him so adamant about something that didn't have to do with making more money."

Linda laughed sarcastically.

"I can't deny that I'm excited. I've always wanted to go to Italy, and we'll go to your father's hometown. It's been too long since you and I had a vacation. Dare I say that I might even be excited to see your brother."

That made Gabe laugh.

"I'm excited too and I'm sure we'll have a great time as long as my mother doesn't find a way to break her neck to stop us from going."

"Speaking of which, what the hell happened today?" Linda asked.

"She's driving me crazy. The outbursts are more erratic."

"Tell me what happened." Linda insisted, turning back to the computer.

"I was presenting the sales analysis and projections to the division managers in our meeting. For twenty minutes, all I feel is my pocket vibrating. Boss has been on my ass too, so I just ignored it. There were nine missed calls and four messages, one was crazier than the next."

"What did she say?"

Gabe handed her his phone and watched her mouth open wider as she listened to the voicemails.

"This is crazy!" Linda said in astonishment.

"It gets even better." Gabe told her the rest of the story.

"She called your aunt and just blatantly made up a story right in front of you?"

"Yup." Gabe sighed with resignation. "As the trip gets closer, I'm more and more worried about getting her out of the house without a fight. What if she refuses to go?" Gabe asked.

Linda turned away from the computer again and said earnestly. "Honey, we have to start talking about a more permanent solution for her."

"I know… I know." Gabe said wearily.

"What if you take too long to decide and her bad judgment ends up killing her?"

4:7

"You've learned a lot about wine."

"—And from an American no less. That's almost embarrassing."

"Remember my father was born here, smart ass."

"You would've never survived being a teenager in Italy. You hate being teased."

Giancarlo curiously listened as Marc went on about Florence, particularly Giovanna's farm. The yard was filled with herbs and large rosemary bushes. You could smell it from over the hill and even taste it in their wine. There was basil, thyme, oregano, parsley and many other herbs growing, a vineyard, livestock, fruit trees, and vegetables. Giuseppe lived in the main house with his wife and two sons. Giovanna lived in a smaller house on the south side of the property. They had an outdoor kitchen with a fireplace where they had a late lunch.

"Can you believe they produce so much for the restaurant themselves?" Marc marveled.

"That salami was ridiculous. I'll bet you can't find food that tastes like that in the states." Giancarlo said.

"That's very true. You go to restaurants and some are really good, but you can tell that it's not the same. My father always spoke about that. He used to make pizza a lot when I was little and complained about the quality of the cheese and the tomatoes. We had Jersey tomatoes and he still complained."

"What are 'Jersey tomatoes'?"

"People watch Hollywood movies and think New Jersey is all like Jersey Shore. It's also known as the garden state—our tomatoes are some of the best in the country. My father would wait for them to come in season and we'd jar them. That was something even my mother liked doing. He used to say that it was the closest you could get to a San Marzano tomato in the US."

"My grandparents did it too. I remember they had a garden. I used to eat the marbleized tomatoes with a little salt like apples. I ate so many once I got diarrhea." Giancarlo laughed.

"We should explore Florence. It has so much tourism and there's a big exchange school. There's a lot of demand for apartments. We should start researching."

Marc had never mentioned Florence before, which made his new infatuation with Giovanna all the more obvious. Giancarlo played along not to embarrass him. Marc got so exuberant that he woke Sara from her nap. She raised her middle finger, grinning with her eyes still closed, insisting they would both be walking home if they awoke her again.

Later, they pulled into the neighborhood and stopped in front of the apartment. They woke Sara and got out of the car while Giancarlo went to park. Marc rode the elevator with her and kept noticing how tired she'd been lately. No sooner were they home and she and Giancarlo went straight to bed

Marc, on the other hand, didn't sleep. He made himself a caffé and tried to freshen up for his appointment. The kids were right, he did like Giovanna, and he felt guilty about it. He'd been thinking about Hannah a lot, but something had changed. Was he allowed to like someone else after how he behaved?

The screen came into focus and Dr. Rossellino was

wearing red. Her manner was often predictable by her choice of color. Though therapists were charged with impartiality, she wasn't above human idiosyncrasy. When she wore gray, she wasn't patient. Red meant she was in a lively mood and perhaps that was appropriate.

"I met someone. Her name is Giovanna and she's from Florence."

"I'm pleased to hear this because it means you are moving on from your marriage."

"Before we left, she said she wants to come to Rome."

"How does that make you feel?"

Marc hesitated. "Terrified, actually."

"Why?"

"All I could think about was how I was afraid she would see me limp. I think I was limping at some point, and I know she must have seen me but never asked. I was surprised."

"Why would that surprise you?"

"Obviously it would mean that there's something wrong with me. That usually turns people off." Marc said.

"Have you considered that not everybody is like that? So, will you see her again?"

"Like I said, she wants to come to Rome."

"Did she say when?" Dr. Rossellino pressed.

"Not yet but she asked me twice."

"That obviously means she's interested in coming."

"I know that." He dismissed her.

"Are you afraid to see her?"

"Why would I be afraid?"

"I think you'd better answer that question because you already know the answer."

Marc was silent.

"Come on, you can just say it." She taunted.

"I haven't been with another woman in a long time. I'm also not feeling very virile. I guess it's a confidence issue."

"So, this is about your manhood?" She asked.

"No, it's not… Well, maybe it is?" He looked away from the screen awkwardly.

"Marc, since your recovery you're learning to trust and rethinking your view of the world. Honestly, I'm surprised something like this hasn't come up sooner."

"Why do you say that?"

"You're a very successful and, might I say, a very attractive man. When you're not acting like an angry ogre, you're also very charming. Why should it surprise you that somebody notices?"

"It's my illness. I feel like it's written all over my face." He said somberly.

"Marc, you're in your 40s. Most people by your age have some kind of major life setback. By the time you reach my age, a common dinner party topic is what medications you take."

Marc laughed.

"Yes, people in their 60s talk about meds as small talk. Eventually, issues of virility no longer matter so much. People aren't really looking for the passion of twenty-somethings. After 40, they also want companionship. Perhaps she saw qualities in you that she liked? Is that so hard to believe? Were Sara and Giancarlo with you?"

"Of course."

"Did they make any observations?"

"Immediately. When we told her Sara's pregnant, she thought I was her father at first. I felt proud."

"You really don't understand women." She asked again. "Do you want to see her?"

"That's not the—"

She cut him off. "Do you want to see her?"

"I can't stop thinking about her."

"Finally! I'm surprised that I still have to remind my middle-aged patients that the rest of your life will pass with the blink of an eye. Tomorrow you'll be 50. Next week you will be 60. That's how fast it goes. I think you should indulge this little intrigue."

Marc paused contemplatively and then abruptly changed the subject to Hannah.

"You feel guilty, don't you?"

"Yes. I just wish we could resolve things. It's not about getting back together. I just want to make amends with her, and with Paul."

"Do you feel like you need her permission? Because you don't. As for making amends, some people have breaking points and you need to respect their need for time."

"I know that. I wish I could undo what I've done to both of them, but I know I can't."

"That might change. Time has a funny way of righting old wrongs. The nicest thing you can do is let them be for now."

4:8

Sara usually browsed novels, but she was now searching books about newborns. She stood with her hand on her belly in the Feltrinelli bookstore inside Termini station waiting for Giancarlo. As she thumbed through a book functionally titled "Day to Day Issues and Challenges of Newborns," she was shocked to see best practices for things like wiping. The graphic account of one mother's experience made her wince. *Motherhood must be an expression of true love*, she thought.

Then a familiar hand caressed its way around her waist. "If you're going to read the entire book, you should buy it." She leaned back into Giancarlo's embrace.

"I should buy this for you so you can read about all the poop and vomit we have to look forward to."

"Sounds romantic."

"Remember my dear, I'm not an old-fashioned Italian woman who will dutifully change all the diapers and wash the dishes."

"I will do my share, my love."

"We will see. You can't even handle the smell of old food in the refrigerator."

"I already have a solution. I'll just breathe through my mouth and wear rubber gloves."

Sara cackled.

"It's almost time. Let's get a caffè first."

They headed to the bar. Sara ordered her caffè latte and Giancarlo a double espresso. She also ordered two cornettos with cream and Nutella filling. Giancarlo wasn't paying attention and when the barista brought two separate plates and placed one in front of him, he was about to say he didn't order it. Then Sara stopped him because they were both for her.

She could eat a whole pizza and suffered from cravings for creams and sweets. She also desired salami and sat in quiet desperation when Giancarlo or Marc ate prosciutto or mortadella.

Giancarlo sipped his caffé while Sara marauded through her snack. She was crazed. When she finished, Giancarlo stopped her to clean the powdered sugar off her cheek before she stepped away from the bar. There were also flakes that looked like snow contrasted by her black hair.

"I'm hopeless." She said regretfully.

"No, you're beautiful. Let's go."

They weaved their way through the sea of people swimming in and out of the station. Termini was where both subway lines intersected. It was Rome's equivalent to 34th street.

"The train arrives on track 7." She said.

Sara and Giancarlo pushed their way through the congestion to the end of the platform.

The train arrived and the passengers exited. Giancarlo remarked on the differences between the wealthy and everyone else. People with thousand-dollar suits, 500-dollar shoes, bad plastic surgery, and November tans stood out. The immigrants and working-class Italians were noticeably different from their debutante compatriots. Then there were tourists who noticed neither. Italy had not changed much from its ancient past. There were still plebeians and patricians; yet despite their differences, they all sat together, packed like hamsters as they did on ancient Roman latrines. There they were equal in their discomfort and reminded of who really ran the country: the Mafia.

Sara and Giancarlo peered through the crowd. Giancarlo's height was convenient because he noticed Giovanna's frosted blond hair bouncing as she walked half-way down the platform. She was dressed plainly in jeans, black boots, and a gray sweater with a long black, fitted wool coat. Giancarlo waived to her over the crowd.

"Ao!" Sara said.

"Ao? You are learning Roman dialect!" Giovanna remarked.

"How was your trip?" Giancarlo asked.

"It was okay, apart from sitting across from a man who snored and slept most of the way. Thankfully it was short."

"I'm glad you made it here safe." Sara said.

"And how are you feeling my dear?"

"Nervous."

"I'm sure everything will be fine." Giovanna said.

"We hope so." Interjected Giancarlo.

"Do you mind if we stop at the bar? I need a caffè to wake up." Giovanna requested.

"We were just there but I never say no to caffè." Giancarlo replied.

"Can we go to one outside the station? I need to pee."

Sara's sudden urges to urinate became more frequent. They exited the station and were accosted by street peddlers. One sold scarves, another selfie sticks, and another knock-off designer handbags. The sidewalks also had gypsies kneeling in penance right on the asphalt, holding tin cups and clasping rosary beads. They turned down a quieter street and stopped at the first café they found. Sara went straight for the bathroom while Giancarlo and Giovanna waited at the bar. A few minutes later Sara returned to them sipping cappuccinos.

"Can I also get a latte with a cornetto." She said.

"You just had two of them!" Giancarlo said in shock.

Sara looked up in embarrassment and Giancarlo poked fun. Giovanna leapt to her defense.

"Fetuses are resource-consuming machines. Don't tease her about her appetite. Let me look at you. Pull your shirt tight. You are showing a little and that beautiful face of yours is a little plumper. Your cheeks are rosy and gorgeous."

Giovanna had a classic Italian beauty and manner like Sofia Lauren. Her vowels were exaggerated and her words full of emphasis. She was direct, yet serene, which Sara found comforting.

"My parents are coming in two weeks and not a moment

too soon. That is when we're telling them. This is part of my uncle's master plan as he likes to call it."

"I'm starting to feel confident about it." Giancarlo added.

"My father knows we're both working with Marc, so the plan is to show we are making money and then to tell them we're pregnant and getting married."

"Ahh, so you're luring them here to show you are prepared to support a family and that you are ready to start one. Smart plan. I don't know Marc well yet, but he strikes me as a clever man."

"He and my father are very different. My dad is a lot less intense."

"We should get going," Giancarlo said.

Back at the apartment, Marc compulsively monitored the pork loin temperature. It was exactly the same the last time he checked it two minutes earlier. What could be taking so long? Her train had arrived almost an hour ago. Did she not come? There was no message from Giancarlo or Sara to say otherwise and he resisted the urge to text to not seem eager. He walked towards the living room and opened the front window to look down at the street. November was not high season, and the streets were quiet. He checked the room that had been prepared for Giovanna and then stopped in the dining room on his way back to the kitchen. Everything was in place. Giancarlo and Sara had done a thorough job of cleaning the apartment in anticipation of her arrival, but that was no longer a lot of work. Now that Sara and Giancarlo were living there, the apartment never came close to the squalor of when Marc lived alone. Back in the kitchen, he checked the temperature twice more and then heard the door opening.

"Ciao bello." Giovanna said warmly.

Marc smiled shyly and then leaned in for the customary two-kisses.

"Smells fantastic." Giovanna exclaimed.

Marc smiled. "You and your brother own a restaurant. That is a high bar to meet."

"You didn't have to go through all this trouble."

"Who said it was trouble? I enjoy cooking, more now than ever. And now, since Sara is always hungry, her appetite keeps me busy."

Giancarlo burst into laughter. "She had two cornettos with me before the train arrived and then another at a different café after we met Giovanna."

"Both of you? Stop giving this lovely girl a hard time!" Giovanna scolded them.

Marc opened the wine and then passed glasses to Giovanna and Giancarlo. Sara looked on bitterly as she leaned into Giancarlo's glass to take her customary large whiff.

"Don't worry my love, when the baby is born, I will spoil you with every culinary delight forbidden to you now." Then he took a sumptuous mouthful of the wine while teasing Sara with an exaggerated expression of pleasure. She responded by slapping his arm.

"Are they always like this?" Giovanna asked playfully.

"Yes, and worse. I never knew how much of a tease Giancarlo is."

Giancarlo disputed, to which Marc responded by detailing other incidents to which he had tortured poor Sara about food.

"You terrible boy." Giovanna said adoringly.

"He is terrible sometimes." Sara said, leering at him. "I am admittedly OCD. Giancarlo, for all his gentlemanly qualities, can be a slob."

"He is a man." Giovanna said as if stating the obvious.

"He always takes his pants off with change in his pockets. They go everywhere and it drives me nuts!"

Giancarlo and Marc began to snicker.

"What did you do, you evil little boys?" Giovanna jested.

"I glued some of the change to the floor."

"It was not just one either! There were eleven!"

"If you did that to me, I would put double stick clear tape on the toilet seat and unscrew the lightbulb!" Giovanna asserted.

"Creative!" Marc said.

"I grew up with a brother and four male cousins. I had to learn to defend myself. So, what's for dinner?"

Marc didn't answer right away. A few clicks and pops from his phone and out from the speakers came saxophone jazz.

"Charlie Parker!" She said.

"Yes!" Mark responded happily. "So for the primo piatto we will have pasta with wild boar meat sauce and for the second, pork loin marinated for two days with special salt, fresh rosemary, thyme, and pepper."

"He also made steamed artichokes." Sara interjected. "You're going to make that gravy from the broth?"

"You made artichokes al vapore?" Giovanna asked. "What sauce?"

"I used a vegetable bullion on the bottoms of the artichokes. It makes a very nice broth. I add flour and some drippings to it and make a gravy that complements meat very well." He said.

"I'm impressed." Giovanna admitted.

Giancarlo and Sara looked on and kept looking back at each other. They were becoming spectators.

"I'm a little tired." Sara said.

"Do you want to lie down for a while?" Giancarlo asked.

"Yes, but we have more to do for dinner." She said.

"You silly girl. I own a restaurant. Go and rest, both of you."

After Sara and Giancarlo retired, there was an awkward moment of acknowledgement that they were alone together for the first time. Marc was nervous. Giovanna knew and broke the silence by asking what she could do to help. He told her she could prepare the antipasto plate. She sat at the kitchen table while Marc remained at the stove.

"It's nice to have you here." Marc said quietly.

"Thank you for inviting me."

It was not exactly the response Marc wanted but he turned and saw her smiling as she laid out the serving plate.

"I love this building and the apartment." She said.

"We do too, and we love the location, but I'm not sure how much longer we'll be here. With the baby coming, we'll need more space. We're actually thinking of getting out of the city. I'm looking at a few properties in Sabina."

"Sabina is beautiful. Best olive oil in the world in my opinion." She said.

"Is that really true?"

"Sabina oil was documented by the Babylonians in the 17th century BC."

"I never knew that."

"Do you know we have a few dishes at the restaurant that use Sabina oil specifically? There is a peppery and buttery quality that the Tuscan oil lacks. It's really unique." She said.

"Now I have even more reason to consider living there." He finished at the stove and sat down at the table, pouring another glass of wine.

"This wine is lovely and expensive, even in Italia. My brother would be impressed."

"How is he?"

"He's fine, the other day he pissed off another American tourist when he denied her Parmesan cheese. He does that all the time with Bolognese sauce. I keep telling him to let people eat what they want."

Marc burst into laughter "He did the same thing to us!"

"That's my brother. He's known in the town for this and some tourists come just so he will tell them no. I remember reading you had someone in New York called the soup Nazi. Giuseppe is the pasta Nazi, and he's proud of it."

Marc could not contain himself. "That's exactly what I called him before you got there!"

"And you didn't know about him?" She said with eyes wide open.

"No!" Marc laughed harder.

"That is too funny, but in all seriousness, it's not a gimmick. My brother really cares about tradition. The Americans and British drive him crazy. I have to admit it amuses me, but I admire that he cares so much."

Marc enjoyed the pleasure on Giovanna's face as she sampled the antipasto.

"I remember how my brother was furious when the first McDonald's opened in town. He could not believe there could even be a market for such food. It was expensive and he could not fathom how a kid could want that instead of good salami, mozzarella and fresh bread for 3 Euros at any salumeria. He feels like American culture is slowly encroaching on Italy."

"He's right."

"How can you be so sure?" She asked.

"Name some of your favorite bands."

"I love Led Zeppelin and the Doors." She said.

"Two of my top five favorite bands. What about TV shows?"

"The show with Bill Cosby was the biggest show in Italy when I was growing up."

"The Cosby Show!" He said laughing.

"We called it the Robinson."

"Singular?"

"Yes."

"That's hysterical. My point is that we are from two different countries. We grew up listening to the same music and one of your most popular TV shows was also ours. Was it dubbed in Italian?"

"Of course it was!"

Marc laughed harder.

"Yea, how many American black dentists who speak Italian are running around Italy? Nothing was more Americana than that show. Crazy he turned out to be a scumbag, but every saint turns out to be a sinner if you wait long enough. Anyway, I even noticed the influence of American culture when I first got here. I'm going to tell you something that I hope doesn't make you lose respect: I like McDonald's here."

Giovanna laughed. "Me too but I would never admit that to my brother."

"I know, but seriously, I saw a group of kids stuffing their faces with fries. Three of four were overweight and one had a NY Yankees jacket on. I couldn't believe it."

"How do you know they were not American?" She questioned.

"I thought the same thing, then I listened. They were Roman."

Marc got up to check on the sauce. "Son of a bitch!"

Marc burned himself. Giovanna got up quickly and pulled him to the sink. She turned on the cold water and grabbed his arm, studying it as the water poured over it. He felt her touch more than the pain. As Marc looked down at her arm, he noticed it was filled with scars and blemishes.

"Are those all from the kitchen?" He asked.

"Yes, and that's how I know you will not die."

Marc grinned contemptuously.

"How did you get this scar?" She asked.

Marc was so busy enjoying her attention that he didn't realize his scar from his suicide attempt was in plain sight. His face turned red and his enjoyment transitioned to anxiety. He stuttered. "It's a long story."

His eyes looked out the window above the sink and then broke off to staring at nothing. Then he mustered the courage for prolonged eye contact with Giovanna. He was terrified to speak. She grabbed his hand and kissed it. He felt like a boy who had never been kissed. They held hands silently as Charlie Parker's horn sparkled.

Meanwhile, Giancarlo snored while Sara laid there half-awake, frustrated and envious. Giancarlo could sleep through an explosion and worse yet, he could fall asleep during one. Since she had been pregnant, Sara had more trouble sleeping. Giancarlo stretched and groaned into wakefulness. Sara raised his shirt and kissed his stomach.

"Shouldn't I be doing that to you?" Giancarlo asked.

Sara slid up the bed and wrapped her arms around Giancarlo. They laid locked in a tender but urgent embrace. She whispered, "Please promise me we'll work hard and make enough money to bring my parent's here eventually?" Their embrace loosened and she looked at him with doubt.

"My love, of course, but I also don't think this is that grave either, at least not yet. We aren't working day jobs and we can travel. There's nothing stopping us from going back and forth." He said.

"Giancarlo, when I have the baby, I'm not going to be able to travel for a while. I would love to be able to just bring them here. Promise me."

"I promise. Just relax and it will be okay. Let's just get through these next few weeks. At least we find out the sex tomorrow!" He said enthusiastically. "We need to talk about names."

"Not until after we know the sex. Coming up with one name is hard enough." She dismissed. "Let's get ready for dinner. Remember that gallon of Brunello you promised me?" Giancarlo smiled back at her. "You will go to Montalcino and bottle it yourself. I saw what he bought. You fuckers are going to drink really good wine tonight." Sara said dejectedly.

"Sadly for you my love, yes we are." Giancarlo teased.

Sara grabbed a pillow and proceeded to beat him with it, laughing as she did. Giancarlo was cornered and she taunted him as she pelted him with the bag of down feathers.

"Think you can escape? You wouldn't push a pregnant woman, would you?"

The harder she hit, the harder they laughed. It echoed off the tiles through the apartment.

"I love young laughter," Giovanna said quietly from the other room. She and Marc looked on as Sara and Giancarlo frolicked.

"They are fortunate to have found one another and to have grown up in good families. It is nice they are still so playful." Marc commented.

"Still?" Giovanna asked. "They are still kids."

"I was already too serious by 16 and by 23, I was out of college and had a company. There wasn't much laughter in my house because there wasn't anyone to laugh with."

"I am very sorry to hear that. I couldn't imagine living without laughter. It's like air for me. At least you laughed with friends?"

"I did, but I've always been overly serious and reserved. My ex-wife and I laughed often and my friend Paul too, but that's about it." He felt a pang of remorse as their names parted from his lips.

"Your brother seems light enough with the way you speak about him."

"Gabe and I are making up for lost time. Until very recently our relationship was difficult." He seemed regretful as he got up from the table and returned to the stove.

"Better late than never?" She said.

"I agree."

"What about your parents?" She asked.

Marc momentarily avoided the question as he exaggerated his inspection of the artichoke leaves. He placed the lid back on the pot with more force than necessary and then stood rigidly with his back to Giovanna. He turned and sat back down and gulped down the remainder of wine in his glass. "My father died when I was 13 and I haven't seen my mother in some time."

Giovanna's face sank and her gaze grew compassionate. She grabbed his hand from across the table. "I'm so sorry about your father. That must have been terrible for you."

"It was." He squeezed her hand. "I don't want to get into this now. I would like a fun evening with some laughter. We also better intervene between my niece and future nephew."

Sara and Giancarlo entered the kitchen. Giancarlo's hair was still disheveled from sleep.

"It smells so good in here. I'm starving!" Sara said. She aggressively grabbed the baguette, tore off the end, and stuffed it in her mouth.

"Obviously." Giancarlo remarked.

"I told you to behave!" Giovanna snapped playfully.

The apartment on Via dell'Orso was a home like none Marc had ever known. Dinner proceeded splendidly. Conversation sped through matters of food, history, politics, satire and personal stories: hallmarks of any exceptional evening with good company. Several hours later, Giovanna and Giancarlo took charge of clean up on the insistence that one was pregnant and the other had cooked dinner. After dessert, Giancarlo and Sara went to bed, leaving Marc and Giovanna in the living room.

"You drink grappa like a man." Marc remarked.

Giovanna laughed, "My father said the same thing to me once. It's such a cliché that the women gather in the kitchen for coffee and the men in the living room for grappa and amaro. My father gave me my first sip at 12." She said.

"Me too! I hated it."

"I loved it." She fired back. "Italy has become a tourist economy. Foreigners want to savor everything about our culture, but there are certain places they can't go, and our liquors are one of them. Americans especially cannot acquire a taste for grappa unless they move here and make an effort. I must say I'm happy about that."

"Why is that?"

"Our bars after hours are one of the few places Italians can enjoy the company of other Italians without the tourists. You find the Germans, Brits and Americans in pubs, but the bars mostly belong to us. It is not that I don't like tourists, but sometimes I'm just tired of them. I know my brother and I make our living from them but a part of me misses the Italy of the 80s and early 90s, when we still had something resembling an economy. Sometimes I think no one understands us except each other."

He loved the sound of her voice and how she spoke. She made the simplest things sound so fascinating. He also couldn't help but notice how different she was from Hannah. For the first time, he considered that maybe their split was for the best. He felt a comfort with Giovanna he had never felt with Hannah.

"What are you smiling at?" Giovanna interjected.

What Marc thought was a subtle grin grew into a full smile to which he blushed and looked away. He had so many thoughts, none of which he could say.

Giovanna smiled back, grabbed the bottle and poured both another glass. "You are a fascinating man, Marc Diodato."

Marc chuckled in what seemed disbelief and could only mutter a simple thank you.

"I'm serious. Most men are overgrown teenagers. You think with your cocks and mistake passion for love. You agree with us during conflicts because you can't be bothered. It's nice to spend time with a man who doesn't speak with the assumption he is a genius without knowing he is an idiot."

"That's a relief, I'm glad you aren't scared yet."

"Not one bit." She said.

"Be patient, I just got started." He warned.

As they spoke, Giovanna's eyes moved about the room. The small painting near the window continuously distracted her. "You have quite an art collection. Is that? —That looks like a Picasso. Did you pay for a reproduction?"

Marc grinned but said nothing.

"What is so funny?" She asked.

Marc began to laugh.

"Wait, that's not? Are you kidding me?" She got up and inspected it closely. "You own a fucking Picasso?" She said contemptuously.

"Four actually. I also have three prints in my bedroom."

Chapter 5
Love and War

5:1

Dear Marc,

After reading your email, I was too jealous to feel happy that you are doing better. New people in your life seem to be getting the best of you while we got the worst. Why? My parents regarded you as a son. That my father is dead makes it worse because your behavior is an insult to his memory. Now you say you need my friendship, yet you didn't seem to regard it when you had it. I remember how much you suffered during the years following your father's death. I remember my mother hugging you while you cried when things with your mother were so bad. My father shared our time with you because you didn't have a father. I shared my father with you! You practically lived at my house in high school and to think of how our friendship devolved really imbitters me.

Our history was why I was able to look beyond your flaws because I held on to who you once were. But your lie and what happened when I came to Rome are bridges too far. Believe it or not, the lie is actually the worst of the two and that's why I can't pardon what you've done to Hannah. What kind of a man lies about an affair, to abandon his wife to inadequacy, just because he is too proud to admit weakness? Though I'm no longer your attorney, take my advice: don't contact her.

As for me, I have my own problems. I'm still dealing with my divorce and trying to put my life together. Frankly, you are the last person I want around while this is happening. If I had to be privy to your problems, I would have no time for mine because it's always about you, Marc.

I saw the truth about you in your apartment. To think I was enjoying seeing you like that is incomprehensible, as if I am in some kind of competition. Then I realized that you are the competitor and you enjoyed making me a subordinate. When I left your apartment, I understood the extent to which our relationship had become one-sided. When I was on the plane, I asked myself if you would have come to check on me? I didn't even need to think about it. I knew the answer was no and that was when I realized I've had enough.

If I ever want to reconnect with you, it will be on my terms and I'll reach out to you. If you want the door to remain open, respect my wishes. I don't want to hear from you. I hope you treat the new people in your life better than you treated me.

Paul

5:2

A scream launched Marc from his bed to find Giovanna consoling Sara. She tried to speak but could not. Giancarlo's gaze was blank.

"The clinic just called with the test results." Giovanna said.

Sara's crying intensified.

"There's a chance the baby has a serious genetic defect." Giancarlo said.

"Like Down Syndrome?" Marc asked.

"Worse."

Giancarlo's big eyes wandered the ceiling as tears fell from them. Marc reached out and grabbed his hand. He squeezed and Giancarlo squeezed back.

"So… what does this mean and what happens now?" Marc asked apprehensively.

"I need a drink." Giancarlo said. They went to the kitchen for the grappa but also because Sara didn't need to hear the details twice. Every sound was irritating. The glasses clanking together, the door of the cupboard closing, the sound of the liquor pouring and the thud of the bottle on the table were tedious.

"We have to go for an amniocentesis tomorrow. They want to do it right away." Giancarlo explained. "If this is confirmed, they advised terminating the pregnancy."

"Okay, back up for a second; why aren't we sure?" Marc asked.

"The doctor said there's a 50% chance based on the prenatal testing. They can't be sure without the procedure tomorrow because it's the only way to confirm it." Giancarlo explained.

"Why should we doubt this test?" Marc inquired.

"He said these tests can generate false positives. Hormones could throw off the result, they are less accurate in younger mothers and there could've been a twin who died."

"How long do we have to wait for the results?"

"A week."

"At least we'll know before her parents get here. Look at me. We're going to get through this together."

Marc raised his glass. Giancarlo looked at him puzzled. "Raise your glass." He ordered him.

"I don't feel like a toast is appropriate." Giancarlo protested.

"No, this is important because we're drinking to spite." He said.

"Spite?" Giancarlo asked wearily.

"Spite can be a virtue. I learned this after my suicide attempt. It is a good old-fashioned fuck you because that beats despair."

"Don't you mean defiance?"

"No, spite is a step further because it's not only thumbing your nose at your hardships. It is taking pleasure in their displeasure that they are not getting the best of you. There's something satisfying about that!"

Giancarlo reached across the table and placed his hand on Marc's arm. "If I only had known how much the crazy guy at the restaurant would've changed my life."

It was a needed moment of levity.

"To spite then!" The men touched their glasses like two soldiers about to depart for battle. Giancarlo leaned back in the chair, emptied his glass and said with conviction, "Let's go in the other room."

The sun was shining brightly through the windows. Sara laid on the couch with her head on Giovanna's lap who caressed her hair gently. Marc sat alone while Giancarlo went to Sara and leaned over to kiss her forehead. Quietly he said, "Ti amo." Sara lifted her feet and Giancarlo sat by her with her legs across his lap.

"There's still a chance it'll be okay. We can't despair yet. We just have to make it through tomorrow and next week until we get the results." Marc reasoned.

"But what if the results are bad?" Sara said and started to cry again.

"Then we'll deal with it once we know. For now, all we can do is wait. We have to resist despair and remain neutral. I know that's hard, but we have to try." Marc said.

Sara turned to Giancarlo. "If... if we lose this child, would you still want to marry me?" Her wet eyes were filled with fear.

Giancarlo pulled her face to his. "I absolutely want to marry you."

"No matter how this turns out, neither of you will ever doubt that you love one another again." Marc interjected.

"That's true, Uncle." Sara was solemn.

"I'm really proud of you both. This does not in any way detract from what you have accomplished."

"You're both young and you already know you can get pregnant." Giovanna said. "My ex-husband and I tried for years only to find out he couldn't have children. Then I got diagnosed with cancer."

Marc didn't know.

Giovanna pulled out her phone. "This was me three years ago."

She was pale, gaunt and wearing a red bandanna on her head. Marc gently grabbed her phone. As he gazed at her picture, his heart filled with dread. Now he knew why she didn't care about his limp. Dr. Rossellino was right.

"I still need to get checked every six months. There's a chance it'll come back. I really wanted to be a mother. Sometimes I struggle but I always remind myself that this is hardly the bottom. I have learned to find pleasure wherever I can. After my ex-husband left and I got diagnosed, I was so disgusted with men I wondered if Catherine the Great had the right idea about sex with her horses. Then again, maybe not, only because she was supposedly impaled by one. Maybe it wasn't a good idea after all."

The mood of the room suddenly tripped and fell like

a fool with his shoelaces tied together. Giancarlo and Marc looked dumbfounded. Sara lifted her head and fired, "It's a joke, you idiots!"

Sara's head fell back to the pillow and with her eyes still damp, she smiled admiringly at Giovanna as they giggled together. Giovanna had marvelous wit and impeccable timing.

Marc whispered to Giancarlo, "This is what spite looks like."

For the rest of the day, everyone did their best to function. Sara and Giancarlo mostly slept. Marc and Giovanna kept tabs on them but tried to give them their space. Marc spent most of his time online doing research.

"You've been reading for hours. Why don't you take a break? Do you want caffè?" Giovanna asked.

Marc refused and then spun in his chair. "There's a chance this will be okay."

"Marc, if you keep this up, you're going to drive yourself crazy. There's nothing we can do but wait."

"Giovanna, I really want this child." Marc's eyes teared up. "Thank you for everything today. Thank you for being here." He whispered.

"You really love those kids."

"I do; I can't get the sound of her sobs out of my head. And poor Giancarlo."

She got up and hugged him from behind pressing his head against her chest.

"Do you want me to stay longer?" Giovanna asked.

"Yes, it will be really good for the kids."

"And you?"

"Not only do I want you to stay, I want you to come to San Pietro al Tanagro." His answer rushed out of his mouth. "Can you be away for that long? What about the bed and breakfast?"

"My brother is there. I can stay here as long as you need me."

"I'm so sorry you were sick." He said.

"It was one of the scariest things I've ever been through, but I'm still here. I still think that for something that was the worst experience in my life, nothing has made me stronger. I know what's really important, which is why I don't care that you have suspicious scars on your arms and why I don't want you to be afraid to tell me why."

"Last year, I got some really bad news. It was so bad that I started to work with a therapist who specializes in people with my issues. Dr. Rossellino is an extraordinary woman. When I first saw her, I couldn't talk about my past, or my situation. She suggested I started writing memoirs. She would read them out loud to me and then I understood that hearing myself say things was therapeutic. Letting it out really helps. I'm starting off with this because I want you to know just how hard it is for me to talk about myself."

Giovanna waited patiently and he felt himself run out of distractions and preludes. His heart quickened. How would she react? He spun again and turned his back to her staring at his phone. Suddenly Giovanna's phone sounded an alert. It was a text from Marc that said, "I have MS." She stared at the phone and then looked at Marc. He looked terrified. She got up from the bed without saying a word. She drew her mouth to his and kissed him lovingly. She responded without words because they would never have sufficed. The meaning of a kiss is unmistakable.

5:3

Sleep was a good way to sublimate anguish, but for Marc, it was barely adequate. His eyes opened and he saw that the sun had shifted. It was later in the afternoon and while Giovanna, Giancarlo and Sara slept, he laid in bed with uncontrollable thoughts. He tried to fall back to sleep but couldn't, so he took his laptop into the dining room and closed all the doors. He went back to his research and after reading one article that was more horrifying than the previous, he looked at more pictures—which were even worse.

Realizing he was finally alone; he froze to listen, just to make sure no one else was awake. As the silence hissed, the sound of his breathing was amplified. Then a feeling started in the pit of his stomach, spread to his back and down his arms. His breath quickened and a very needed release befell him. He could finally cry properly. As he wept, he realized what he hated the most about relationships, and understood why he avoided them. They hurt. When you care for others, their suffering becomes your suffering and as he sat at the table, every image he saw was a nightmarish flipbook in his head. He remembered the sound of Sara's cries and his heart sank even further. *I wish we could talk, papa.* He reached across his chest to hold himself.

This is when people pray, he thought. Marc never prayed but he found himself envying people who did, because of its power to give hope. For the first time, he felt himself a fool for the years of condescension and ridicule. He thought people of faith were just cockroaches, but now he would rather have been a cockroach himself.

He decided he needed to get out. He quietly put on his shoes and coat, closing the door slowly. Instead of taking the elevator, he took the stairs, remaining conscious of the lightness of his steps. He made a right out the door and headed towards Via di Santa Maria dell'Anima. A few blocks down was Via della Pace, Peace Street, and thinking he needed some peace, he turned left and there was the church.

He stared up at the round edifice supported by Doric columns and decided that he would visit the cockroaches, hoping they would accept his company. He entered and was consumed by the smell of incense and candle wax. The interior of the church was supported by rose marble columns and by the looks of the art, it spanned from the medieval to the baroque. It was a gorgeous church but modest by Roman standards. He had visited it once before, but as a tourist. Now he was a guest and instead of critiquing the paintings, sculptures and interior architecture, he hoped something more would touch him, something esoteric that might alleviate the anguish coursing through his veins.

He sat down in one of the aging wooden pews. It was very worn from generations of worshipers. The main part of the church was circular and was crowned by a vaulted ceiling with a painting of Christ above the oculus. The painting was surrounded by windows that were concealed by the edge of the oculus making the light more mysterious. As the ambiance of the church saturated his senses, he realized he felt a little better; but why? What was it about this place? Was it really some mystical ethereal energy? Perhaps it was the elegance and grandiosity, but that seemed cynical. Then he wondered if it might be the energy of the devotion of every artist and believer who ever entered that church. Maybe some of it lingered like the faint aroma of perfume after a woman leaves a room? As he studied the worn benches and marble floor, his imagination brought him to visions of peasants from centuries past. Could one of his ancestors ever have visited? He imagined what it was like for them and suddenly, he understood.

People faced disease, hunger, squalor and war every day. They toiled for their living, without any heat beyond a fireplace, if they were lucky enough to have one. They had no dentists, vaccines, antibiotics or running water. Children died more often than they lived and that was when it clicked. Here, everything was okay. Mothers felt closer to the souls of the children they lost, and their beliefs assured them they still had a connection. The church was clean, beautiful and safe, opposite the cruel world just beyond the threshold of the door. For the first time in his life, Marc Diodato had what one could consider a spiritual experience. Was it God? He didn't know and didn't care. He only knew what he felt and that he liked it.

He thought maybe he should pray, but didn't know how or to whom. Then he remembered that people didn't just pray to Jesus or God, they prayed to saints, and ancestors. Marc didn't believe in God, but he believed in his father and in that moment, it was the closest he felt to him since his experience.

He wasn't alone in the church, there were about half a dozen other people, mostly older women praying nearby. They were in stark contrast to the tourists taking selfies in front of master paintings. He turned his focus back to those actually attending the church and there was one dressed in black, clutching rosary beads, muttering to herself as she rocked back and forth. She seemed in a trance. Were she and the others also affecting him? Even if a God who listens to the prayers of the faithful was some kind of fantasy, prayer was real and what if people created energy when they prayed? What if there was a force that was amplified when people came together in common intention? *What if meaning has mass?* He wondered.

Marc began to pray to Antonio. He kneeled, with his hands clasped and his head bowed. He told Antonio he loved him and missed him. He asked him for strength and suddenly a soft smile mused across his face followed by tears. In the back of the room, an older priest heard Marc's sniffles and approached.

"Are you okay, my son?"

Marc slowly lifted his head and above him stood a priest in his 70s. He was short, a bit stout, with curly white hair and thick glasses. His cheeks puffed slightly as he looked kindly on Marc who was worn and tired. "I'm having a rough time," was the best way he could say it.

"What is your name? I'll pray for you tonight." He said.

Marc introduced himself and the priest called himself Father Antonio. Marc's eyes lit up.

"What is it?" The priest asked.

"My father was Antonio, and I was praying to him just now."

"That's a sign." He said warmly. Father Antonio placed his hand on Marc's head, closed his eyes and asked God to give Marc strength. His touch was sublime.

"Father, can I ask you something?"

"Of course, Marc."

"How do you feel about questions?"

"Our Lord Jesus almost always answered questions with questions. Questions have driven the most profound thinkers throughout history. Men have dedicated their entire lives with pens in-hand, wrestling with the deepest mysteries of life. I think contemplating questions is the highest form of prayer." Father Antonio explained.

Pens in-hand? He wondered.

"Father, are you saying that writing is a form of prayer?"

"Of course. We believe that the gospels were divinely inspired. They were written down by men communing directly with God. There is no one closer to God's secrets than writers."

Marc grabbed Father Antonio's hand, squeezing it intently. He exited the church and headed straight home. When he arrived back at the apartment, he felt a renewed sense of purpose and courage. Everyone was still sleeping and he decided that if no one knew he was gone, he would save his encounter with Father Antonio for himself.

Dear Papa,

I think Father Antonio might have been some kind of angel. I love the idea that he was, and I was meant to meet him. It is just too coincidental to dismiss. If writing is prayer, my prayers will be letters to you. I don't know much about God, but there is a life behind all life and I don't have to understand what it is to experience it.

I need you to help me not be so angry! Why Sara? Why her, of all people? Please give me strength.
Love,
Marc

Giancarlo was the first to wake and Marc said nothing about his walk or Father Antonio. Soon Giovanna and Sara awoke as well. The mood of the apartment was almost rigid, as though they were holding on to each banal gesture as a link to normalcy on a day that was anything but normal. Even when they ate dinner, they sat at the table and said very little. Sara was pale. Giancarlo's attention was solely on her. As she picked at her sandwich, he rubbed her back. She rocked back and forth gently and neither showed any emotion.

Though he was reenergized by his visit to the church, Marc's anxiety and sadness returned. He was trying so hard to be strong, but he was roiling with anticipation. Giovanna was the only one with enough distance to be everyone's anchor.

"While you slept, I've done nothing but read about this. I'll leave out the bad parts because we don't have to discuss them until we know for sure. That said, I think we have a good chance."

Sara turned her head away and clenched the table with

her hand. "I can't listen to speculation, Uncle Marc. There's no point!"

"Sara, listen to me, after the scan we'll have a better idea of what to expect. Giancarlo, you should let me go in with her. I have studied the symptoms and know what to look for. If you get a clean ultrasound tomorrow, we have reason to hope."

"We want to have hope, Marc." Giancarlo asserted. "We're still just getting through the shock of the news."

"Maybe it's better to not talk too much about this until tomorrow?" Giovanna suggested. "Let's just get through today. We should go for gelato."

At first, Marc and Giancarlo scoffed. Then Sara showed a slight hint of a grin. Giovanna looked on curiously, almost confused as if her suggestion were a foregone conclusion.

"I'm serious, what could make anyone happier than Gelato? I don't know about you but when I'm sad, nothing—and I mean nothing—is better."

"Okay, fine, but I don't think I can leave the house." Sara said.

Marc interjected. "Giovanna, why don't we just take a walk?"

"Do you know what kind you want?" Marc asked and Giovanna interrupted. "I'll choose the most decadent chocolate flavors they have." She insisted.

Giovanna and Marc departed. The distress on Marc's face was evident.

"I know you must be so worried." She said.

"I am, but it's not just that. I'm in some pain today. It's the stress. I really internalize it." He explained.

"Are you sure you're up for the walk?" She asked.

"I'm fine but some days are better than others. The doctor says I might be going into remission. Over the last few weeks, I've had more good days than bad. Probably helps that I drink a lot less and have been eating much healthier."

"What is it like?" She asked.

"Pain, stiffness, and a lack of strength."

The elevator door opened and they departed for the Gelataria.

"Something occurred to me, I just talked to you about my disease. I don't think I've ever said this much to anyone about it other than my therapist. I didn't even realize I was talking about it until I did."

"Why is that such a big deal?" She asked.

"Let's get through this mess with Sara and then I promise I'll tell you."

"You don't need to promise me, Marc. You have no obligations to me. You share what you want."

"Really, I want to tell you. Honesty feels good."

"What, were you some kind of liar? I know, you're a conman who uses his good looks and charm to get people to invest and then leaves town with their money. That's why you're in Italy. You're wanted by the American authorities."

"You've found me out."

"I thought so." She teased.

The Gelateria was packed. The high ceilings echoed with chatter. The smell of caramelized sugar, chocolate, vanilla, nuts and espresso was overpowering. As they waited, the workers prepared gelato orders like acrobats wielding their flat paddle tools to pack cones with the various flavors. That was one distinction with gelato. The attendants didn't use scoopers like in the US. Gelato was lopping and pulling like toffee in every direction. They got to the register and Giovanna asked for five large containers. They handed her the receipt and gave it to the attendant when it was their turn. Marc just watched as she ordered chocolate varieties, one more self-indulgent than the next. Their order was packed and bagged within a few moments and they left.

"That place is even busier in the morning."

They elbowed their way through the crowd to reach the street. "Makes me a little claustrophobic."

"Me too," she agreed.

"You were right, just buying gelato makes everything better, let alone eating it. It's good Sara stayed home though. There were a few babies there. Probably not good for her."

"At least she's going through this in Italy. It's the country you're least likely to see a child because Italians don't have children anymore. At this point, they're so rare, you'd think they're exotic pets on the endangered species list. We have the lowest birthrate in Europe."

"I don't even know how to react to that."

"Neither do we." Giovanna said regretfully.

The couple strolled back through the streets and returned to the apartment. Sara and Giancarlo were back in their room with the door closed. Marc and Giovanna exchanged glances. She handed Marc the bag and told him to put the gelato in the freezer. She knocked on the door and Giancarlo answered. She gestured for him to come out.

"Her father called while you were out. She didn't say anything and tried to make it seem like she was busy and couldn't talk for long. I could tell she wasn't going to last long. Her voice started to shake and as soon as they hung up, she burst into tears and ran to the bedroom. This is going to be harder than I thought. How is she going to keep this a secret for a week, especially with them coming?"

"Perhaps it's worse because today is the first day?" Maybe tomorrow will be better?"

Giovanna sent Giancarlo to the kitchen and knocked gently on the door.

"Please dear, can I come in?"

Hearing a faint and breathy yes from the behind the door, she entered. Sara laid on her side facing the wall. Giovanna sat at the foot of the bed looking down at her. "I heard your father called."

Sara rolled over to face Giovanna. She pushed her long hair from her face and rubbed her eyes.

"Forgive me for being forward, but can I ask you something? Is this the worst thing that has ever happened to you?"

"I think so, yes." Sara wondered.

Giovanna put her hand on Sara's foot.

"Do you remember your worst day?" Sara asked.

"My cancer diagnosis, and a lot of other things are close seconds."

"What was that like?" Sara asked.

"Other than feeling like you got hit in the stomach by a cannonball, your skin turning to glass, and an indescribable sensation of fear, it's not a big deal."

"I can't imagine that."

"No, you can imagine it. You're feeling it right now and I'm going to say something that might just surprise you. Welcome to adulthood, the real adulthood. Honey, life is hard, brutally hard. We get to enjoy the day-to-day pleasantries and if we're lucky enough, we'll have some joy too. However, tragedy will not be denied its day, and everybody pays. I hate to tell you this but, you're young and it's just the beginning. You're not old enough to have funerals be a regular thing. Wait until your parents get old or when the day comes that financial crisis might leave you homeless. This is the real shit, the parts they leave out in the fairytales."

Sara's face lightened a bit and her expression softened. "I see what my dad goes through with my grandmother. I can see how much of a burden it is for him and then he has me and my mother to worry about. My dad always tries to be strong but now, for the first time, I think I know how he feels."

"All things considered; you're doing great. I'm proud of you and so is your uncle. I haven't known you for long, but I can tell how much he adores you. It was probably one of the things I liked most about him from the beginning."

Sara finally smiled. "My uncle is..." She paused. "Unique. I probably know him better than almost anyone and that's saying a lot because he's so private. What has he told you?"

"About what?" Giovanna pondered.

"In general, about himself."

"I know about his illness."

"You do?" Sara's eyes opened wide in surprise. "He told you about that already? That's huge. What else do you know?"

"Never mind that. Let's focus on you and I want you to listen very carefully. There are five large containers of sinfully good chocolate gelato in the freezer. We have a moral imperative to eat until we cannot swallow another bite!"

5:4

Dear Papa,

I can't sleep because I can't stop thinking about worst case scenarios. My thoughts are so dark, but I'm comforted at the idea that I'm being more like you.

I have been thinking a lot that family matters most and how Sara is the future. Individuals die and family continues like a play that just changes characters from generation to generation. This is why parents sacrifice for their children, why men die on the battlefield, and others devote their entire lives to causes.

2000 years ago, this city was home to millions. We still know the names of leaders and a few prominent figures, but what of the countless who lived and died each day? They contributed to establishing western civilization, yet we only remember the battles they fought or the structures they built. As my eyes pour over every brick, I can only imagine the hands that placed them. These streets were packed with six times the population density of New York and we'll never know any of their names. So many lived and fought just so I could be born. Every one of them had stories and histories. We are their beneficiaries and just like they are mysteries to us, so will we be mysteries to our descendants. Like them, we will fade to oblivion.

I remember when you spoke of your grandfather after your Aunt Magdelena died and you said that she was the last person who really remembered him. When she died, it was like he died all over again because his memory died with her.

But right now, all that matters to me is your granddaughter and the child inside of her. Pop, I feel like I could explode. A few moments of distraction here and there offer me anemic relief. Then it all comes rushing back.

I know you want me to talk to mom and I can't believe I'm actually considering it but with everything I just wrote, I must. I have been nagged by a thought. As bad as she was, you remained loyal and like it or not, she is part of this family too.

I keep having this recurring dream and know it must have something to do with unresolved issues. I find myself in total darkness bumping into obstacles. Then I realize that I have a flashlight in my pocket. As soon as I hit the switch, I wake up. I've had it three times. After the second time, I was troubled because I've never had recurring dreams. I hope you can help me understand?

Love,
Marc

The bottle of grappa emptied slowly. He drank more, feeling oppressed by how Elaine could reject the child she had when they might lose one they wanted. It seemed cruel. Then he thought of Giovanna and a more familiar emotion overcame him. For the first time, he felt distrust. How could she be interested in a sick guy? Was she seducing him with a motive? *Love really is a luxury affordable only by the poor,* he thought.

Then he realized that his suspicion wasn't even about his money. It was a lie, just a diversion to deceive himself, because it was really about his mother. Their relationship shaped the rest of his life, particularly with women. He knew then, he had no justifiable reason to distrust Giovanna as he recalled the countless incidents with Hannah that involved the same issues. How many things did he blame on her when in fact, it was just about himself? This made him feel guilty.

He heard the faint sound of footsteps and then a light tap on the door. He said, "Come in," and the hinge made the characteristic creak as the door slowly opened. It was Sara.

"You can't sleep?"

His speech was slurred.

"I'd offer you a drink but probably not a good idea."

"You're drunk." Sara was concerned yet understood considering the circumstances.

"I am, my dearest. I'm so fucking angry that you're going through this."

Sara smiled. "If it helps, Giovanna said something to me that really put this into perspective. She welcomed me to adulthood. It sounded absurd, but after a few moments I thought it was brilliant. She helped me understand that hardship is inevitable, and we have to believe that good can come of tragedy because that's the only way we can bear it.

Look at what you've become in spite of your diagnosis. Look at what you've done for me. You and Giovanna inspire me."

"She really is something, isn't she?"

"Yes. I like her so much."

"Me too."

"See, not everything happening now is bad. We can't ever forget that this is beyond our control now. Not for nothing, Giancarlo will be my husband and he'll be the father of my children either now or later."

"I'm really glad to hear this. You should try to sleep, honey. Tomorrow is a big day."

"You're right. Hopefully Giancarlo isn't snoring."

"Lucky you." Marc joked.

She got up and gave Marc a kiss on the head. "Don't drink too much."

Sara turned to leave, and he stopped her.

"One more thing. You think your dad would be happy if I went to see your grandmother?"

He expected her to be dumbfounded but she was poised and confident.

"Yes, I do." She said plainly.

"Thought so. Go to bed."

A few moments later there was another knock at the door.

"I thought you said you were going to bed."

This time it was Giovanna and his heart jumped as soon as he saw her. She was wearing a green robe and her hair was pulled back. He wasn't expecting her and her arrival both excited and scared him. Giovanna raised her finger and left the room. He heard the clank of a cabinet door and the tinkle of glass and she returned a few moments later. She took the bottle from him and filled hers, placing it back on his end table.

"What're you doing up?" He stammered.

"I woke up to go to the bathroom and I heard you and Sara talking. I overheard some of what you were saying so I thought it best to give you some privacy."

"What did you hear?"

"I heard enough to know you two were having a moment,

so I let you be. So, how are you feeling?" She asked.

"A little drunk, a little angry, a little sad, but okay I guess."

"Drunkenness could be advantageous. You could be more truthful, and it'll be easier to seduce you."

"I was afraid you would say that."

"Are you nervous?"

"Yes." He said plainly.

"Don't worry, I'll go easy on you." She promised.

"I keep having visions of Sara and Giancarlo weeping. I keep hearing it, over and over. It makes me so angry."

"When I found out my ex was cheating, I had visions of gouging out his eyes with a knife while he slept. I wanted to hurt him physically so much that it actually scared me, so I understand."

"If you must know, I never cheated on my wife."

"Did she cheat on you?"

"Nope."

"Then why did you get divorced?" She asked.

"It's quite ironic actually."

"Why?"

He didn't answer and by convenience and compulsion, he was distracted by his arousal.

"You know, you are so beautiful."

His eyes poured over Giovanna. The skin on her legs was smooth. Her robe wasn't tightly bound, and part of her breast showed. Giovanna placed her hand on his leg, and he let out a gentle moan. She leaned in and her scent thickened the air between them. He felt the faint touch of her lips on his. Their breathing quickened. Giovanna pulled his cock from beneath his pants and then her lips descended on it.

It was exhilarating but then distraction crashed upon him. He thought of his lie. He thought of Hannah and was corrupted by guilt. To feel such pleasure and regret at the same time was maddening. Giovanna slipped off her robe and her satiny skin glistened in the light. She pulled his hands to her shoulders. She moved closer as his hands descended to her waist. She opened her legs, and he could feel her desire. Then he thought of his lie and he yelled, "Stop!"

They froze. She could feel his cock throbbing against her.

"What is it?" She asked.

"I want to fuck you so badly right now."

"So then fuck me." She said sweetly.

"No. I can't fuck you until you know certain things. It just wouldn't be right. I don't want more secrets in my life. Put your robe back on."

Giovanna did as he asked. Marc laid there with his eyes closed and slowly his cock relaxed. He pulled up his underwear and put the sheet over himself.

"I need to tell you what happened in my marriage and what I'm doing in Italy. I don't want to be burdened with the memory of your sex only to have you leave because of what I'm about to say."

He divulged his lie to Hannah. She listened intently and to his relief, he didn't see judgement in her eyes.

"You actually aren't freaked out?"

"Yes, a little, but I've heard worse. Why did you choose Rome?"

"In therapy I realized how much I needed some kind of connection with my father and I thought being here would help. I didn't realize how much his death still had so much of an effect on my life. Between that and my mother, I became very deficient in communicating my feelings."

"It's common for us to continue our patterns of rejection. There were a few short-lived relationships after my ex that continued mine." Giovanna said.

"It wasn't only about that for me. I've come to realize I have an overdeveloped sense of self. You know I was a fitness junky—if you could believe it? That was another reason my diagnosis was so difficult. I couldn't be weak or sick for anyone, even myself."

"I can see by your build that you were very active. It must have made it harder to accept your disease."

"Exactly, but I didn't get to the really crazy part of the story."

"Marc, your scars look recent."

Marc then told Giovanna about his suicide attempt, near-death experience and existential crisis.

Giovanna gasped. "I think this might be the most

fascinating story anyone has ever told me. You got a glimpse of the afterlife and it scared you. That's not a common reaction. Most become serene."

"I'm more serene now, but I wasn't at first."

"You really think you saw him?"

"Yes, and I was so tortured at the idea that he knew the truth about me. I have a lifetime of bad behavior. You don't even know how I've treated my brother. That was why I wondered how the fuck something like this happens to an atheist like me? It's a bad joke."

"So, is this everything you needed to tell me?" She asked.

He said yes as if stating the obvious.

"Okay, well just so you know, it's fine and I feel special that you thought it important enough to stop. If you have nothing else to add, I want you to fuck me now."

5:5

Gabe was leaving in four days and Elaine was merciless.

When he arrived, she was watching A Streetcar Named Desire, for the 465th time, give or take twenty. It was one of her go-to battle-cry films when she needed inspiration for a fight.

"Are you ready?" He asked. She still didn't answer. The volume was blaring. Gabe grabbed the remote to turn it down.

"This is my favorite part! I know it doesn't matter to you, but I happen to love this movie!"

"Mom, it's recorded."

"Where the hell are we going anyway?"

She forgot again.

"I told you, we're going to see Doctor Levy."

"What the heck for? I didn't make the appointment."

"Mom, I told you about it twice."

Always the amateur psychologist, he muttered tactical encouragements while he helped her put on her coat and wool hat. They exited down the ramp and he pushed the wheelchair to the car. Getting her in it was an increasingly strategic routine. Once Elaine was seated, he lifted her legs over the car door threshold and closed the door.

After folding her wheelchair and putting it in the trunk with her walker, they were off. He had her Elvis CD playing. She adored the King, but Elaine's mistrust diminished the effect of the music. She had already convinced herself that Gabe's trip was just a ploy to institutionalize her.

Gabe insisted the visit was just routine. As they drove through the streets of Ridgefield, the Christmas decorations abounded. Though they helped cheer her up, she didn't miss the opportunity to use every display and ornament to passive aggressively provoke Gabe. He still hadn't put up her decorations.

"Oh would you look at those cherub statues! I just love them. Can't wait to see mine."

"They're very nice mom." Gabe's voice was tight.

"Love Me Tender is my favorite. Your father and I had our first dance to this song."

Not only did Gabe know this, but he knew she was going to say it.

Gabe was anxious. He and Marc had worked out a scheme to take Elaine to the doctor's, get her prescriptions and to have a chat with Dr. Levy about her stay in the nursing home. He spoke with the doctor earlier that week and explained the situation. As soon as they got into the waiting room, Elaine lit up, because she had an audience.

"Hello!" She shouted to the girl behind the counter.

"Hello Mrs. Diodato."

"Your office decorations are just lovely. You should see mine. They aren't up yet, but I have over 100 angel decorations."

That was another soft jab for Gabe. The office phone rang, and Elaine kept talking. The girl didn't want to seem rude, so Gabe intervened.

"They're very pretty, mom. The receptionist has to work."

Elaine was in a better mood because she was in public. The volume of her voice increased too because she was intent on everyone in the room hearing her; it always made Gabe and Marc uncomfortable.

"Dr Levy is such a good doctor. I've been coming to him

for 18 years."

The man sitting next to her just nodded and grinned. That was classic Elaine. She made open-ended statements that left little room for response. Perhaps it was because Elaine was often the only participant in her conversations. Marc used to joke that they could be on the phone and in the middle of one of Elaine's monologues, he could go to the kitchen, make dinner, eat, do the dishes and then go take a shit and she would never know he was even gone by the time he got back.

The door opened, and they were called. Gabe was grateful to get her out of the waiting room. They got to the examination room and Gabe caught his breath in the chair while the nurse took her vitals. By the looks of him, she should have also been checking his blood pressure.

"Have you ever seen A Streetcar Named Desire? It is such a great movie! It has Marlon Brando."

The girl looked at her kindly but blankly, so Gabe came to her rescue too. "You don't know who Marlon Brando is, do you?"

The nurse giggled cutely and shook her head. Elaine was shocked.

"He was so gorgeous! You gotta watch this movie." She asserted.

"Mom let her do her job. She's too young to know Brando's work."

"Well she should know it. That's the problem with kids today, they don't know history!"

The nurse smiled politely and assured them the doctor would be there shortly. No sooner did the door click shut then Elaine started right in on Gabe.

"How does she not know who the heck Marlon Brando is? Greatest actor of all time."

"That may be true mom, but she can't be a day over 30. Brando died when she was a little girl. Younger people have their own movies and their own stars just like you had yours."

"Brando was not just generational! Everybody has seen the Godfather."

"No, they haven't, mom. I have such a headache."

"My hip is killing me, you'll live."

Elaine was the star of her own game show called *Can You Top This?* If you were hungry, she was hungrier. If you were tired, she was more tired. If you loved a show, she saw a better one. Gabe waited desperately for the doctor. The impending trip really had her wound up so everything was exaggerated.

Dr. Levy entered. He was a short and fit man in his 60s, with a shaved head and a pristinely trimmed white goatee.

"So how are you feeling, Mrs. Diodato?"

"Everything is great! Feeling great! It's gonna be Christmas soon."

"She fell a few weeks back." Gabe interjected.

"Oh it was nothing!"

"Actually, it wasn't nothing, mom. You did something you weren't supposed to do and weren't wearing your life-alert." Gabe said.

"Always trying to make me look bad."

"What did you do, Mrs. Diodato?"

"I just tried to change a record and I lost my balance. It was nothing, I tell you."

Gabe had a different version. "I came in the house and found her on the floor, and you were on the floor for at least two hours."

"It was less than an hour." She said.

"No mom, it was longer."

"Elaine, we've talked about this, you have to stop taking unnecessary risks. It's not going to end well. One bad fall could spell disaster. I want to weigh you." He asked.

"I don't know, she's a bit stiff today."

"Don't speak for me. I'm fine. Get the chair close."

With the help of Doctor Levy, she stood and precariously got on the scale. Gabe balanced her while the doctor moved the counterweights.

"I need you to focus, Elaine. Keep your balance." He said as he adjusted the weights, and the final tally was 256 pounds. Elaine was 5 foot 7. He then took her blood pressure: 155 over 95.

"I don't like your blood pressure and you've gained 13 pounds."

They went back and forth. Dr. Levy asked about her diet to which Gabe was resigned because she refused to eat certain foods.

"So, are you excited about your vacation?" He asked.

"What vacation? I get to go to a nuthouse. He's the one going to Italy." She said resentfully.

"Twin Pines is hardly a nut house. It's nice and you could choose to see it as a vacation. They have fun activities and you'll meet new people." Dr Levy explained.

"He's trying to put me away. That's what this really is. Aren't you?"

Gabe looked at the doctor in desperation.

"Elaine, people at your age do this sort of thing often. You're the third patient of mine this week going there for a temporary stay."

Elaine tried to keep her poker face, but she showed signs of wear. Dr. Levy's reassurances were resonating, even if only a little. "Have you ever been there?" Dr. Levy asked.

"Of course I haven't!" She said nastily.

"Why don't you go now so you can see it first. Gabe, when do you leave?"

"Saturday. She's supposed to check-in Friday."

"It's Tuesday. They have a visitor center. Gabe, do you have time to bring her there?"

Dr. Levy was like a snake charmer. They shook hands and he bid them goodbye.

No sooner did Gabe close the car door and Elaine insisted she didn't want to go. Gabe's patience finally wavered, and it caught Elaine off guard.

"Your son almost died, and I need you to cooperate. Just the other day you were bragging to your friend about him and yet you don't care he's in trouble. No wonder he doesn't— never mind."

"I used to clean your backside."

Gabe interjected, "And I've since cleaned yours!"

"This is all nonsense. You're trying to put me in a looney house." She repeated.

"No, I won't have to because you'll do that all by yourself." Gabe then turned up the volume of the music.

They turned into the driveway of Twin Pines senior facility. It had white wooden columns with an overhang at the entrance. The landscaping was impeccable as the bushes were trimmed precisely and evenly. The trees were not particularly tall which was evidence that the facility was fairly new.

They parked in the handicapped spot and Gabe hung the tag from his rearview mirror. "Much nicer than Halford Manor where you did rehab for your hip."

Elaine wasn't impressed.

Gabe positioned Elaine's walker and her wheelchair customarily and stood staring down at her.

"Am I supposed to get out now?"

"Mother, get out of the car, please, now."

Gabe hovered in exasperation, and Elaine began to pivot towards the door. Linda worried the stress and aggravation would result in a heart attack and she had no intention of losing her husband because of his mother. She was no less impossible and her capacity to hide her madness diminished as she aged. When she was younger, it was easier for her to appear normal, if only superficially which was why she didn't keep friends.

Despite all this, faint moments of clarity provided insight into Elaine's pathologies. If she somehow understood, was she really crazy? If not, was it malice or poor character? If there were moments of lucidity under extreme duress, it still didn't discount the extent of her irrationality and hysteria. Awareness of her mental illness made her bearable because she couldn't help herself and like his father, Gabe had a strong sense of duty, even to his detriment.

He wheeled Elaine through the automatic door into the foyer. The walls were white at the top with a room border and mid-tone green at the bottom, decorated with ordinary landscape paintings probably manufactured in Chinese sweatshops. The carpets were neurotically busy, similar to those typical of Atlantic City casinos. Since Elaine liked casinos, he hoped that would help.

He approached the receptionist as Elaine looked around suspiciously. A few minutes later, they were greeted by Mrs. Wilkens. She was African American with salt and pepper hair, a warm smile and a kind voice. She had a tinge of an accent and a formality suggesting she was from the south, maybe Georgia. Gabe called her Mrs. Wilkens because she never volunteered her first name.

"Hello Gabe, nice to finally meet you in person."

"You too, Mrs. Wilkens. You've been very helpful. This is Elaine, mom this is Mrs. Wilkens."

"Hello Elaine. We are very excited to have you as our guest."

"Nice to meet you. Guest, huh?"

"Yes, of course. By the way, I love your blouse." Mrs. Wilkens said.

She was very good at her job. Took her less than thirty seconds to figure out flattery always worked with Elaine. She thanked her as the expression on her face softened. They toured the halls, the common room and the physical therapy center. Despite the cleanliness and politeness, there were also the unsettling sounds of unanswered buzzers and patients calling for help. One woman was gutturally screaming for water. This didn't help assuage Elaine.

"What's going on with her?" Elaine lacked her usual grandiosity as her need to perform was offset by her distrust. She maintained the same cold expression.

"That lady has dementia. She yells like that all the time. Unfortunately, some people here are very sick."

"People don't seem like they're having too much fun here." Elaine said crossly.

"Like I said, Mrs. Diodato, some people here are permanent residents which will not be the case with you. You'll have the option to move about the facility. Some of the ladies like to play cards. Do you?"

"Does she ever." Gabe said enthusiastically. "Mom has spent more than her share of time in Atlantic City."

"Yup and I'm damn good at poker!" She said.

"Good!" Mrs. Wilkens exclaimed. "Perhaps you'll bring a new level of competition. Let's go down the hall, I want to show you where you'll be staying."

They went about another thirty feet down the hall and came to an empty room. There was a large window that looked out to a garden.

"This room is empty now so unless someone comes for subacute rehab to fill the bed, you will have the room to yourself." Mrs. Wilkens explained.

Elaine grew quiet and her eyes began to well up with tears.

"Mrs. Diodato, there's nothing to worry about. We promise we will treat you very well here and you'll be back home before you know it."

Elaine's tears broke into a full cry. "My son is trying to get rid of me." She was sobbing. Then she turned to Gabe. "You bastard! I'll sue you! You can't do this to me. You don't love me!" Her sobbing grew louder still.

Gabe's face turned red. "Mrs. Wilkens, can I speak to you outside?"

"Mrs. Diodato, I promise we'll be right back."

"See what I mean?" Gabe asked.

"Unfortunately, I do. I'm sorry."

"I think we need to go forward with what we discussed." She nodded in agreement. "Let's go back inside."

"Mom, I need you to calm down."

"Don't you dare tell me to calm down! I know what you're doing and I won't let you." She screamed.

Gabe pulled over a chair and sat across from her. "Look at me."

She continued to look away. Then Gabe said even louder "Mother!" That got her attention. "You leave me no choice. I've just spoken with Mrs. Wilkens and your vacation here already started. I'm not putting up with this or giving you the opportunity to refuse to come back here. I'm going home to get your clothes."

Elaine's sobbing became uncontrollable. Gabe, even in the thick of his frustration, gave his mother a kiss on her forehead, which she didn't acknowledge. Mrs. Wilkens helped her get the TV turned on and showed her how to use the remote. They found a channel she liked and after a few minutes, the drama wound down a bit. Mrs. Wilkens called in an aid who brought coffee and water. With the phone within reach, Elaine composed herself.

"Mom, I'll be back in about an hour."

"Make sure you bring my phone book."

He and Mrs. Wilkens exited the room. "I really want to thank you for playing along with this charade." Gabe said.

"Not a problem. There's nothing I haven't seen here."

"I need to warn you again, she's a handful. Keep an eye on her because she's very prone to willful behavior. She's fallen more often in the last six months because she tries to do things she can't do anymore."

"That's half the people in here." She joked.

"That makes me feel a little better."

As soon as he got outside, Gabe called Marc.

"So how did it go?"

"Terribly, but your plan was brilliant. She did exactly what we said she would do, and the admissions person couldn't have been any better. How's my daughter? I tried to call her earlier and she hasn't called me back."

"I told you, she's really busy on a project. I'm working her ass off and best of all, she's doing great. She's a natural."

"That's good to hear but why doesn't she have time to talk to me?" Gabe asked. "It's not like her."

"She's 22 and having fun with Giancarlo when she isn't working. She actually told me to tell you she loves you and can't wait for you to get here." Marc said.

"I guess I understand. Tell her to at least answer my texts."

"I will." Marc assured him.

They still didn't have the results back and Sara was laying low. It was too emotional for her to talk to her parents.

"Email me your flight info. I'll arrange transportation for you." Marc said.

"How're you feeling?" Gabe asked.

"Believe it or not, I feel great. The doctor said I could make a turn for the worse at any time but as long as I take the medication and don't behave too badly, I might be alright for a while." Marc explained. "So, what else happened?"

"Great news about you. Mom, on the other hand, was impossible. She actually got me to lose my temper today."

"Jesus, call the fucking pope and ask for a novena. You

never get mad."

"My temper has been flaring up with her more lately. Force is the only thing that seems to work."

"Gabe, why don't we just go forward with putting her in a nursing home permanently?"

"I told you, she's still too sharp. Going into a home now will kill her."

"From what you've been telling me, she may kill herself before we get that far. You should think about that."

"Linda keeps telling me the same thing."

5:6

Giancarlo came back alone. Sara and Giovanna were still out. Waiting for the news made him want to sleep. He couldn't handle the anxiety.

Marc put his hand on his shoulder.

"Sara is worried about me."

"I know. She told me."

"Sometimes I wonder if she is withholding the secrets of the universe."

"You're not the first man to wonder that about a woman." Both chuckled. "I was saying the same thing about Giovanna."

"Things are getting serious then?" Giancarlo asked.

"In one word, yes." Marc admitted.

"Really glad. There's no doubt she has been a big help through all of this. You know, I'm thinking about doing my PhD. Now that you've helped us get started, I think we know what we're doing now. We're learning what to look for and how to invest. There's no reason I can't do both."

"That's great news. I think you'd be great." Marc encouraged him. "Best part is that at this point, you don't even need the money."

"Exactly. I can do it because I want to and that'll give me freedom to do the kind of work I want. It's such a dream to be able to say that."

"Be a great example for your children." Marc said.

"My children." Giancarlo paused. "You know I think

back to my initial reaction when Sara first told me she was pregnant. I was afraid and not sure if I wanted to be a father yet. In hindsight, there's nothing I want more. I've been trying so hard to find that middle ground we talked about. Sara has been better at it, but I go back and forth between extremes of hope and despair."

"Listen to me. Whatever this situation will be, it already is. You're just going to find out tomorrow. You know Dr. Rossellino told me that pregnancy complications are a common issue with her patients."

"I guess it's easy to forget that life is not promised. You even know what it's like to want death, even to choose it. I've not had much time alone with you lately and there are some things I've wanted to ask you." Giancarlo said.

"Like is there really life after death?" Marc said with a grin.

"Actually no, I wanted to ask about you. You've been a completely different person since your experience. You're a father figure for us and a few months ago, I couldn't stand you."

"I can't attribute all of it to some big moral revelation. Part of it is because I take my meds. They turn down the volume of the noise in my head."

Giancarlo fired back, "Yes, your meds stabilize you, but it's so much more than that, it's your values, your character."

Marc reflected, "I don't know what to say, but that's not what's on my mind now. I'm thinking about Sara. Even if this child doesn't live, another will. You'll be the father of my father's great grandchildren and the cycle of life continues. Just like how we're talking, my father and his brother sat and had conversations just like we're having now. Your children will have the same conversations and speak of us just as we are speaking of them. Their children and their children's children will do the same. Looking after our family has brought me joy. Reconciling *my experience* had a lot to do with that. I chose to believe I saw my father because it made my life better. Since then, I've been kind of approaching everything with that same logic. I love looking after you kids. My happiness depends so much on you."

Giancarlo listened intently to every word.

Marc continued. "Sometimes I wonder if our worst fears somehow bring out the best in us. When I hit my head on the stone the night of my suicide attempt and I watched everything go dark, I really thought it was over and I've never felt a deeper regret. I've been given a wonderful gift. That is why I am different. We are like frequencies of meaning. Our DNA is a frequency of consciousness and that means we're not just vessels of meaning; we are meaning itself and my meaning is now this family."

"I never thought about it along those lines but what you say makes perfect sense. I wish my brother were here. Do you think he still is? It's funny how you're more of an authority on this than most." Giancarlo jested.

"I told you, I cannot and will not say for sure that I saw my father but, I really believe I did. At first, I was terrified. The thought of being conscious eternally seemed exhausting."

"Only you would react that way. I've read accounts of other people becoming so serene from near-death experiences. You had an existential crisis." They laughed more. "I guess I can make it through this one way or the other."

"Yes, you can, and you will. I'm really proud of you."

"I'm proud of you too, for many reasons."

"Spite is a lot of fun, isn't it? If we had a drink, we'd toast to it again."

"I'm starting to understand what you meant about it." Giancarlo said.

"Beauty, love and hope are sublime revolutionary acts in trying times. I didn't know this before my incident, but it's one of the most consequential things I've ever learned. Life is going to keep throwing bombs at you. The only way to stop them from exploding is to have the courage to catch them and the strength to throw them back!"

They heard the sound of the elevator and Sara and Giovanna burst through the door. "The doctor called with the results."

Chapter 6

The Prodigal Son

6:1

"Sara, are you sure you're okay?" Linda persisted.

"I'm fine mom."

The elevator car slowly muddled upward. Marc was waiting at the top. He wore a black dress shirt with dark gray pants and had returned to his normal body weight. He was clean-shaven and smiling. He embraced Gabe sincerely. Linda was caught off guard when he kissed her.

"Please come in." Marc said graciously.

They entered and in the living room Giancarlo and Giovanna were waiting.

"It's very nice to see you again, Mr. Diodato."

"Call me Gabe. It's good to see you too, Giancarlo. I'm sorry I had to leave abruptly when I was here. Thank you again for everything."

"It's my pleasure."

"It feels weird to speak English." Sara mused.

"How is her Italian?" Gabe asked.

"Exceptional actually." Giancarlo attested.

"You must be Giovanna." Gabe went to shake her hand and she stopped him.

With a big smile and in her very suave manner, she kissed both cheeks customarily and did the same with Linda.

"Your daughter is quite something." Her accent was heavy. Giovanna's English was reasonably good, but her diction remained firmly rooted in the Italian vernacular. Her vowels were more pitched. Picture was pronounced peekture. English was Eengleesh. It was demurely sexy.

"Your English is good too." Marc interrupted.

"Thank you, your Italian isn't bad either."

"He lets you make fun of him?" Gabe remarked.

"He doesn't have a choice." Giovanna responded.

"What would you like?" Marc asked.

Gabe and Linda said "coffee" in unison.

Giancarlo and Sara wisped out of the room to prepare beverages.

"So how are you, umm?" Gabe stammered.

"How am I feeling? Don't worry, she knows everything.

I'm responding well to the new medication. It's a weird disease. The thing about MS is that when you walk up a hill or try to walk too fast, it feels like you're walking through a pool. The worst is the muscle aches but other than that I'm fine for now."

Gabe wasn't used to Mark being so forthcoming. "I feel like I haven't seen you in years."

Marc smiled faintly. "Years? It's been decades."

Gabe knew it was metaphorical. Sometimes it takes siblings so few words to say so much. There was no animosity between them.

"It's really good to see you."

"You too. How was your flight?"

"Thanks for the business class seats. Really made a difference. Listen to this. There was a young man across the aisle whose chair was broken. He told the steward, and his answer was 'everything's broken in Italy.'"

"That's not what you want to hear before you're ten thousand meters in the air." Giovanna replied.

"My thoughts exactly." Linda responded.

Sara and Giancarlo returned with a tray of small demitazza cups and saucers, coffee, anisette cookies, glasses and a big bottle of water. They were curious about the laughter and Gabe repeated the story but was impatient to know more about his daughter.

"What's going on with you, Sara? You haven't returned my texts and calls. Your uncle says you're working on a big project." Gabe was adamant.

Marc answered for her. "Sara and Giancarlo just finished their first project and I calculate they will make around fifty thousand Euros in profit."

Gabe and Linda were stunned. "That's wonderful! Why didn't you tell us?" Gabe asked.

"I wanted to surprise you."

"Fantastic, honey." Linda said.

Gabe's face grew perplexed which Linda noticed and it seemed that both were reaching the same conclusion.

"So, does this mean you're not coming home?" Linda asked nervously.

Sara sat rigidly on the edge of the couch. Her father asked the same question even more urgently.

"Gabe, Linda, please. There's more and I'm asking you to keep an open mind." Marc pleaded.

Sara started to breath heavily. The mood and color of the room changed quickly, and humor passed to formality. Giovanna noticed and attempted to calm her. Gabe and Linda grew defensive. Sara was unable to speak and Marc took the lead.

"The kids want to get married and I support them."

The room fell silent.

"You support them?" Linda fired back. "You planned this! This is why you insisted we come." Linda shouted.

"No. Gabe, I'm begging you both to trust me and just listen."

"Stop it!" Sara shouted and then began to sob. "Everybody stop it and sit down."

Sara sprang from the couch and into her mother's arms. She held her tightly as Linda comforted her as only a mother can. Linda softly begged her to share her troubles.

"Mom, I need you to listen to everything I'm about to tell you." Then she reached over to grab her father's arm. "Daddy, promise me you'll listen."

Marc intervened. "Do either of you honestly think I would condone this under anything but the best circumstances?"

Their expressions relaxed and Gabe leaned back in his chair.

Though he asked him to call him by his first name, Giancarlo continued to use his surname out of respect. "Mr. Diodato, I love your daughter. I want to marry her, and I want to be a good husband and I ask for your blessing."

Gabe didn't immediately respond.

"Mom? Dad?" Sara's eyes were fixed on Giancarlo. Anxiety overcame them. "Now I have to tell you the most difficult part." Sara got up from her mother's lap and went back to sit next to Giancarlo. Gabe was contentious. Sara regained her composure, wiped her eyes and sat up straight.

"I'll start at the beginning but you're both going to swear to let me finish."

The two parents nodded auspiciously but Sara wasn't convinced. "Say it!"

Gabe and Linda obliged.

"OK, I'm pregnant."

Their faces reflected excitement, dread, shock, disbelief and joy all at the same time.

"When the kids found out, I asked them what they wanted. They said they loved one another. I think they'll make a great team and good parents. I've deliberately acted as a buffer between you because there's more." Marc said.

"Why did you keep this from us?" Gabe asked.

"Sara was so afraid that you'd be disappointed. We decided that I was going to partner with them and teach them my business. They really stepped up because they knew that they needed to show you they were serious. Gabe, you're going to be grandparents!"

Gabe could no longer curtail his joy.

Marc continued. "That's not the only reason we kept it from you. This was almost a very tragic situation. There was a chance the fetus had a genetic disorder and that would've required an abortion. Three days ago, we found out the baby is fine and it's a boy."

"But why didn't you come to us?" Gabe asked intently.

"Dad, what would have been the point of telling you? We were prepared to face this together. I realized I wanted to marry him even if we lost the child. I also realized how much I want this baby. Uncle Marc was our rock. Dad, you've always been the first man in my life but two other men and soon a third will share that place with you."

"It's starting to get crowded in here, but I guess the company is good." Gabe laughed.

Linda was still apprehensive, but Gabe made it clear there was nothing more to discuss. He turned to Giancarlo. "Do you really love my daughter that much?"

"Yes." Giancarlo said without hesitation.

"And you'll take care of her and your son for the rest of your life?"

"Yes!"

"Then you have my blessing." He turned to Sara. "You

would have really never told us about the baby if the news had been different?"

"I would have later but there was no reason for you to know now. I had support here."

"That's how I know this is real and that you're grown up enough to handle this. That you both stepped up and faced this together is what holds marriages together." He turned again to Giancarlo. "You have taken care of my daughter and you saved my brother. You deserve my respect and approval."

"Bravi!" Giovanna exclaimed.

Then Sara unveiled her surprise for her father and uncle. "His name will be Antonio, after grandpa."

6:2

It was her fifth day at Twin Pines and Elaine got chummy with the daytime receptionist. She continually remarked about how beautiful it was outside. When she was told patients could only be outside near the cafeteria, which had a fence, she said it depressed her. She really wanted to sit under the entirely ordinary trees in the front, near the banal and boringly trimmed bushes bordering the driveway. When she pressed and the receptionist told her no for the third time, Elaine's tone changed, and she defiantly wheeled herself away.

Elaine spent the whole next day in her room. She didn't want to meet other residents or socialize. This was not subacute rehab after surgery. This was different. She didn't belong there, and she wasn't going to gratify anything about Twin Pines under the circumstances. She sat in her chair, brooding and compulsively picking at the cushion on the armrest while cycling through the TV channels three times in an hour as she fretted about how to escape.

"911, what is your emergency?"

"I'm being held captive at Twin Pines nursing home. I'm here against my will."

"Ma'am, are you in immediate danger and have you been hurt?"

"No, I'm not in immediate danger, but I am being held against my will! Isn't being kidnapped enough of an emergency?"

"Ma'am, you could not have been kidnapped and brought to a nursing home."

"Oh, forget it!" Elaine slammed down the phone.

About ten minutes later, Mrs. Wilkens arrived. "Mrs. Diodato, are you okay?"

"I'm fine." Elaine said angrily.

"Are you sure? I just hung up with the police department. You called 911 and claimed you were kidnapped."

"I, I don't know what you're talking about."

"Mrs. Diodato, I know you called because the officer provided the number. It was your room."

Elaine tried sticking to her story.

"Mrs. Diodato, if you call them again, I'll have to block your phone from making outgoing calls."

Elaine glared defiantly at Mrs. Wilkens.

Undeterred, Mrs. Wilkens asked if Elaine needed anything and she whimsically said no.

"Very well, use your call button if you do need anything."

When she returned to her office, she began a write up of the incident.

"What did she say?" Her colleague asked.

"She denied it. Luckily, she's only here until next week, let's hope she doesn't cause any more trouble."

"Of course, she denied it, they always do." Her colleague said.

No sooner did she start writing her report when the fire alarm went off and there was no fire drill scheduled.

She got up from her desk and went into the hall. Amidst all the hustle and bustle, Mrs. Wilkens had an intuition. She went straight to Elaine's room and when she arrived, she wasn't there. She went back in the hall and noticed the fire alarm a few doors down had been pulled. She rushed around the corner and saw Elaine slowly and laboriously wheeling herself towards the door. Mrs. Wilkens hurried after her.

"Mrs. Diodato, Mrs. Diodato!" She yelled.

Elaine tried to wheel even faster. She just wanted to get to the other side of the door. Her plan did not go any further than leaving the building. She summoned all of her strength.

"Nurse, stop that woman."

"No!" Elaine screamed.

"Ma'am, please stop!"

The nurse stood in front of her chair. Mrs. Wilkens caught up to Elaine who was crying.

"Please don't lock me up here. Please let me go home."

Elaine pleaded desperately and Mrs. Wilkens' frustration transitioned to sympathy.

6:3

Mrs. Wilkens emailed Gabe about the incident and asked him to call her in the morning. She assured him it was not urgent, but he was no less concerned. Linda protested because Gabe promised he would detach and try to enjoy himself.

"Now, I want my Italian breakfast. I want to try that cor-something."

"A cornetto." Gabe said with a worried grin.

"And how are they different from croissants?" Linda asked.

"They are lighter, flakier and sweeter. Croissants have too much butter. You can get them plain or cream filled. My favorite was always Nutella. We can also try a ciambella, which is an Italian donut."

"Okay, now I'm hungry, let's go."

It was perfect jacket weather for December. The sun reflected off the smooth sampietrini stones of the street. Linda thought they were beautiful. They looked like cobblestones but were more tightly fit together and much darker in color. The ones on the footpaths were centuries old and worn down.

They made a few turns and arrived at a café recommended by Giancarlo. It had a wooden bar as long as the room. Linda began to walk towards the counter and Gabe stopped her because you had to order at the register.

Gabe ordered two Nutella stuffed cornettos, a double espresso, a caffé latte and two small blood orange juices.

They waited at the counter and a twentyish young woman greeted them with the customary "prego." Gabe handed her the receipt.

"Okay, let's sip the coffee first." It wasn't just good; it was an experience. They each picked up their cornetto and bit into them together.

"Oh my god." Linda said in amazement.

It was warm and silky. The smell of freshly baked dough mingled with sugar and chocolate was exquisite. When they finished, they cleared their palettes with water for the fresh squeezed orange juice.

"I think I just had an orgasm." Linda whispered.

They left the café and Gabe's mood changed.

"What is it?" Linda asked.

"Being here really makes me miss my father."

She grabbed his arm as they strolled along the street. "I remember how devastating it was for you and I imagine it must've been terrible for Marc."

"Absolutely, but it was different. They were closer, and he was younger."

Linda realized she'd never really asked him about his relationship with Marc as children.

"I feel like I'm meeting your brother for the first time." Linda remarked.

"I think I am too. Have we discussed Sara enough?"

"I can't believe I'm saying this, but I'm not worried. I really like Giancarlo and I believe she really loves him. They…"

"They remind you of us." Gabe said.

"I see how she looks at him and it's how I looked at you when we were young. They're working hard to plan for this child. Honestly, I'm impressed." Linda said.

"I can't believe I'm okay with it either, but not only do I trust Sara, I trust my brother. I don't think he would've let Giancarlo anywhere near her if he didn't trust him. We are going to be grandparents!"

They kissed and squeezed each other's hands as they walked along.

Linda and Gabe spent the rest of the morning sightseeing, but he was occasionally distracted by the coming phone call with Mrs. Wilkens.

Back at the hotel, Linda continued packing but listened carefully to Gabe's call. After a few minutes of yeses, oh noes, okays and thank you's, mixed with sighs of anguish and embarrassment, the call ended. Gabe laboriously recounted the details. Linda felt very sorry for her husband, but also resentful.

She said she would have been surprised if it had been anyone else but Elaine.

"I don't want to talk about your mother while we're here, but when we're home, we need to resolve this once and for all. You can't go on like this!"

"She's fine so there's nothing more to discuss." Gabe said.

"This is our first vacation in years and here we are talking about your mother. She always has to be the center of attention."

"I've put up with it because I think my mother is just crazy. She's not a bad person."

"I'm not so sure. Her gambling problem, the strange men, and her mean-spiritedness suggest otherwise. She's so opinionated about everyone, but no one can have opinions about her. Your brother's illness has got me thinking. He's younger than you. I'm not about to be a widow at my age—especially when we're about to have a grandson!"

6:4

"I had that dream again last night. It always ends the same way. I pull a flashlight from my pocket and I wake up."

"What do you think it means?" Giovanna asked.

Marc shook his head as he chewed his sandwich. He started to tell her about the fire alarm incident but was interrupted by Giancarlo and Sara. It was time to depart for San Pietro al Tanagro.

Marc was jumpy and impatient. "I can't wait to see my Uncle Angelo, Paolina and Renata. They're my first cousins and I barely know them."

Giovanna kissed him on his cheek. They reached the ground floor and boarded a black van. They picked up Gabe and Linda from their hotel and were off. After a lot of stop-

and-go traffic in the city, they finally reached the highway and veered left towards Napoli.

"How long has it been since you were both there?" Sara asked.

"I was about 18 and Marc was 9." Gabe said.

"So, what's it like in San Pietro?" Linda asked.

"San Pietro al Tanagro and Sant'Arsenio are situated in a valley between two mountain ridges. San Pietro is smaller, and its name is derived from the Tanagro river that separates them." Giancarlo explained.

"I can't wait to see Aunt Angela. Wait until you meet her! She's a big ball of energy. I couldn't believe how she sounded so young and sharp on the phone, just how I remember her. She's got to be in her mid-60s by now," Gabe said.

"How old is Uncle Angelo?" Sara asked.

"He's in his early 70s. He was a lot younger than your grandfather. Grandpa would be in his 80s." Marc said.

"How did grandma and grandpa meet?"

"Your grandfather came to the States in 1963. They met at a dance." Marc explained.

"My grandmother was so gorgeous." Sara said to Giancarlo and Giovanna.

"She was." Gabe interjected.

They told stories for the rest of the trip. As they got farther south, the mountains got bigger. They passed Naples and marveled at Mount Vesuvius dominating the landscape. Soon after, they passed the city of Salerno, which meant they were only about 30 minutes away.

Soon, things started to seem familiar. They pulled off the exit and passed over the highway onto a road that snaked through a flat valley flanked by two mountain ridges. As they drove across, they had to stop for a very large flock of sheep crossing the road.

"Can't be the same family." Gabe insisted.

"No, it is." Giancarlo asserted. "They have tended sheep here for generations."

"I'll be damned." Gabe said.

"Things don't change down here." Marc said.

"Well, they do, but very slowly." Giancarlo remarked.

The flock of sheep finally cleared the road and the black passenger van drove on towards town.

"There's the house!" Gabe said.

"And it looks exactly the same!" Marc responded.

The house did look the same. It was terra cotta mustard yellow with a slate roof. They turned right on the side street and pulled up past a large gate that led into the compound. Marc was the first out of the van and stood at the top of the driveway waiting for everyone. The door of the house opened and out walked a very pretty woman in her 30s. She was tall, with short dark hair the length of her chin and very large brown eyes.

"Paolina!" Marc said.

"Cousin!" She responded.

"It has been so nice corresponding with you." She said. "I'm so happy you're here."

"Me too!" Marc said enthusiastically. "You were just a little girl when I saw you last."

The two exchanged a warm embrace.

"Look at this little girl all grown up!" Gabe said.

Marc finally got around to formal introductions. "This is your second cousin, who happens to be the youngest and the first female mayor ever elected in San Pietro al Tanagro."

Sara approached her timidly to say hello. Paolina looked at her and called her a bonazza, which means a hot woman. Sara blushed.

The door to the house opened again and out walked Uncle Angelo. He had lost most of his hair. He was simply dressed and wore fine rimmed glasses.

"Uncle!" Gabe said.

"My boys are finally home." Angelo said. He looked at Marc and squinted his eyes as he peered up at him, smiling warmly. "You look so much like your father. And who is this lovely woman?"

"This is Giovanna, my... girlfriend." Marc said to his own surprise.

"To be young again. If I were, I would steal her right out from under your nose!" Angelo said.

"You would try!"

Giovanna laughed, "I don't know, Marc, your uncle is very handsome. I'm afraid you have some competition."

"I like her already." Then Angelo turned his eyes back to Giovanna "Keep him guessing." His attention went to Sara and he said to Gabe, "how long will you continue to insult me by depriving me the acquaintance of this lovely young woman? I still have every picture you ever sent me. The pictures just don't do you justice."

"Thank you, Uncle Angelo." Sara said as she presented him to Giancarlo.

Then Aunt Angela came bursting through the door. She was all of a hundred pounds with very diesel arms. By the looks of her, it was hard to believe she was a woman in her 60s.

Marc felt like he was back home. His eyes danced across every detail of every face. The property was just as he remembered it. There was the field of tomatoes and zucchini right next to the house and he could hear the goats bleating and pigs grunting out back.

Southern Italy was frozen in time, which was both a blessing and a curse. Tradition reigned out of reverence and sheer stubbornness. Only little things like smartphones showed signs of modernity. Recipes remained unaltered. The fields near the house still grew the same vegetables and every subsequent generation had the same handful of names. His father was Antonio and his brothers were Angelo and Francesco just like their parents and uncles before them. Marc and Gabe didn't reflect the tradition because Elaine refused to name Gabe Arsenio, who was Antonio and Angelo's father.

They had about an hour to freshen up before dinner. Giovanna wanted to take a nap, but Marc was restless. He headed straight for the outdoor patio. It was covered by a roof with gas heaters so it could be used for gatherings during the winter. In the spirit of things never changing, he was eager to see if the hammock still hung from the old wooden beams. It was still there. Nobody was on the patio yet and Marc wasted no time to lay in it. He stared at the ceiling rocking back and forth, remembering being in the exact same spot when he was a boy. He remembered the men sitting on one end of the long table, drinking and smoking cigars, while the women sat at the other end drinking coffee, eating pastries and making fun of the men without them ever catching on.

The air was fresh with the smell of slow cooked meat and charcoal. Angela was roasting a pig for the evening banquet.

"You couldn't wait, could you." Angelo's voice bellowed suddenly from the house behind him. "We couldn't get you off the hammock when you were little."

"I'm surprised and yet not surprised it's in exactly the same place." Marc said.

"Of course, it is. It's the perfect place for a hammock, so why would I move it?"

"Yes, indeed, uncle." Marc said, as he sat up and put his feet to the floor. "It's so good to see you."

"I look at you and I see a ghost."

Marc smiled. "I couldn't help but notice there are more table settings than just us. Who else is coming?"

"As observant as ever, my boy." He remarked. "I have a surprise for you."

"What surprise?" He retorted.

"If I tell you, it's not a surprise!"

"Ciao papa," a demure voice sounded from the stairs that led to the driveway. It was followed by a much younger voice that yelled out "ciao nonno!" The child's yawp was accompanied by the sound of footsteps running. His grandson Francesco had just arrived with his mother Renata and father Luigi.

"Who is that?" Little Francesco asked inquisitively with his big brown eyes.

"That's your cousin." Angelo said.

"How could he be my cousin if I've never met him?"

Francesco was a very adorable and precocious child. His mother picked him up, nuzzling him with a kiss, and asked him to stop giving his cousin such a hard time.

"Ciao Renata. You are as beautiful as I remember you."

"Marc! So nice to see you, thirty years goes by so fast."

"Too fast." Marc said regretfully.

Renata was thin like her mother, with jet black hair and very dark skin. She looked almost north African.

"My father has been talking about you coming for weeks." She said.

"Your son is extraordinary."

"That's one way of saying it. I swear he can already read people. We were in a store in town and after we left, he said to me that the person at the counter was bad. I asked him how he knew, and he said he just did."

"God help you." Marc joked.

"So papa, did Francesco and Stefano confirm?"

"Who?" Marc asked.

"Your surprise." He rolled his eyes. "Francesco and Stefano were close with your father when they were in school together. They want to see you."

"Wait, I remember them! That's great!" Marc said.

"How is your mother?" Angelo asked.

"Cannot say for certain but from what I can see, not very good." Marc was evasive.

"How do you mean?" Angelo responded.

"It's probably better you ask Gabe."

Marc was grateful when the door to the house opened and out came a parade of family members with platters of food. He didn't have to elaborate. Angela was first with a large plate of salamis and prosciuttos that were hand cut. Then Sara, Linda, Giovanna, Paolina, Gabe and Luigi brought more food, bottles of wine, and pitchers of water. The table exploded with color and aroma. Everyone took their seats, and the wine went around the table. Everyone raised their glasses for a toast and Angela noticed Sara only had water.

"We make the wine here, you have to try some!" Angela said. All of a sudden, an awkward silence followed. Then Sara and Giancarlo started to laugh which made everybody more confused.

"I can't have alcohol because I'm pregnant."

The whole table chorused in rejoice.

"And by the way, we're also getting married."

The celebration grew louder still. Everyone came around and congratulated them and Marc looked on feeling very pleased with himself. Then Paolina said "I told you I can keep a secret."

Angelo protested. "So you knew?"

Paolina nodded mischievously.

"Can't trust any politicians, not even my own daughter!"

Then Angelo stood up and asked for everyone's attention. Marc imagined his father as if he were still alive.

"I am 72 years old and I've lived long enough to know that days like these are very rare and that it is important to acknowledge them. Two of our sons returned and our beautiful Sara will have a child and be married. I'm such a lucky man to share this moment with you."

They raised their glasses in celebration. A moment later, Francesco and Stefano arrived.

"You're late!" Angelo joked.

"We're old." Stefano joked back.

"I remember both of you well." Gabe said. "You look great!"

"Wish I felt great, but I am 82. At my age you take what you can get." Francesco said.

"Come on, let's sit and eat. You just missed the toast." Angelo said.

They all took their places and began the feast. By accident, or not, the men and women were at opposite ends. Angela held court on one side and Angelo on the other. Marc, Gabe, Angelo, Francesco and Stefano sat together. Marc and Gabe were eager to learn new things about their father. They chatted as plates of meat passed around the table.

"So how did you two meet?" Angela asked Sara and Giancarlo.

"I still can't believe we're from neighboring towns." Giancarlo said.

"You are from Sant'Arsenio?" Angela asked boldly.

"My father is."

"What is your last name?"

"Graziano." Giancarlo said.

"Was your grandfather Pietro Graziano?"

"Yes, as a matter of fact."

"Oh my god, your aunt Vera had such a crush on him!" Angela said in astonishment to Paolina.

"What a small world." Giovanna remarked. "Did you two

make sure you're not related?" She asked Sara and Giancarlo.

"No, they're not." Angela said. "But it's not that far-fetched. People go back many generations." Angela turned her head. "Angelo! Giancarlo's grandfather was Pietro Graziano!"

"Your grandfather was a good man. He died just a few years ago."

"Yes, he did." Giancarlo said regretfully. "I miss him."

"So, you worked for Marc and met Sara. Sara, when did you get here?" Angela asked.

"A few months back."

Marc overheard again and said, "Aunt Angela, I'm sorry I didn't get down here sooner."

"Don't worry Marc, you must've had a good reason." Angelo said.

Marc's first reaction was to agree but as he sat and saw the trusting expressions of his family, he started to feel angry with himself. He felt like a liar. Conversation at the table resumed and as their afterthought for his benefit seemed a foregone conclusion, he yelled out "Aspetta!" Everyone stopped talking and all eyes were on him. Marc stood up, grabbed his glass and emptied it.

"I have something I need to say. I didn't expect to say it like this, but I can't let you think I had a good reason for being away so long."

"Marc please, you don't have to be so hard on yourself." Angela said.

"No! You're wrong. I do. I have so much to be sorry for and so much that I still have to make right. I'm not deserving of your understanding. The truth is, I didn't want you to know I was here. I am ashamed of that. My father would be ashamed of me for that."

His eyes welled up and his voice cracked. Gabe grabbed his arm. "You don't need to do this now."

"Yes I do!" He shouted. "Please let me finish. How many times did you call, Uncle Angelo, and I didn't call you back? It's terrible and sometimes I think I got what I deserved for being a self-pitying ass."

Marc shared the news of his illness. Gasps could be heard at the table. What were joyful faces a few minutes earlier sank with concern. His eyes locked with Giovanna's. He saw love—real love in her eyes and it filled him with hope, but also shame.

"If we are to have a beautiful time together, it has to be honest or it won't be real."

His head sank as he stood at the table. Angelo stood, grabbed him by the shoulders and turned him to face him. "It's okay."

Marc started to resist, and Angelo forcefully stopped him. "Basta! I only care about one thing: that you are here now. Look around you! You have people here who love you. Your father wouldn't be ashamed of you! Don't you ever say that in my presence again!"

Marc tried turning away and Angelo slapped him in the face. "Never! Do you understand me? You are my brother's son and to have you back is all that matters to me." He pulled Marc to him and held him. Everyone applauded. Angelo pulled back, looked him in the face and said, "Not another word. Your aunt prepared a glorious meal that has taken days and we're going to celebrate. Have I made myself clear? This is my house!"

"Yes uncle." He said quietly.

"Then let's have dinner! My brother loved music. Let's put on some music."

Angelo's command had restored levity to the evening. Paolina queued up some traditional Napoletana music and the feast commenced, but not without Giovanna moving her seat next to Marc. No discussion about his outburst was needed. She just sat with him. It was one of the many things he appreciated about her.

The first cured meats were buttery but not too salty. The taste was perfectly complemented by the aglianico red wine that was made locally from one of Campania's signature red grapes. It was hearty enough to mature in the hot Campania summers. There were also pickled foods like artichokes, peppers, olives, sundried tomatoes and eggplant along with an assortment of cheeses.

This must be what food tasted like a century ago, Marc thought. He savored every bite as he looked around the table at everyone enjoying themselves. He kept looking at Gabe. His expressions seemed youthful as he and Sara flanked Linda to aid the translations.

Out of nowhere, Angela stood up like a General. "Time to get the pig! You want to see it?"

"Of course, we do!" Sara blurted.

Angela and Paolina led them down the back stairs of the patio. There was a large smoker made of a dark metal. Paolina put on some gloves and heaved the top open. They looked on at the golden red skin of the pig that had been slow cooking for many hours. Sara was a bit shocked because she didn't expect the pig to still have its head.

"He was a young pig?" She asked innocently.

"You're probably not used to seeing a whole animal cooked. All things must die, my dear, but if it makes you feel better, this animal had a leg injury. That's also why we slaughtered him young."

"*You* slaughtered him?" She asked timidly.

"And who else do you think is going to do it?" She was playful and sarcastic. "This animal had a good life. He never suffered and was never hungry. How many times have you eaten pork and never once questioned where it came from?"

"You're right." Sara admitted. "I've eaten bacon, prosciutto, sausages, pork chops and I've never once thought about it because I never had to face that it was actually an animal. That's what I get for growing up in America."

"You think it's just Americans? Kids in the big cities are the same, especially if they don't have roots in the small towns." She said.

Marc and Gabe asked what they could do to help.

"Both of you put on gloves. We have to lift out the bar."

It was clearly a home-made cooker, but it was rather ingenious because the main bar that skewered the animal had a gear that attached to a motor. It turned continuously. Marc and Gabe got on either side and lifted out the pig. Angela instructed them to lay it on the large platter. She took a knife and cut off a piece of the skin and gave it to them. At first it crunched then it melted in their mouths. Then she and Paolina removed the rod from inside the pig. Marc and Gabe picked up the tray and the two carried it up to the patio. They arrived at the top of the stairs to the sound of more applause. Linda had a similar reaction as Sara because she also had never seen a fully cooked young pig. Angela followed closely behind and had them place it down on a large counter that was against the house. Angela opened the drawer and pulled out some very impressive knives and cleavers and proceeded to butcher the pig like a Samurai warrior. Marc, Gabe and Sara looked on with respect. Giancarlo came up behind Sara and said, "Never seen that before, have you?"

Angela was like a surgeon explaining every detail of the process. They all stood about watching. Giancarlo and Giovanna were more interested in watching the family in amusement because this was nothing new for them.

"For the first time in my life, I'm realizing how much I don't know about survival." Sara said in bewilderment. "If civilization breaks down, can we come here?" She asked Angela.

Everyone laughed.

"You're welcome here any time, my dear."

"I remember seeing my first pig slaughtered when I was a child." Giovanna said.

"How young were you?" Sara asked.

"I was five. When my father cut the pig's throat, I cried and begged him to stop. He told me to keep quiet and leave, but I wouldn't. Then he did something that really surprised me. He cradled the pig's head in his arms and caressed it as he died. I stood there weeping as my father cleaned the blood off his hands in the sink. He walked over to me and kneeled down. When I asked him how he could be kind to the pig as he killed him, he said that an animal doesn't need to die in terror. Killing him had nothing to do with any kind of malice. It's just life. I continued crying and he grabbed my chin and smiled at me. He said, 'You know that prosciutto you love so much, where do you think it comes from?'"

"What a story." Sara said. "It really does put everything into context. We go to the store and we buy steak or chicken and it never occurs to us they were walking and breathing until very recently. It never bothers me and because I make it a point to buy meat that's pasture raised, I absolve myself, but the truth is, I should have the courage to kill and butcher an animal if I'm going to eat him. It's the right thing to do."

Now she had Giancarlo's attention as her mother's face reflected sheer horror, but Sara pressed on. "No, wait a minute. The pig that Giovanna's father slaughtered had a peaceful death. The animals we eat do not. By comparison, he had a great life compared to pigs that are in industrial farms. This is as humane as it gets."

"I think about this a lot. We try so hard to run from any hint of violence but in the end, it's unavoidable. The violence itself is not always bad. It's why and how that matter." Marc said.

Sara agreed.

"You know, I was planning on slaughtering another next week, but it doesn't have to wait. I could use the help." Angela said and before she could even finish her next sentence, Sara said "Yes, I'll help."

Linda cried out in protest, "Why in the world would you want to do that?"

"Because I want to know what that kind of remorse feels like. I'm about to bring a life into the world, I should also know what taking it feels like. Perhaps if humanity had to face what we kill directly, we would do it with less frivolity?"

"Wait, you're pregnant, you can't be in contact with blood." Giancarlo interjected.

"He's right." Angela said.

"Then I'll watch." Sara insisted.

"Okay, time to eat." Angela interrupted. She asked Giancarlo to bring the platter to the table. Everything was so neatly sliced but he couldn't help but notice the bucket of bones next to the counter. He placed the platter on the table by Angela. Plates were passed in her direction and she and Paolina prepared them for everyone. As soon as the last plate was placed, Angela gave the equivalent of a horse bell to signal the start of a race. Everybody dug in and no one said a word. All you heard was the banging of forks and knives, the subtle sound of chewing, nostril breathing with pleasurable groans, and the music. Finally, Angelo looked across the table and said, "My love, this is beyond spectacular." Everyone agreed. Every mouthful of pork didn't need to be chewed. It just dissolved.

"So, what was it like growing up with my father?" Marc asked Stefano and Francesco.

"Depends on whether we're talking about youth or adolescence." Stefano answered.

Francesco interjected, "When we were young, your father compulsively took apart everything he could. He had to know how everything worked."

"Oh my god, you have to hear the carburetor story. I was playing with my toys and your father was under the hood of Grandpa's car. I didn't know what he was doing. Then grandpa comes out and starts screaming at your dad."

"What was he doing?"

"Your father decided taking apart the carburetor on his engine was a good idea. Problem was, Grandpa needed the car to go to work in three hours and your dad had never put one back together. He assured Grandpa that it would take him less an hour. Your grandfather stormed back into the house and your father kept working. I soon got bored with my toys and went in the house to watch TV. My father kept watching the clock and saying, 'your brother will be pulling a cart if he doesn't fix this mess.' A little bit later, we heard the sound of an engine roaring. My father and I ran outside and there he was, less than an hour later, standing next to the car, looking very pleased with himself."

Everyone started laughing. "Your grandfather tried to seem serious, but it didn't work. Soon he started to laugh even as he playfully berated your father. Eventually he couldn't hide that he was impressed. What was even funnier was that your father knew it."

Marc and Gabe delighted in the story.

"Can you imagine dad doing that?" Gabe imagined.

"You probably could not imagine a lot of things. Your father was rebellious. He and your grandmother always argued about religion. He would quote Marx calling it the opiate of the masses. This incensed your grandfather. Every Sunday there was an argument about church. He never wanted to go but your grandparents always forced him to keep up appearances."

"I can't imagine any of this!" Marc gasped. "Did grandma and grandpa force him because they were religious?"

"No. In those days, if you didn't go to church, there was talk." Stefano explained. "You wouldn't believe what he'd say when he dipped his hands in the holy water. He would say under his breath, 'Hail Satan.' Sometimes he said it just loud enough for the nuns to hear. It was all a joke to him. He thought it was silly."

"Can you believe dad was such a smartass?" Gabe commented.

"Are you really asking me that question?"

"Your father used to get in trouble in Catechism on Saturdays because he'd ask questions the nuns didn't appreciate." Francesco said.

"He and your grandmother battled about this and she insisted he continue until his confirmation. Afterwards, he never went again." Angelo said.

"What kind of questions?" Sara interjected.

"One day, our teacher was talking about eternal damnation. We were all terrified. Your father was less affected. He interrupted the nun and asked how God could be all-forgiving and yet condemn us without any chance of redemption? Then he added insult to injury when he asked why Lucifer was so powerful if God was all-powerful? Sister Maria stood mortified at the front of the room." Stefano explained.

Francesco was laughing. "She was as white as a ghost and Antonio just sat there. All she said was for him to go see the Monsignor."

"Oh my god, I remember that. Your grandmother was so horrified when the Monsignor called." Angelo added.

"It's weird I have so much trouble imagining dad like this because I'm exactly the same way. Considering how religious my mother is, I still can't understand their marriage. How could he have changed so much?"

"He didn't want you boys to hear arguments that weren't necessary." Angelo explained.

"That sounds like dad." Gabe affirmed.

Angela and Paolina, with the help of Linda and Renata, cleared all the plates and returned with trays of desserts, caffè and liquors. As a point of order, she set a tray with three bottles of dark after-dinner liquors on their side of the table with more than half a dozen small glasses. Of course, they were homemade too. Angelo passed the glasses around and all the men and Giovanna toasted. It was smooth and bittersweet with flavorings of almonds and herbs.

"This recipe has been in our family for generations. I learned it from your grandfather."

"You could sell this." Giovanna said.

Marc held hands with Giovanna sipping his drink. He listened to Gabe continue to quiz Francesco and Stefano about Antonio, enjoying every smile of Gabe's plump face. At the other end of the table, Angela, Renata and Linda gave Sara a litany of warnings about the trials of a newborn while Paolina, Renata and Luigi played with little Francesco. Marc had a quiet and serene smile on his face. *This is what happiness feels like*, he thought. There was no philosophy required. It was just good, intrinsically good.

6:5

Elaine's room was now next to the nurse's station. She was under 24-hour surveillance. There was an alert sensor beneath her buttocks that sounded if she tried to get up. She hadn't entered Twin Pines as a prisoner but turned herself into one within a few days.

She found this very difficult but was comforted by her newfound celebrity status. The fire alarm incident was the talk of the nursing home. She would get a thumbs up from each passer-by for sticking it to the man.

Her fame emboldened her. Most of her aids and nurses were black so she assumed Fox news would annoy them. When they changed her bedding, she commented about the glory days of Reagan. She indirectly criticized welfare mothers, but the nurses and aids were unaffected having already heard every insult in the book.

Chapter 6 - The Prodigal Son

Meanwhile back in San Pietro al Tanagro, Gabe finally had some peace knowing Elaine was under lock and key. It was the next morning and everyone congregated in the basement. It had a long table that was covered with trays of pastries from the local bakery. The room bloomed with the scents of sugar, dough, cream and espresso coffee. Angela was always up first, followed by Angelo. Then Renata came with Luigi and little Francesco followed by Paolina. They were all accompanying Paolina to a town function later that morning. Breakfast was efficient but no less self-indulgent. Sara ate five pastries provoking Giancarlo's usual ribbing.

After breakfast, everybody got ready. Giovanna came out of the bathroom to see Marc dressed stylishly.

"You packed a suit?"

He glanced back at her in the mirror while he trimmed his sideburns and nose hair with a grin.

"Why didn't you tell me this is formal? I don't have anything nice."

"It isn't, don't worry."

"Then why are you wearing a suit?"

"Habit. In business, you never know who you'll meet."

Giovanna conceded but the questions continued downstairs.

"What are we doing this morning?" Sara asked her father.

"Not sure exactly. I know your cousin is making a speech in town."

They arrived at a large courtyard in front of the town hall. There was a podium on a small stage and seating for about 150 people. Paolina spoke to a gentleman who proceeded to lead the family to the front two rows which were marked reserved. This inspired more grumbling about being underdressed. Marc was busy shaking hands with men who seemed like town officials accompanied by Paolina. Shortly after, he sat and joined the family. A gentleman with greyish hair introduced Paolina who was greeted with applause.

"Thank you. So many of our sons and daughters are leaving our towns for either the cities or leaving the country entirely. I campaigned on finding ways to keep them here, so our town and our culture has a future."

She paused for a resounding applause.

"Look around, there are not many young people and there should be. It's my pleasure to announce we are establishing a fund for young entrepreneurs. The benefactor is a son of San Pietro and my first cousin. Ladies and gentlemen, it is my honor and privilege to introduce Mr. Marc Diodato."

"That explains the suit," Giovanna whispered to Sara.

Marc and Paolina exchanged two kisses and he took the podium.

"It's an honor to be here. I notice the expressions of disbelief on my family's faces. I wanted this to be a surprise.

"First, I want to thank my cousin, your mayor Paolina Diodato. She has an unwavering commitment to the people of San Pietro al Tanagro and its culture. She expressed a lot of regret about the prospects of Italian youth in the south. She cried about our town as though it were a person dying. I was very moved, and I would like to applaud her for it.

"Today, we find new hope in the establishment of the Antonio Diodato fund. It is named after my father who was born and raised right here. While he lived in America with my mother to raise my brother and me, his heart never left this place, and he came back as often as he could. My success is an extension of the values of this town. They are ultimately my values and why I must give back.

"My father insisted we learn this language and maintain this culture. Sadly, he passed away far too young, so my time with him was cut short, but I never forgot the lessons he taught me. Thankfully, my father was also a man with foresight. He'd always say to prepare for the worst-case scenario, and he did that by making sure I'd be taken care of if he died. On my 18th birthday, I started my business because my father was able to leave something behind for me. By the time I graduated college at 23, I was already a millionaire. Though I worked incredibly hard, I also had a head start. I want to give others the same chance I had.

"While I do this for others, it's also for me. I guess you could say that I have to make up for lost time. In the last year, I've had some significant personal battles and I'm so fortunate to have a family who cared enough about me to look past my shortcomings and come to my aid when I needed it most— even if I didn't deserve it. Through them, I learned something about myself: family means more to me than anything. So, I stand before you today as a man acting out of gratitude and good will. Success is not worth having if you have no one to enjoy it with. I'm so lucky to have learned that.

"The Antonio Diodato fund will provide grants to entrepreneurs of San Pietro, Sant'Arsenio and the surrounding towns. Young entrepreneurs will submit business plans to be reviewed by a board chaired by my cousin Paolina. I have faith this money will be well spent because I have faith in Italian youth who are stifled by bureaucracy and a lack of opportunity. This fund will encourage them to keep dreaming and give young Salernitani a reason not to leave. It is my belief that those who leave, do so not because they want to, they think they have to. My goodbye to my father was final because he died. Families should stay together because we bring out the best in one another and we don't know how much time we have. Since I'll never have children of my own, I will take care of the children of others. The people of this town are my extended family and I'm sorry I didn't come home sooner. Thank you."

Marc's speech was answered with a standing ovation.

Marc stood on the stage with Paolina doing photo ops. Paolina hugged Marc and said, "I think you just got me reelected."

Gabe was the first to greet him on stage. "You are unbelievable."

He approached Giancarlo. "Remember what you said about me starting a foundation? You were right."

From behind he heard Giovanna. "I don't know what turns me on more, what you've created or that you were able to keep this a secret from everyone."

"I wanted to stand up there and see the expressions on your faces."

"You really kept this from us just for that?" She asked.

"Of course." He chuckled.

6:6

"I remember this park," Marc said. "I almost got killed by one of those super wasps here. What are they called?"

"Calabroni." Gabe answered. "Never heard you scream like that before."

"You couldn't stop laughing at me." Marc joked.

"Could you blame me? Dad warned you."

"And of course, I didn't listen."

"I can't believe they still have all the old timber fences and rails." Gabe said.

"Let's sit, my leg is bothering me."

"Does it bother you often?" Gabe asked.

"Often enough. It's not all related to my condition. It's sciatica and it's probably the biggest nuisance on a day-to-day basis with my health. Let's go a little further up to those rocks. It's a nicer view."

They walked slowly up a small hill. The park was quaint and well kept. It was surrounded by large trees with a brook and the remnants of an old mill.

"I remember being so impressed by the mountains." Marc said.

"Enough about the mountains. You said you had something urgent to tell me."

"When I was dead, I saw dad."

Gabe's face froze.

"I see Sara didn't tell you."

"No, she definitely did not." Gabe said nervously.

Marc finally told Gabe everything. He was very emotional.

"I haven't seen you cry since you were a child." Gabe said.

"He said you would be there for me, and you were. He spoke of mom too and said I don't have much time. I am still not sure what that means. Then there was a bright light and I felt like an anvil was dropped on my chest. Defibrillators fucking hurt."

Gabe had the chills.

"Why didn't you tell me any of this sooner?"

"I felt really strongly that I needed to tell you here."

"Well, I'm glad you finally did. So does this mean you believe in God now?"

"Not exactly."

"Then how do you explain dad?" Gabe asked.

"I didn't see God; I just saw dad."

"Always the skeptic." Gabe remarked.

"I have a lot of reasons to thank you but of all of them, Sara staying here tops the list. You should know that I could have never come out of this without her. When I left the hospital, we had a conversation about it. She didn't know what happened, but I asked her the same question you asked me. She helped me understand that I didn't need to understand. Believing means not knowing." Marc explained.

"I think I understand what you mean." Gabe pondered.

"This is a cigarette conversation. I wish we had a pack." Marc said.

"Where did that come from?" Gabe laughed.

Marc shrugged his shoulders like a teenager.

"You aren't going to believe this." Gabe reached into his pocket and pulled out a pack of Marlboros.

"You've gotta be fucking kidding me." Marc blurted out.

"I had a craving this morning. Paolina gave me a pack."

"Give me one of those motherfuckers now. We'll have to find a bathroom and wash up before we get back, so we don't stink." Marc said.

Gabe laughed again. "It's like hiding from our parents all over again. So, finish your story."

"When I came home from the hospital, I realized dwelling on it felt stupid. I just wanted to have dinner with the kids or do something pleasant with my time. Every time I felt like I could get into it, I would stop and eventually realize that I wasn't avoiding it, I just couldn't be bothered. That I didn't want to figure it out was the answer."

Gabe wearily pulled a drag from his second cigarette. Marc lit another.

"Gabe, I thought a lot about you, and I need to tell you something that might surprise you. Of dad's two sons, you were the success, not me."

"Marc, stop it. That's ridiculous."

205

"No, you stop. Your wife and daughter worship the ground you walk on. Until recently, I wouldn't know what that was like if it hit me over the head with a brick. You may not have had financial or professional success, but you lived a good life. I realized that for the remainder of mine, I should try to be more like you."

"Thank you for sharing all that."

"Honestly, I couldn't wait to tell you. You know, I'm so mad at myself for taking so long to come back here. I intend on coming back here regularly. I want to spend more time with Uncle Angelo and I'm sure Stefano and Francesco have more stories. Who knows how much time they have?"

"Marc, you have to come home to see mom. She's declined a lot. You need to deal with this for your own sake."

"I already decided that I will. I'm just not ready yet."

"Don't procrastinate!"

"Let's walk," Marc said.

"Have you discussed mom with Giovanna?"

"She thinks I'm waiting for some kind of grand inspiration that'll never come so I should just do it."

"Marc, she's right."

They walked out of the park into the town. It was quiet and most of the streets were empty.

"You want a drink?"

"That's a good idea." Gabe said.

They walked a few blocks into the one café in the neighborhood. It was right on the piazza where Marc made his speech. They sat at one of the empty high-top tables and the barista came. She was thin and muscular with a lot of tattoos and some piercings. When she approached the table, she recognized Marc.

"You're the man who spoke this morning. I really liked what you said. My name is Marta."

"Thank you. I'm Marc and this is my brother Gabe."

"Pleasure to meet you both. What can I get you?"

"Two brandies and two caffés." Marc said.

"I'm actually hungry." Gabe interjected. "What do you have?"

"We have sandwiches, cornettos and other pastries."

"Angela is cooking, don't eat too much." Marc said.

"Just give me a cornetto—no wait, you have gelato?"

"Of course."

"I'll take a small hazelnut." Gabe said.

"Make that two."

The bar had the feel of a place that was a hodgepodge of four decades. There were Coca-Cola signs from the 70s, a Pacman video game from the 80s, 90s music was playing and, on the wall, hung an autographed picture of Diego Maradona. Marta brought their caffé, the liquor, and the gelato to the table.

"We very rarely see Americans down here."

"There should be more tourism." Marc answered.

"Who would want to visit here?"

"Have you ever lived anywhere else?" He asked.

"No, I've lived in this town my whole life and one of my goals is leaving. It's always exciting just to see a new face."

"Every inch of this country is beautiful and historical. All it needs is some investment." Marc said.

"The first thing it needs is new men. I'm not even 25 and I'm already resigned to the idea of never getting married and having a family. There is nobody interesting."

"That is a broad statement. I wouldn't give up hope. You are pretty." Marc said.

A few other men, all clearly above the age of 60, came in. "See what I mean? The geriatric club just arrived. I'll check on you in a bit."

Gabe took a large sip of his brandy and got back to Elaine's past.

"Marc, mom was a normal mom. She was pretty and playful. I had a normal childhood with her." Gabe recounted.

"Did she and dad fight when you were younger?"

"Yes, but not until after I was 5 or 6 and it was usually over the same thing. Come to think of it, they'd argue most when dad was coming back here." Gabe explained. "Dad came back more often when I was young, a few times a year. By the time you were born, she hated when he came here."

"That's weird. Why would she not want papa to see his family?" Marc wondered.

"I don't know why it got a lot worse when you were born, but it did."

"Why haven't you told me this before?" Marc asked.

"You never cared to know. By the time dad died, your relationship with her was already so bad, you weren't interested. You already called her Elaine. I couldn't figure out how to tell you."

"When did she start drinking a lot?"

"After you were born." Gabe hesitated. "Dad mostly took care of you. I even changed your diapers."

"You never told me that either!" Marc said.

"Dad and I use to laugh because you had a really big dick for an infant. Dad used to joke and call you cazzone."

Marc burst into laughter and Gabe followed. "But I have to say I'm not surprised; I still have a pretty big cock."

The laughter increased. Gabe asked for two more drinks. Then he noticed somebody smoking.

"Wait, we can smoke here!" Gabe asked her for an ashtray and pulled his pack of cigarettes out of his pocket. Both men lit up.

"I'm not really supposed to be smoking but a little cheating never did too much damage."

Gabe didn't directly respond because he assumed Marc was referring to his condition.

"I never knew any of this about mom and I really wish you had told me."

"You just didn't want to hear it and whenever I tried defending mom, you got hostile. I stopped trying." Gabe confessed.

"I guess I can't hold that against you." Marc pondered.

"Sometimes it was hard for me to believe you were her son."

"I don't know why the fuck she hated me. I was a fucking child and I hated her because of how she treated me and how she treated dad. As I got older, I saw how other mothers were with their sons and I couldn't imagine mom being like that with me. Thankfully I had Paul's mother."

Saying his name still stung and to make matters worse, Gabe asked about his divorce.

"I treated Hannah fucking horrendously and I wish I could change that, however, now that we're divorced and I'm with Giovanna, I really see that she and I were wrong for each other. I wish we could've figured that out sooner and with a lot less pain and suffering. It was really ugly."

"Divorces happen all the time. How was what you did any better or worse than what happens with other marriages?" Gabe asked.

Then Marc explained his lie. Gabe was flabbergasted.

"I'm going to need a stronger drink for the rest of this conversation. This is really hard to listen to, Marc."

"I know that was a little selfish."

"A little?" Gabe snapped back.

"Gabe, when is the last time we sat together like this? Have we ever?" Marc asked.

"No, but that was on your part, not mine. I hoped one day you'd wake up and want to be brothers."

Gabe sipped his whiskey and lit another cigarette.

"We're going to need another pack soon." Marc said.

Gabe finally smiled slightly. "I would give anything to go back and be around more after dad died."

"Should have, could have, would have. We can't go back." Marc said dismissively. "Speaking of which, it's getting late. How drunk are you?"

"I probably need another coffee. Let's wait about fifteen more minutes."

Gabe sipped his coffee, hoping the booze would quickly wear off. Marc went to the counter to pay the bill.

"I know it's not customary to tip but, here you go."

He left her 20 Euros. The barista laughed and thanked him.

"Marta, do you love your parents?"

"That's an odd question to ask a stranger." She said.

Marc agreed but still wanted an answer. She said yes as if the answer was obvious. Then he asked her if her parents loved her. She answered the same.

"We always risk undervaluing what we have at our disposal. If your family has love, consider the alternative and maybe your life with them will mean more, even if it means

209

staying in this boring town. They would be heartbroken to see you leave or worse yet, to see you unhappy." Marc said.

"Thank you for coming here."

"My pleasure, and one more thing, this isn't the only town. I'm sure the boys down here feel the same way as you. Maybe you should discuss it?"

"Maybe we should?" She smiled.

Marta walked out from behind the counter and gave him a kiss on the cheek.

"What was that all about?" Gabe asked.

"Nothing." Marc acted coy.

"My brother has turned into Mr. Rogers."

6:7

Giovanna finished packing what she didn't need in the morning and laid down on the bed. Marc was on his back staring at the ceiling with his hands clasped behind his head. Giovanna laid on her side with her head resting on her arm.

"Why are you with me?" Marc asked.

"How do people decide their favorite food? We've talked about this, Marc."

Marc sat on the bed looking perplexed. "I'm like your favorite food?"

Giovanna let out a hardy laugh. "You are delicious, now that you mention it."

"Seriously though. My condition makes me feel like less of a man. I could wind up an invalid."

"Well, right now you're not one. When you're a cancer survivor, you learn that the future might not matter. Right now, you make me feel desired and interesting. You ask me things no man has ever asked me before. You're very handsome and I love your mind. So, Marc Diodato, while I have you, I'm going to enjoy you, if that's okay?"

"That is perfectly fine with me. I keep asking you because I'm happy. I never thought I would be in a new relationship at this stage of my life. I don't want to lose it."

"Why is that so strange?"

"I always expect good things to end badly." Marc was

regretful.

"Marc, look at me. I have a confession to make."

Marc looked panicked.

Giovanna hesitated. "There's another reason I'm with you." She leaned closer and whispered. As her breath could be felt on his face, she slid her hand down his stomach. "It's your large, gorgeous cock. I also measure a man's value by the quality of my orgasms, and I make no apologies for being greedy."

"I was scared you would mention my money."

"Well, I had no idea just how much you had when I decided I wanted you."

"That's one of the reasons I really trust you." Marc explained.

"I'm very happy with my business. My brother and I do well and life is good. Your money has no affect on me either way." She dismissed.

"But I guess my cock does." He said devilishly.

"That, my dear, is far more important."

"Both my cock and I really want to fuck you."

"I'm glad you are both in agreement." She surmised.

Though marble tiles amplified every sound, as far as they knew, their copulation went undetected. After their orgasms, they whispered themselves to sleep. The next morning it was time to leave. Everyone gathered in the driveway for a final goodbye when Giancarlo asked Marc why he had no bags. Marc was staying in San Pietro.

"Uncle Marc, don't you want to be with us while mom and dad are here?"

"Listen, I think it's important for the four of you to spend the last few days together. You are marrying Giancarlo and you need time alone."

"But you're talking like you're not family." She said.

"Of course I am, but your parents are your parents."

"I didn't think we would be saying goodbye here." Gabe said.

"I'm sorry but I need to stay." He turned to Giancarlo. "I leave everything to you."

"I'll take care of everything."

He turned to give Sara a kiss and then approached Linda. "I can't believe I am saying this, but I'm actually sad you won't be with us for our last days." She said.

Marc laughed quietly and shrugged his shoulders and then got to Gabe.

"I'm going to make you a promise. I will be home, very soon and we'll deal with mom." The brothers embraced properly. It was an embrace that made up for lost time and said what words could not. He saved Giovanna for last.

"So my dear, I want you back in Rome as soon as possible."

"You are coming to Florence for New Year's. How long do you think you'll be down here?" She asked.

"I don't know, I was planning on being back for Christmas, but I could stay here. Haven't decided yet. Gabe and Linda leave in a few days and the kids can spend Christmas with Giancarlo's parents."

Marc looked straight into her eyes as if he had something important to say but he remained quiet. Giovanna stared back looking satisfied. She simply said, "I know," and they kissed.

Amidst their long romantic moment, there was a flurry of double kisses and hugs as everyone said goodbye. Paolina and Renata were also there to see everyone off. Angelo smiled quietly and Angela was giving orders about when everyone was obliged to come back. The engine rumbled and they pulled away. Marc watched the van as it grew smaller and disappeared against the landscape.

He savored the smell of the country air that was a mixture of livestock and burning brush from a nearby farmer. The December chill was more evident in the mountains. Though he would be spending time with his family, he'd also have time alone. He had almost none since waking from his coma. Eager to indulge himself, he told everyone that he was tired and wanted to rest. He climbed the marble stairs up to his room. He listened to the faint hiss of silence accompanying the rustle of leaves outside. He could hear the drone of the pipes as Angela turned the water downstairs on and off. His body sank deeper and deeper into the mattress as he enjoyed recalling every word of his conversations with Gabe.

He drifted to sleep but found himself back in the dream. He was in the darkness stumbling through clutter with the pain of small objects beneath his feet. The air smelled like stale cigarette smoke as he bumped into object after object. He knew he was dreaming. "Papa!" He yelled. There was no echo, no acoustics of any kind. "Papa?!" He yelled louder again. Still nothing. He moved suddenly and fell to the ground, hitting his head on what felt like a wooden object. He felt the flashlight again and took it out. He felt his finger poised on the button and instead of turning it on, he threw it forcefully. It never hit anything or landed. Was Elaine there? Was Gabe? Then, with no clue or intuition, he closed his eyes and with all the force he could muster, he screamed, "MOM!"

The sound was like a large book slamming to the ground. He opened his eyes and saw his clothing. He was glowing. He yelled, louder again, "Mom!" He felt his throat tear and the light grew brighter, but it was not from the space, it was from himself. He was tripping on the matchbox cars and Legos from his youth. He glowed brightly enough to see a few feet around him. Familiar things came into focus. "Mom, where are you?"

With each call, the light got brighter yet he couldn't see the end of the room. He saw pieces of furniture from his house, piles of Avon makeup, household cleaning products, decks of cards, empty bottles and poker chips.

He heard the faint sound of a woman weeping but couldn't tell from where it came. He listened intently and then climbed over piles of laundry, books with all the pages torn out and cigarette butts. Then his light illuminated a woman sitting on a bed. It was Elaine. She was crying and rocking back and forth. He called to her, but she couldn't hear or see him. She held a picture of his father. He was young and so was she. Then she spoke. "Why don't you love me?" She said it over and over again. Then he heard the sound of a young boy.

"Mommy, mommy?" The boy said and Marc realized it was himself. Elaine ignored him and the child began to cry. The cries grew louder and shriller with each heaving breath.

Marc wanted to console the child and went to pick him up, but he couldn't touch him. The crying grew deafening and she continued to repeat the same words. Marc felt the sensation of spinning. "Stop, stop, stop, STOP!!!"

He sprang up in bed and was covered in sweat. The room was dark and he hurried to turn on a light. He fell back down onto his pillow, covering his face with his hands. There was a knock at the door. It was Angela.

"Are you okay? I heard you scream."

"I was just having a nightmare."

"Can I get you something?" She asked and then came into the room. She felt his forehead. "You're soaked! Are you sure you're okay?"

"No, I'm fine Aunt Angela." Marc repeated

She left and Marc grabbed his phone to text Giovanna.

"I had the dream again. It was different this time."

6:8

Dear Papa,

Why would mom think you didn't love her? I actually felt sorry for her in the dream and I'm still not used to calling her mom. Gabe doesn't like when I call her Elaine. I wish you could tell me more about your relationship with her. I'm struggling with everything Gabe told me. Though it could justify why I may have judged her harshly, it doesn't change how she rejected me. It couldn't have been just some form of post-partum depression. She was too calculated in front of strangers. If it was just about her mental health, she would've been less deliberate. This dream was as real as seeing you. You have me chasing a breadcrumb trail and I don't know where it'll lead.

I intended to write to you tonight, but I never thought this would come up. Do I need to hurry home?

Maybe this is about you? You never told me much about your childhood and you never spoke of our family in-depth. Thinking about it now, that's a little weird. You came here at least twice a year no matter how much mom protested.

Maybe I'm reading into this too much?

Love,
Marc

Marc was pulled by smells meandering up from the kitchen. Angela stood at the stove with a cigarette burning in the ashtray. He took one from her pack and lit it.

"I'm making frutti di marc."

"One of my favorites. White wine broth, right?"

"Of course. You taste the mussels, clams and shrimp more than with red sauce. Sometimes it overpowers."

"Can I steal a mussel?" He asked with a grin.

In the other room, Angelo was sitting with a big brown box of pictures.

"Wash your hands if you just touched food. I didn't take them out with everyone here. Some pictures are very fragile. Look at this." Angelo grinned.

"Aunt Angela, you were hot!" Marc blurted out.

"Were?" She shouted from the kitchen. "I think I'll just freeze this, and you can have sandwiches instead." She joked.

Marc shuffled carefully through the pictures. "*This* is what the town looked like?"

"Look at these," Angelo said. "These are my grandparents! They must have been in their 30s."

"They look twenty years older than that." Marc commented.

"Life was hard, Marc."

"I haven't seen enough pictures of my father. He was really handsome."

"Yes, he was." Angelo exclaimed.

"I haven't seen any of these! Dad wasn't one to keep pictures around. In fact, now that I think about it, there were no pictures. I never realized that. Why would dad never have pictures?"

"I don't know and sadly he's not here to ask. Maybe he didn't need them? Your father had a photographic memory."

"Maybe it was because of my mother?"

"I've only been in your mother's company once."

"What was your impression of her?" Marc asked.

"I can't speak English and she couldn't speak Italian, so there wasn't much opportunity to talk. It was in America when I came to visit. It was before you were born."

"I guess the language barrier would be an issue, but still, you had no observations?"

"Your mother was loud." Angelo commented.

"Who is this woman with papa?"

"She was his high school girlfriend. Angela, is dinner ready?"

"She was very pretty." Marc remarked as he glanced at the picture. "Isn't it something how time changes us. Are you okay? You seem nervous."

"I'm fine, I get distracted by the pain in my knees. Arthritis is the curse of this family."

"Dinner is ready." Angela sounded.

"Does dad have any other friends here?"

"I would talk to Stefano and Francesco. They were with him a lot more than I was."

He changed the subject to begin discussing an issue with the house. As Angela and Angelo went back and forth, Marc checked the time to estimate when Giovanna would arrive in Florence. He missed her already and since they met, they remained in constant communication. He never felt like he needed space. He was as relaxed with her as when he was alone.

"So, what do you think of Giovanna?" He asked.

"She is lovely, and you two make a nice couple." Angela said.

"She really seems to understand me, and I never knew how important that is." Marc responded.

Angela and Angelo looked at one another the way that all couples who non-verbally communicate do.

"That's what I mean." Marc said. "I saw how you looked at each other. It was a whole conversation in a glance. I never had that with Hannah."

"That's why you are no longer married." Angela said.

"I'm starting to understand that."

He savored the last mussel and Angela cleared the table.

Angela placed the small espresso pot on a slab of stone and small demitasse cups in front of Angelo and Marc.

"Dinner was wonderful. I need to share something with you, and it might be a little intense, so I hope you don't mind."

"Why would we mind?" They asked contentiously.

"I want to show you something." He raised his sleeve revealing his scars. Angelo and Angela looked on but neither broke the silence. Marc revealed the specifics about his attempted suicide and finally divulged his subsequent near-death experience. Angela made the sign of the cross and Angelo just reached and grabbed Marc's hand.

"Do you think the experience was real?" Angelo asked.

"I was very convinced of my atheism. At first, I couldn't even enjoy it because of the possibility that there is life after death and that papa knew everything I had done. If it wasn't for Sara and Giancarlo, I don't know what would have happened."

"So, I guess you aren't an atheist anymore?" Angela asked.

"No, but not necessarily a believer either."

"But you believe you saw your father so that means you've seen proof of life after death. How can you not believe in God after that?" Angela probed.

"Do we know there is a God from our existence here?"

"Hard for me to say because I'm a person of faith." She said.

"Exactly, you have faith, but do you know God exists in as much as you can show me God?" He asked.

"Every time I go out of the gate and I see the sun on that mountain, I feel like I see God." Angelo said.

"You see something majestic as evidence of God, but you don't see God himself. Considering that God is so unfathomable, who's to say that papa in his dimension is any closer to the answers than we are? How do we know that death is the last unknown? I see no reason to conclude there is anything definitive. I didn't feel that different when I was dead than I do now. I wasn't overwhelmed by some grand revelation. If anything, I have more questions now than before."

Angelo looked on in awe. "You sound exactly like your father when he was young. Your grandparents thought every other thing that came out of his mouth was heresy. 'Why' was your father's middle name. Remember the story of the holy water? That was one of the funny ones. Others were not so funny."

"Ok then. While I *believe* my experience was real, I don't *know* anything about the secrets of the universe. However, the biggest change was not in my faith, it was my outlook. I'm no longer a nihilist. I really saw the world as this brutal monster with no morality or hope. It was a very biological view. I saw life as a genetic competition that had no intrinsic purpose. When we die, we are dead, and it is all meaningless. I must admit, it made me miserable." Marc took a long drag from his cigarette.

"Your old view was pretty awful now that you mention it." Angela said as calmly as one asks the time.

"I agree. Before my diagnosis, I condescendingly dismissed faith but now I know it was a reaction to my mother. Her faith always led her to bad decisions with very grave consequences. I grew to detest it, but since my experience, I understand that my reaction was just as irrational."

"Wait though, you can't show me your experience with your father just as I can't show you how I see God in the mountains." Angelo remarked. "How can you call yours evidence?"

"You're more like my father than you give yourself credit, Uncle. That's exactly the point and this is what I came up with after weeks of driving myself crazy. I couldn't look in the mirror and deny that it happened. I couldn't bring myself to dismiss it and even more importantly, I didn't want to and that was when it hit me. I had to make a choice because a conclusion wasn't possible. I finally understood the difference between faith and knowledge. The only option was to choose."

"Then why is it so hard for you to say that God is working through you?" Angela asked.

"I won't make the mistake of second-guessing God because I can never presume to know what God is or what

God wants. That's why I'm very happy now as an agnostic, though sometimes I feel like I cheated. I got a bigger glimpse of eternity than most. Maybe it was just luck."

"I can't say I really understand the difference between agnostic and atheist." Angelo said.

"That's okay, most people don't. I guess the main distinction is certitude. An agnostic might not believe in God but reserves the right to be wrong, whereas an atheist forms a conclusion. You want to laugh? I realized I was no different than my mother with the severity of my views. Sure, she believed in God and I didn't, but the forcefulness of our opinions was the same. I realized that those hard-core communist atheist types are no different than the Taliban. They think they know and how could I be so critical of faith when asserting something I couldn't possibly know either? That's when I understood the joke. In matters of the unknowable, being happy is far more important than being right."

6:9

"You keep having this dream, and for the first time the ending has changed. There was only you and your mother. Again, what else could it possibly mean?" Dr. Rossellino asked.

"I never said it wasn't about her, but how do I know it means we need to talk? I've already said I will go see her."

"Yes, you did, but for your brother's sake; what about yours?"

"I still haven't figured that out yet."

"How will you feel if your mother dies and all this is left unaddressed?"

Marc didn't answer.

"I've been imploring you to stop avoiding this because you aren't considering the worst-case scenario."

"Which is?" Marc was combative.

"The only reason you've been okay with not forgiving her is because you have the option. Once she is dead, you won't. It will be forced on you and for that reason alone, you will hate it. You have to be prepared to live with that, and you need to be honest with yourself about what that'll mean. You can't argue in the cemetery." Dr. Rossellino said assertively. "How did you feel in the dream, listening to your mother continually ask why your father didn't love her?"

"I felt sorry for her and I was confused. I never really considered that. I always saw my father as putting up with her, but I never thought his calmness might be indifference." He wondered.

"Have others shown you forgiveness, Marc?"

"Yes."

"What has it meant to you?" She asked.

"A lot." He murmured.

"Do you feel you deserve their forgiveness?"

"Sometimes no. I have alot to make up for." He conceded.

"And you appreciate the opportunity?"

"Very much." He said.

"Then how can you deny your mother on the basis that she doesn't deserve a chance from you when you admittedly say you don't deserve it from others?"

Before Marc could even answer, she continued. "And what would you give for Paul and Hannah's forgiveness? You mention them in almost every session."

"I would give anything for that. But I'm not my mother and I don't even know if she would appreciate it. She might see my gesture as a victory, as some kind of vindication and the thought of that makes me sick."

"Hasn't your mother called you over the years?"

"Yes." He murmured again.

"When?"

"She always calls me on my birthday and leaves me a message."

"And you've never called back?" She asked.

"No."

"Then how could it be her victory when she has already tried with you?"

His shoulders slumped and he lowered his head. Dr. Rossellino didn't waver.

"Do you ever remember your parents being affectionate?"

Without hesitation, Marc said, "No!"

"What do you remember?"

"They seemed estranged. He took her abuse and blew off her outbursts."

"You mean how your brother blows off yours?" She interjected. Her eyebrow stood at attention on the screen.

"I can't figure out why Gabe remembers my mother being in love with my father. What happened for their relationship to change so much? Maybe it was me?"

"Don't be ridiculous, Marc. You were an infant and all they do is cry, eat, poop and sleep. If you're the reason, then it's entirely irrational on your mother's part. Babies are not responsible, but adults are, for both their indiscretions and their happiness. In your mother's case, she pertains to both and there are only two relevant questions. Can you live with all these uncertainties, and can you accept your estrangement as a final outcome?"

Marc lit a cigarette. "I think the estrangement is easier than the questions. Something isn't adding up."

He knew he needed to go home, and it took less than half an hour for the doctor to convince him.

"What has your uncle told you about your father?"

6:10

Marc was enjoying his time in San Pietro. He spent his days looking at old pictures, going for walks and enjoying the pleasantness of the countryside. He spent a lot of time with Angelo and it was a perfect night for grappa and cigars.

"I saw the Milky Way for the first time when we arrived. It's really amazing. In New York, you barely see a few stars anymore. It even changes the color of the sky. It's like a dull purple. Did you know that every element in our bodies was made inside of a supernova? All the iron, magnesium, copper, zinc, all the heavier elements came from massive stars that exploded. Our real mother is a star that died billions of years ago. We are made of stardust. Makes me wonder if the whole universe is alive."

"That's a beautiful thought. Your father spoke often

about your depth and talent so it's a little strange that you became a real-estate developer."

"I got obsessed with making money because it meant freedom from my mother. When I first started out, I learned a lot of skills, but demolition was always my favorite. I couldn't get enough of it. Swinging a sledgehammer really helped emotionally but building also engaged my talents. I was very good at design and craftsmanship. That kind of work is so cathartic. I always loved building things and I have a head for numbers."

"I guess I shouldn't be surprised because I was a contractor and your aunt and I have done very well."

"Don't you get gratification from it?" Marc asked.

"Yes, I do." Angelo said frankly.

"Is it because you are doing something meaningful? We have a kind of kinship with our ancestors."

"That's very true, and I imagine that so many Italians who went to America found work in construction because everybody knew masonry. It's practically in our blood." Angelo mused. "If you don't mind me changing the subject, how much can you tell me about what happened with your mother after your father died?"

Angelo's question was like an abrupt kick in the gut. Marc knew there was no nice way to explain what happened but he did his best.

"Uncle Angelo, I'll put it to you this way. I haven't seen or spoken to my mother in nine years."

Angelo interjected. "Your aunt and I talked about intervening after your father died. I stayed in touch with your brother and he told me a lot but there wasn't much we could do. Getting custody of you would've been almost impossible. We didn't know what to do."

"I appreciate you saying that. Luckily, I had my friend Paul's house. His parents looked after me."

"What is it?" Angelo said.

"I miss him, and I don't think our relationship is salvageable."

"Have you tried talking to him?" Angelo asked.

"I might reach out to him in a last attempt when I go

home next month, even though he told me not to."

"I didn't know you planned to go back."

"I promised Gabe I would see my mother. He thinks I need to, and I owe him that." Marc said.

"You will do the right thing." Angelo responded.

"You give me too much credit, Uncle." Marc began to tear up.

"What is it?" Angelo asked.

"I'm so afraid to see her." Marc said with a shaken voice. Angelo asked why. "I'm afraid of all that negativity coming back. I know how I can be, and I don't want to feel certain feelings again. If I see her, I will—it might be inevitable."

"Was your relationship with her really that bad?" Angelo asked with hesitation.

"I don't have much memory of her being loving and to this day I don't know why. There are things Gabe told me when he was here that just deepen the mystery. It took her less than four years to burn through all the money after papa died. She had her first boyfriend within a year of his death, and every relationship was short and mostly with younger men. She took lots of trips to Atlantic City and Las Vegas. She loved gambling and there was always a revolving door of so-called friends who came and went. There were people in the house all the time. I hid in my room. When the money dried up, her behavior got much worse. Letters from collection agencies were a regular thing. Between the time when dad died and I left, her looks really went downhill from all the drinking, and the boyfriends got stranger and stranger. She was out of her mind."

Marc was rambling but Angelo thought it best to let him talk it out.

"As time went on, I started having a new perspective on my life with my mother, especially when I started making money. I realized that if I could survive her, I could survive anything. How much of a big deal was risking money or living on my own after her?"

"Yes, but at what cost? This is so hard for me to hear, Marc. I feel more guilty than ever. How could I have left you to this?" Angelo said despairingly.

"It happened and we can't go back. If nothing else, it made me tough. The happiest day of my adolescence was the day I moved out. I turned to her to tell her I was leaving. All she said was 'have fun' and she said it in the strangest way. I couldn't tell if it was indifference or remorse. She was blank. I still remember her with the remnants of her makeup from the night before. There was a cigarette smoldering in the ashtray. Her eyes never left the TV. I walked out and that was it."

"Can I say a few things?" Angelo asked nervously. Marc nodded.

"How do I say this without offending you? Marc, you don't know the whole story of your parents' relationship."

"How do you mean?"

"You don't know all the circumstances of their marriage. Your father died when you were still a boy. Your mother was a widow in her 40s. I can't imagine what that could be like."

"Gabe said after I was born, she changed and he thought maybe she had untreated post-partum depression, but you have to understand, it's really hard for me to make excuses for her. How much consideration does one person get?" Marc retorted.

Angelo looked concerned. His words were cagy. "You don't know what it's like to lose your partner at her age with two sons. I know it was terrible, but I'm forced to think there are serious psychological circumstances behind it, and your father…" Angelo stopped himself.

"My father what?" Marc asked quickly.

"It's about time you knew the truth." Angelo said.

Chapter 7

Elysium

7:1

"Mrs. Freda?"

"Call me Barbara."

She was a small woman who seemed like age and suffering had her worn down. She had light eyes and thin lips. Her hands were frail and trembled slightly. She wore a black dress.

"How much do you know?" She asked.

"My uncle said I needed to come see you." He reached into his jacket and pulled out the photograph.

"Before I say a word, you should know your uncle has been very good to me and he didn't tell you about me at my insistence. You should come in."

They sat across one another in the living room. It was plain and even a bit dreary. Barbara began to laugh and cry simultaneously.

"I knew you were going to speak in town and at first I swore I wouldn't go but when the day came, I couldn't stop myself. Seeing you at the podium filled my heart with joy. Before I begin, there are things I'm going to share with you that will be very hard for you to hear."

"I understand." Marc responded.

"I'll start at the beginning. Your father and I met when we were 16. I had such a crush on him, and I never thought he would be interested in me. One day, I found a note in my desk at school. It said, 'you are so beautiful, and I think about you all the time. I'll be waiting for you today at the footbridge after school at 4pm. Come if you feel the same way.' I was there before him. When I saw him approaching, I hid because I didn't want him to see that I got there first. I watched him check the time over and over again. Finally, I came out from behind the bushes and when he saw me, he handed me flowers and professed his love. He was so nervous, he trembled. I kissed him first and I thought he was going to faint. It was the most romantic moment of my life. I would give anything to relive it. I want to show you something."

Barbara got up and walked to her bedroom, returning

with a picture.

"You both looked so happy. You were beautiful." Marc exclaimed.

"We were inseparable all through high school and university. We talked about getting married and that was what we assumed would happen. Then he got the offer in America. When he left, I was devastated. Worse yet, he didn't want to go. I made him go. That was probably the worst mistake of my life." She cried.

"We wrote letters because talking on the phone was hard. It was very expensive in those days, so the distance was a much bigger problem. Now young people do that facetime thing. My nieces' children talk to all their friends that way. If only we had that, maybe things would've been different, but the distance got to us. Then your father met your mother. When he told me she was pregnant with your brother, I knew what he would do."

"What happened after that?" Marc asked.

"It was strange. There was no big argument. He told me, we hung up the phone and I cried for a week. We didn't speak or write for a long time. We never discussed it but there was this unspoken understanding because the situation was so final. I guess we both knew there was no point. A few years went by and then one day, there was a knock at my door. I opened it and there he was. He looked at me in a way I will never forget. It was his eyes. They were so pained and regretful. His face was covered in tears and he just stood there shaking his head. I wanted to resist him, but I couldn't. I just threw my arms around him and that was when I became the other woman. Before he came back, I tried meeting other men, but I couldn't stop thinking about your father. When I saw him again, I knew I could never love another. Our life together was full of tragedies culminating in his death."

"I was there. I saw him die." Marc said wearily.

"You were actually in the room?"

"I still dream about it sometimes."

"I am so sorry, my dear." There was a long silence. The two just sat in the room together but it was not uncomfortable. Although Marc and Barbara had just met, there was an unexplainable familiarity between them that Marc found comforting.

"So, my mother must have found out about you?" Marc asked.

"She did. We kept our relationship secret for years."

Suddenly Marc interjected. "Who's that girl in the other picture?" He got up and took it off the shelf.

"I was getting to her."

"Who is she?"

"Your sister, Anna."

Marc gasped. "I have a sister?"

Barbara's tears grew larger. "You had a sister."

He felt his heart drop. He had a sister he never knew, and she was dead.

"Why were my brother and I never told?" His tone was sharp, and his eyes changed from sad to angry. Barbara continued to cry, and he felt sorry for her. Without her asking, he fetched her a box of tissues from the other side of the room. He felt compelled to console her but was not sure if he should. He learned Anna was five years older than he. Elaine found out the year before he was born. Now it all made sense.

"That was the year dad came here for a month! Now I know why my mother wasn't happy to see him when he came home or any other time he came back. Now I know why my father seemed so sad." Marc sat with his head in his hands. "I am sorry, but this is very overwhelming. Please tell me how she died."

"It was a freak accident. She and her friends were playing in the woods and she was stung by a bee. Her friends said she started to swell up and within a few minutes, she couldn't breathe. It was a ten-minute run to get back to town. By the time her friend returned with the medics, Anna was already dead. Her throat had closed and she asphyxiated. We didn't know she was allergic."

Through everything, Marc thought he could at least trust his love and respect for Antonio, but his armor had crumbled. Then there was the loss of a sister and the conundrum of having so much sympathy for a woman he should have presumably despised for sabotaging his family life. Every time he looked at Barbara, he couldn't see an enemy. He only saw a woman who had endured unspeakable heartbreak. Every wrinkle on her face was earned by sadness, yet, as she mused about memories of Antonio, the young girl who loved him emerged.

"How did my mother eventually find out about you?"

"Your father told me your mother's spending caused financial problems and she scrutinized money he was sending here. He would send it to your uncle, but she got suspicious and then started looking at phone records. She noticed my number and then began investigating. She finally found a picture of us in your father's desk."

"And this was right around when I was born?"

"Yes, that's correct."

The great mystery was finally revealed. Elaine rejected him because his father rejected her. He was an unwanted child of a relationship torn apart by his father's betrayal. Now he understood why his father took his mother's abuse. It was out of contrition, not indifference. It was his indiscretion and now there was a bridge between the aloof and somber man who quietly drifted through his memory. Marc understood what was behind all the 'nothing' responses every time he asked him what was wrong. He was a man trapped by duty. His heart spanned thousands of miles between two families and two countries. Marc saw that Barbara was Antonio's true love, whom he gave up to protect him from a mother who didn't want him.

"Do you think my father ever loved my mother? Did you and he ever talk about being together?"

"I believe your father's heart was ultimately with me, but I also think he loved both of us. Antonio was a very complex man. He kept so much to himself. As for us being together, we knew that wasn't possible. Once he found out about her pregnancy with you, he needed to stay in America. There was no way for him to earn that kind of money in Italy and he had two families to support. You don't know about me or Anna because your father and mother struck a deal. He was allowed to support us and visit often, as long as he stayed married to her. Your mother said she would divorce him and bar him from seeing you on the grounds of infidelity if you ever found out. As long as she kept his name and we remained anonymous, he was able to care for both of us but under the condition that he was hers."

As Barbara spoke, Marc's despair deepened.

"From what your father told me, I think your mother was very much in love with him and it was the only way she thought she could hold on to him. What's most unfortunate is that you paid the biggest price for it. Your father wanted to take you and your brother away to be here with me and Anna, but he knew that because of his affair, a court of law would never have granted him custody. He knew he needed to stay with your mother to protect you and I settled for having him a few weeks a year. Once he died, it didn't matter anymore. Angelo and I decided it was best to take it to our graves."

"But did either of you ever consider that this might have mattered to me? Barbara, I haven't spoken to my mother in years and maybe this information would have impacted my choices."

"Marc, I'm sorry. At the time, we feared your mother's vengeance would be directed at you. We talked a lot about it but decided it was too dangerous for you and as time passed, it seemed less and less relevant considering Anna and your father were both dead. Angelo was mostly afraid knowledge of this would have made you hate your father and since he wasn't around to explain himself, telling you after the fact didn't make much sense. It was hard for us, but we tried to think of everyone hoping for the best possible outcome."

Marc roiled and yet he knew Angelo and Barbara were right. Who knows what Elaine would have done and regardless of how he might have decided differently, had he known the truth, Elaine's rejection and subsequent abuse of a guiltless child took precedence.

"Wasn't anyone curious about Anna's father?" Marc asked. "Being pregnant was impossible to hide and scandalous without a husband in those days. What about my cousins, didn't they know something?"

"When I got pregnant, I went to live with my aunt and

uncle near Rieti. Since the child was illegitimate, we kept her away. She had cousins there and she was free to tell her friends that her dad was a scientist who worked in America. Had she not died, I think that would've eventually changed, but your Cousin Paolina was a baby when Anna died, and Renata was very young."

"That explains why my father went to Rome alone for a few days when I was here with him! He said it was for work, but he went to see you. I should resent you because your relationship with my father affected my relationship with my mother so much, but I don't. I don't know why, but I don't. All I can think about is the sister I never knew. You suffered enough and you don't need my scorn." Marc said.

"Thank you. That means so much to me. I always imagined what it would be like to meet you and your brother, and this beats even my best expectations. I was so afraid you would hate me and I'm so grateful you don't."

Since Barbara had been so forthcoming with Marc, he requited by telling her about his near-death encounter with his father. She was overjoyed and proclaimed that Antonio had meant for them to meet. This was all meant to happen and instead of any attempt at refutation, Marc entertained Barbara's notion because it made her happy. He was putting his wisdom into practice. What good would it have done to debate philosophy with Barbara? He was learning one of life's golden rules. Sometimes it is more important to be kind than it is to be right. They embraced as friends and he departed.

Marc realized he was collateral damage of an already failed marriage and now he knew why Elaine didn't want to raise another one of Antonio's children. Perhaps Marc's combativeness made matters worse but now, there was no more doubt. He and Elaine needed to talk. He misjudged her not knowing about his father's infidelity, but also resented her even for not giving him the choice to know his sister and for making him suffer for his father's actions.

His head was pounding. *What kind of a person does that to an innocent child?* He wasn't responsible for his father's decisions and this new information reinforced his contempt for her. He thought it verified her narcissism. Perhaps she was just a big mistake for Antonio, an act of passion that became a life sentence? Perhaps he even tried to love her and that was what Gabe remembered? Perhaps she tried harder to make him love her—but was it out of genuine affection or just a challenge?

He headed straight for the house and texted Gabe.

"I'm getting on the next train. Something urgent has happened and I need to see you right away. We have to talk in person."

Then he called Angelo.

"Uncle. I need you to take me to the Salerno train station as soon as possible. I'm sorry but I need to leave now."

"How much did she tell you?" Angelo asked hesitantly.

"Everything."

7:2

When they arrived at the train station, Angelo got out of the car to say goodbye.

"I promise, I don't hold it against you for keeping Barbara and Anna a secret."

"You and your brother are all I have left of your father. Please come back soon."

"Sooner than you think."

They embraced.

"Remember, sometimes good people do bad things. We all need forgiveness." Angelo said as Marc walked away. He turned and waved one last time.

Marc boarded the train and messaged Giovanna that he was arriving at 10:05. He was making a stop in Florence first. A few minutes later, he heard the announcement over the speaker with the departure information. Cellphone usage was frowned upon, but the train car was rather empty. He called Giancarlo.

"How is everything?"

"Sara's back hurts and her ankles are swollen but the doctor said to expect that. She's resting. What's up?"

"There's been a change of plans. I'm on the train to Florence to see Giovanna and then to New York."

"This is unexpected." He responded.

"Giancarlo, can you put me on speaker?"

"Hi Uncle Marc."

"Sara, please don't share this with your parents because I need to tell your father in person. I just found out grandpa had another woman, and we had a sister. When I was four, she died. She was nine years old. I have to confront grandma." Marc's voice trembled.

"How did you find out?"

As Marc recounted his meeting with Barbara, Sara listened in disbelief.

"I don't know how my father is going to take this..."

"I don't know either, but he needs to know. I need to see Giovanna first. I love you both."

"Uncle Marc, please don't let your anger make you say things you'll regret. You are better than that."

"From everything you have told me about her, your mother's sanity is clearly compromised. Hating people for being crazy means you're the lunatic." Giancarlo explained.

"I need to look into her eyes and see her reactions. That's how I will know. I will be in Florence in a few hours."

"You're already on the train?" Sara asked.

"This can't wait. Remember, not a word to your father."

As the train clacked along and the lights blurred by, he felt impatient. He wrestled with trying to sleep to pass the time, but he couldn't relax. He was haunted by thoughts and visions of the loss of loved ones. In scenario after scenario, he was filled with dread and he realized why he fought against attachments. Loving people requires needing them. When you need people, you live with the fear of losing them. For the first time in his adult life, the people in his present mattered more than those from his past.

While leapfrogging through anxious worst-case scenarios, he felt the weight of his new reality. He had always viewed his father as the virtuous protagonist. Elaine was the villain and Marc the martyr. It was no longer so cut and dry.

Just as his past was uncertain, so were his feelings. He was not used to questioning his father nor was he accustomed to reconsidering his mother's cruelty. He never had cause to question either and he felt torn between the rush of urgency to confront her and the paralysis of melancholy. The former left him with insatiable restlessness. Every inch of his skin was cold. The minutes crept along as he sat in that conscious dream state that was only a wishful substitute for sleep. Then time took mercy on him, at least so he thought.

Suddenly, he was back in the darkness of his dream. The same smells, stale air and obstructions greeted him. He yelled for his mother, but this time no light. He yelled for his father and still nothing. This time it was like a maze. He was trapped between tall dressers and wardrobe closets. He could feel boxes and bottles beneath his feet as he stumbled. Persisting, he called to both his parents and still nothing. Then he yelled for Anna and a rage overcame him as he said her name again and again. He punched the object in front of him with all his might, screaming her name louder still. Suddenly, a flash of light assaulted him, and he woke up.

Marc was trembling and saw that his knuckles were bleeding and his hand started to swell. He had punched the wall of the train car and barely missed the window. He reached in his bag and grabbed a sock to clean up his hand and a few minutes later, an attendant approached him. Marc's outburst scared the other passengers. He assured the attendant that he had a nightmare and that he was fine. Finally, after assuaging his concerns, the attendant left. To Marc's relief, he checked the time and saw they were less than an hour from Florence. Now even fearing sleep, he waited in a daze.

Not a moment too soon, he felt the train start to slow down and welcomed the announcement of the conductor. By then, his hand had swollen up more and there was dried blood. He no longer cared about cleaning it off. It hurt but he ignored it. He got up from his seat and apologized to the other passengers. They looked on with smiles as if to gesture that it was okay, yet he knew they only smiled from the nose down. Their eyes said, "Get me off this train away from this fucking lunatic." Not giving a fuck whatsoever, he grabbed his bag and exited.

He was stiff and his feet hurt as he walked. He passed the end of the platform and headed for the exit. It was raining.

He walked across the quad with no umbrella to the line of white taxis. There were only two and both drove away. As he waited, the rain soothed him and felt good on his swollen hand. He made no attempt to cover his head and just allowed the rain to bathe him, hoping it would wash away his sadness.

He got into the next taxi. They swerved through the city streets and crossed over the Arno river. He was more impatient than ever and then he recognized the road and saw the house up on the hill. The car pulled down the driveway and before it even stopped, the front door opened. Giovanna stood with her silhouette lit by the backlight.

Marc paid the driver and exited the car but instead of rushing for the door, he just stood there in the rain. Giovanna waited. As he neared, his tears were masked by the rain drops. His feet squished in puddles. She extended her hand and pulled him into the house, sitting him down on the chair near the door. She helped him remove his shoes and wet clothes and brought him into the living room to the couch. She cleaned up his hand and dried his hair, finally covering him with a blanket. She left the room and returned with a cold pack for the swelling. She wrapped it in a paper towel and placed it on his hand and finally sat down next to him. He shifted his body so they sat leaning towards each other. Marc breathed in and out heavily, inhaling Giovanna's scent. It calmed him more than words could.

She looked into his eyes and saw his suffering. Gently, she caressed his head. Her hand slid down to his shoulder and she pulled him towards her. As he felt her body, he felt weak and soft. His defenses crumbled and as she pressed him towards her, he began to convulse as he sobbed. He let out a groan as he clasped at her shirt. Giovanna held him tight like a mother hushing her child after a nightmare. Not a word was spoken.

7:3

As Gabe jumped from one foot to the next, playing musical chairs with Christmas ornaments, Elaine was in the best possible mood as she gave directions. The tree glistened with lights and tinsel and Elaine's crystal collection sparkled. "You did a decent job," was about the best compliment Gabe could hope for. As Elaine snacked on her water crackers, she recounted the story behind every ornament.

Gabe was playing a much more subtle game, timing the decorating with telling her Marc was coming to see her. Elaine tried not to act surprised.

"I'll be here so it's not like I have anything else to do."

"Good thing you aren't busy." Gabe joked but Elaine chose not to acknowledge it. She sorely lacked a sense of humor. She couldn't understand irony and especially didn't grasp sarcasm. Gabe did his best.

"Wait 'til you see him. He looks so much like dad now. That was what everybody said in Italy."

"Means he's good lookin.'" She said with her heavy Jersey accent. "Your father was a stud."

"Mom!" Gabe said.

"He was! And I was his princess. He could never keep his hands off me. I'm surprised I only had two children." She bragged.

Gabe was due at work for a late-night shift. It was the last week of the Christmas season and he had to go. Elaine's evening nurse wouldn't arrive for a few hours, so he got her some diet coke and a new box of tissues before leaving. Elaine quickly took her remote and restarted Miracle on 34th Street. It was already on while Gabe decorated but there was always a reason to watch it again.

Having seen the film hundreds of times, she was easily distracted by the thought of Marc's visit. Now that Gabe was no longer there to pretend for, she grabbed her mirror and studied her face. She kept thinking she looked old. She didn't even have time to get her hair done. Then her eyes wandered the room. Was it presentable? Despite her sincere enthusiasm, her pride crept in and slowly her joy was sabotaged by ego. What kind of a son doesn't talk to his mother for nine years? Why should she be happy about seeing him? Why should she care? He had all this money and success and who raised him? She did. He didn't even know about his philandering father. He didn't know how she protected him from the horrible truth that could destroy their family. If he only knew the sacrifices she made. For his sake, she stayed with a man she should've divorced. She felt magnanimous for having done the right thing despite being betrayed.

If only Marc could have been inside her head. He would've known beyond a shadow of a doubt that people can remember things how they want to remember them. Never mind that she didn't divorce Antonio because she loved him, and she used her son to keep him. None of her indiscretions after Antonio's death stopped her from seeing herself as the victim. She looked in the mirror and behind her wrinkles, she saw the remains of a woman who had survived infidelity and the death of her husband. She lived through the loneliness of widowhood while raising a son who disrespected her, and look how well he turned out. He had more money than the rest of the family combined. Though she thought she had to have done something right, she still believed his absence was indicative of his flaws, not hers.

Elaine decided he wasn't going to see a thing out of place. Nothing was wrong in her life and he was the one who lost out during their estrangement. This gave her a sense of power. Since he was the one who was really deprived by their hiatus, she justified pitying him. He was coming home because he finally realized he needed her, and though she would be in the right to demand an apology, she was above that. She would take the high road and why shouldn't she? She was a good person who fell on hard times because of misfortune. Had Antonio not cheated, everything would have been perfect. They would've been the perfect family and Antonio might even still be alive. If only he had loved her as much as she had loved him. None of this would have happened.

She imagined scenarios of him falling to his knees to beg for her forgiveness. Elaine was feeling emboldened and determined to put forward exactly what she wanted her son to see.

As she critiqued every detail of the tree, she was confronted with an unpardonable horror: the star was crooked. It goaded her like a splinter in the ball of her foot. Her urge to fix it became irresistible. She could reach it, so why not try? It was tragic that such a beautiful tree had to be shamed because of a ramshackle star at its summit. This would not do, and it could not wait. It became the only thing that mattered.

Elaine wheeled herself over to the tree, dragging her walker in tow. As she neared, the tree seemed bigger. Could she reach the star? She had doubts but it didn't matter. She would not be deterred. Sure, she promised her son Gabe that she wouldn't take unnecessary risks, but this was different. A crooked star on her Christmas tree was like an upside-down cross in a church. The severity took precedence over any promise, and who was Gabe to dictate what she can and cannot do in her own house?

What could happen? She wondered. She was only in the wheelchair as a matter of convenience. She didn't really need it, so Gabe's worry was just routine overreaction. As she accumulated notions of reinforcement and justification, they nullified any capacity she had for restraint.

She placed the walker in front of her, locked the wheels and pressed hard on the armrests. As she raised herself from the seat, her arms shook, making the fat deposits jiggle. Once on her feet, she grabbed the walker with her left hand and balanced herself. She felt stable and reached up to the star but couldn't. She tried and tried and could not get close enough. What could she do? The stepstool! She sat back down and wheeled herself into the kitchen. The stool was used daily by her aids to reach the top shelf of the cabinets. For a moment, she considered waiting for her evening aid to arrive, but that wouldn't do either. It had to be fixed immediately. She placed the stool on her lap and wheeled back into the living room.

She adjusted the walker to make it stand taller to account for the height difference. The stool was only a foot high, so she didn't need much. Despite the recklessness of the endeavor, Elaine was very intent on success so she had the option to tell her son later that she did it all by herself. However, the immediate plan was to keep it a secret because straightening the star was the priority and if Gabe knew what she was doing, it could become inconvenient. He had already threatened to install cameras. That meant total surveillance and the loss of whatever freedom she thought she had left. This was a delicate negotiation and every precaution needed to be taken. Her only real challenge was the narrowness of the stool. She didn't have a lot of lateral space, so she had to step onto it properly.

All the preparation was done. She grabbed the arms of the wheelchair again and stood up a second time. Her arms shook even more. Now she was on her feet and she waited to balance herself. She grabbed the walker and placed her left foot on the stool. That was her good leg. The right knee was a problem. She needed another joint replacement but refused to do more surgery. Her hands clenched the handles of the walker. She counted 1, 2 and on 3, she heaved and pulled herself up on the stool.

Success! She could reach the star! With her arm extended, she clutched the star like a geriatric statue of liberty. After she removed it, she saw the problem: the top branch was bent. She carefully rested the star on a branch so her one hand could be free to hold the walker. Reaching up again, she pinched and pulled at the branch until it was vertical. She placed the star back on top and again it drooped to the left. "You son of a bitch!" She yelled. Now she knew the branch had to be bent to the right to offset the lean. She went back to manipulating the branch but this time, she had been less careful when resting the star on the lower branches and it fell.

"No, no, no!" She screamed. The star had gotten snagged on an even lower branch she couldn't reach. She had to get down. She held the handles again and stepped off the stool. Her breathing was labored as she collapsed back in her chair.

She felt winded and for a moment, she doubted her ability to repeat the climb, but the star was removed. She would be found out. Gabe would never believe the star just fell so he would know she removed it. As she deliberated, she realized there was no option. She had to try again. She waited to catch her breath and began her calculated ascent for the second go. She placed the star on the stool and when she stood, she put it back on the branch where she could reach it. All the pieces were now in place. She tentatively placed her hands again on the handles and raised her left foot. She hesitated as she felt sweat drip down her forehead. Then she counted off and on 3, she heaved again but this time her foot was too far to the left. The stool upended! She tried catching herself with the walker, but the weight imbalance caused it to tip and the entire engineering project came crashing to the floor.

Elaine's body made the sound of a 100-pound bag of cement dropped from the ceiling. She heard a loud crack and felt a stabbing pain in her lower left leg. She looked down and saw her foot was hanging off and her bone was exposed through the skin. She let out a scream but there was no one there to hear her. As she looked in horror, she noticed the blood accumulating on the wood floor. She tried thinking fast in her panic, but she had overlooked one very important safety detail: her life alert. It was still on the charger. That and the phone were more than ten feet away on the table where she couldn't reach them. Her best hope was to get close enough to pull the table over so they would fall on the floor. She frantically tried pulling herself across the floor, but the exertion made the pain worse and hastened more blood loss. Still, she tried and as she inched along, there was a smear of blood that followed. She looked like a snail leaving its slime trail behind her as she slithered across the floor.

Elaine's heart raced dangerously causing her to bleed even more. She began to feel cold and started to cry. Was she going to die? She laid there praying, crying out over and over. "Please don't let me die, Jesus. I want to see my son! Please let me see my son." She kept repeating it as she wailed and sobbed.

Was Elaine finally facing the truth about Marc? There were no more rationalizations to hide behind because she knew this might be it. If only her aid would arrive. If it wasn't soon, this would be the end. It was a race against time. All she could think about was staying alive to see him. For all her defiance and proclamations, the real truth was that she loved her son. As the minutes passed, her screams grew fainter, finally diminishing to almost a whisper. She felt numb and sluggish, and finally lost consciousness.

7:4

After seeing Giovanna, Marc departed for America. He exited US customs and smelled the New York air again. Being happy to be back was unexpected and he felt courageous. The Marc Diodato who left America died by the Tiber river in Rome. The universe had shown him favor and his gratitude filled him with an urge to give back, even to his mother. He was no longer angry and wanted to address his father's secret gently and kindly.

As he walked, he spotted Gabe who wasn't supposed to pick him up. He planned to take a car service to the house. At first, he thought it was a surprise, but as he approached, he saw Gabe looked awful.

"What happened?" Marc asked plainly.

"There's been an accident." Gabe said.

"What do you mean 'an accident?'"

"I spent the whole night at the hospital, and I haven't been to bed yet. Thank God mom's aid arrived early. She went in the house to find mom unconscious on the floor. She must have been trying to mess around with the ornaments. She said there was blood everywhere." Gabe's face grew pale.

"Is she going to die?"

"We don't know. What was it that you had to tell me?" Gabe asked.

Without thinking, Marc said it could wait and wanted to go straight to the hospital. They went down the escalator and exited Terminal B of Newark International Airport. Soon, they were on the New Jersey Turnpike headed for Hackensack Memorial Hospital. On the way, Gabe explained that their mother had already had the first surgery to reset her leg. She had been in post op since early that morning. As they drove, the thought of mentioning Barbara and Anna was incomprehensible. He was already worried about how Gabe would take the news before he got off the plane. Gabe was 14 when Anna died. He actually had the chance to know her. How would he feel knowing he never would?

Instead, Marc chose to tell him about how he had decided to forgive Elaine and as he spoke, he couldn't restrain his emotions knowing that he may never have the chance to make amends. By the time they parked, both men looked like zombies. Gabe's gray curly hair was disheveled, and Marc's five-o-clock shadow was no less impressive.

They entered the hospital and made their way up to the 5ᵗʰ floor. They stopped at the nurses' station and Gabe introduced Marc. There were no updates since Gabe had left. Elaine was still unconscious, but she was stable. An indescribable feeling overcame Marc. Nine years of his absence was about to end but this was not at all the reunion he had anticipated on the plane. As they walked, the feeling intensified. He and Gabe didn't speak. They veered into room 523. Elaine was near the window and the curtain was drawn.

Marc was greeted by a grisly sight. Elaine's leg had an armature, and it was elevated in a harness. The skin was yellowed from betadine with black stiches pocking her ankle and foot. The skin was raw and her toes white. She also had a bandage on her forehead and her arm was black and blue. She had oxygen tubes in her nose as she laid unconscious. The brothers stood somberly over her bed like mourners at a funeral. Suddenly Marc found himself without any discernable emotion. He kept noticing how she had aged. As ghastly as it was, it occurred to him that he couldn't remember the last time he looked upon her without anger. If nothing else, that was a welcomed thought.

"Mom, what the fuck did you do?" Gabe said with exhaustion and disgust. "How many times did I tell you?"

Marc pulled Gabe by the hand to the chairs against the wall at the foot of the bed.

"I'm really starting to hate hospitals." Gabe said half in jest.

"Starting to?" Marc replied. "Did you tell Sara?"

"No." Gabe said emphatically. "Best not to until we know what's going on."

"Good. If you were planning on telling her now, I would've tried to persuade you otherwise. As tough as she is, she's also sensitive. When we weren't sure about the baby, I never saw her suffer so much. She tried not to show it but to me it was obvious." Marc said.

"I believe that." Gabe responded.

"I can't fucking believe this has happened. I told you, I was actually looking forward to seeing her."

"What has changed Marc?" Gabe inquired.

Marc took a deep breath and with a big sigh he responded, "I'm not sure you want to know."

"Does it have anything to do with what you said you needed to tell me?"

"Yes."

"Then tell me. Now is as good a time as any." Gabe said.

"Once I do, I'm not so sure you will agree."

"Is it that bad?" Gabe asked.

"I don't even know how to answer that." Marc mused.

"Honestly, I don't know how this day can get any more fucked up than it already is." Gabe said dismissively.

Marc told Gabe everything about Barbara and Anna. Gabe burst into tears and Marc put his arm around him.

"I want you to know something. When I first decided to come home, I was ready to confront mom, but Giovanna helped me understand that maybe it was better not to. What would have been the point? I know how I feel about it and what else is necessary? Asking her about it will accomplish nothing and I promise you this, if she survives, I'll never ask her. This stays between us."

Gabe agreed.

"There's something else; I had that dream again on the plane. I've had it twice this week. The last three times have had different endings and this last time it was happy. I fell asleep and the dream started the same way it always did, but for the first time, I wasn't afraid. I felt totally calm and I called to dad, then mom, you, Sara, Giovanna and with every name, I got brighter and each one of you appeared. Uncle Angelo, Aunt Angela—and I even called Barbara and Anna. We were all there and with every name, I kept getting brighter and the room got bigger and bigger. Then I realized what it means. I illuminate my life through love. The room is my life and all the clutter and darkness were from my anger. All I had to do was let it go."

They were interrupted by a faint groaning sound. It was

Elaine. Gabe sprang from his chair.

"Mom? Can you hear me? You're in the hospital. You had an accident."

She started to mumble, and Gabe could faintly make out, "I'm sorry, Gabe."

"Mom, I have a big surprise. Look who's here." He motioned urgently for Marc to get up. Marc cautiously approached the bed and they made eye contact. Her arm slowly raised towards him. "Anton, Antonio, my love. Antonio you're here."

Marc reached down and touched her hair. He told her she was beautiful and that he loved her. Elaine's eyes lit up like he never saw before for just a few moments. Then they grew heavy and slowly she drifted back to sleep. She thought he was his father, and his benevolent act of kindness was to let her believe it.

Marc laughed and then he cried because he reconciled his entire life with her with one simple gesture. He didn't even know if she would remember it but that didn't matter. The truth came through about how she really did love Antonio. Marc's conclusions were right. She was a wounded and desperate woman clinging to the marriage she wished she had. Like Uncle Angelo said, sometimes good people do bad things.

7:5

The brothers returned to Gabe's house after Linda arrived. The plan was to rest but Gabe couldn't.

"Why are you making coffee?"

"I have to go over to mom's house. I haven't been there yet."

"You stay here. I'll go. I insist."

Marc took Gabe's car and it was a long drive across town. He pulled in the driveway and saw the glow of Christmas lights through the bay window. He got out of the car and lumbered up the driveway. The motion sensor triggered the light revealing how the house looked the same, but different. The aluminum wheelchair ramp for Elaine gleamed under the flood lights. He went up the stairs and carefully slid the key in the lock. He opened it hesitantly expecting to see the remains of a massacre. The starless Christmas tree flickered but instead of presents underneath it, there was just a floor covered in dried blood.

Overwhelmed, he was distracted by memories, some pleasant, others not. He removed his coat and proceeded to clean up the mess, his mess. He took cleaning supplies and a garbage bag from the kitchen and went back in the living room to eradicate the remains of the event. The bloodstains didn't clean easily. He got a scrub brush and continued cleaning on his hands and knees. His muscles hurt. The blood was stubborn, just like Elaine, and himself.

The regret finally overcame him, and he began to weep. The scratching of the brush grated his nerves. He rinsed the mop, sobbing as he wrung it out in the sink. As much as one finds perspective, hurt is still hurt. Though he now understood his suffering with Elaine more profoundly, it didn't erase the years of rejection the little boy in him still felt, especially knowing they had still not spoken properly, and she could die. Her injuries were extensive, and she still needed more surgery. Anesthesia at her age was dangerous and even if she did live, there was no telling what her mental state would be. Did she suffer brain damage from blood loss? There were a lot of variables and none of them good.

He finished by washing his hands and face. He looked back at the living room. He noticed the star on the floor. He walked over to it slowly and as he picked it up, he remembered it because he was with her when she bought it. After he placed the star back on the tree, he looked at some of the other familiar ornaments. There were a few that he remembered on every Christmas tree that ever stood in that house. One in particular caught his eye, it was made of pasta glued together and painted. He made it when he was seven. It said, "I love you mom and Merry Christmas."

This pushed him over the precipice of grief. Perhaps he too had warped the memory of his life with her into something of a pseudo dark fantasy. It wasn't all bad and he realized the painful truth, that he had played a part in how things turned out. It wasn't just Elaine's rejection of him, he also rejected her. By the time he was twelve, he didn't respect her and had no shame about showing it. As his eyes erratically jumped around the room, he remembered his father asking him not to be mean to his mother. He would belittle her when she drank too much. Now he knew she had just lived in a state of sadness and after Antonio died, she behaved incomprehensibly just to cope.

Even after his nine-year absence, she saved that ornament and it was on the tree, right at the top all those years later. She had to have loved him, even if it was in her own strange way. Marc was overwhelmed by how much of his life was marred by misunderstanding and unfortunate circumstance. There were so many "if onlys" that pounded inside of his skull.

Unable to bear the weight of his emotions, he looked in the cabinet and found a bottle of scotch. He took a few gulps, filled a flask from the china closet and hastily left the house.

He got into Gabe's car and his thoughts unexpectedly turned to Hannah. He felt a growing urge to go to the apartment. He knew he wasn't supposed to, but so much had happened. He no longer cared about consequences. If she just gave him the chance to explain himself, maybe there was a chance for something to come of it. He backed out of the driveway and drove up the street. When he reached the end, he could either go left to go back to Gabe's or go right to head up the palisade. He sat at the stop sign and finally jerked the wheel to the right. He sped through the side streets and then headed down route 1 and 9. He made haste and began his climb up the hill and arrived at the familiar corner of Bergenline and 79th street. It was at the corner of James J. Braddock Park. He drove along the perimeter and could see the light of his building through the trees.

When he arrived, he parked in the visitor spot and briskly got out of the car. As he came through the foyer door, he said, "Hello Hector" as if he had just seen him yesterday.

"Mr. Diodato. It's good to see you sir. It has been a long time."

Hector was noticeably nervous. Marc owned the building, but he no longer lived there, and visitors were not allowed to enter unannounced. Hector clumsily asked whom he was there to see as a formality. Marc of course said he was there to see his ex-wife, so Hector customarily picked up the phone to call. Marc reached over the counter, grabbed it from his hand and hung it up. He peered across at Hector who looked back very anxiously.

"Hector, you can say I threatened you, but you are not to call, and I am going upstairs. Is that clear?" Marc was very intent.

He nodded, looking very uncomfortable. Marc shook his hand and went straight to the elevator. The car raced to the top floor. He exited and made his way down the hall arriving at the door that used to be his apartment. The smell of the hall was unmistakable. Of all he had faced in the last week, perhaps this scared him the most. Should he have come? He hadn't thought it through, however, there he stood, with the sound of his heavy breathing flaring his nostrils. Mustering all the courage he had, he knocked.

"What are you doing here?" The voice yelled from behind the door.

"I need to talk to you; it's urgent." Marc insisted.

"This isn't a good time; you should leave." Hannah said frantically.

"Hannah, please open the door." Marc repeated.

As Hannah ordered him to leave, Marc said forcefully, "Paul, I know you're here."

Hannah fell silent.

"I'm begging you. Please open the door." This time he didn't yell, and Hannah watched him begin to weep through the peep hole. Paul stood behind her. She looked back at him waiting for a signal for what she should do.

"How does he know I'm here?" Paul whispered. He reluctantly nodded but then he raised his finger for her to wait. He gestured for her to stand behind him and turned the lock slowly. A very haggard Marc stood in the hallway. His clothes were untidy and he smelled like detergent.

"Can I come in? I want to talk." Marc was timid and almost dry in his manner of speech. Paul looked over his shoulder at Hannah for her approval. She was trembling.

"I promise I'm not here to fight." His shoulders were slouched forward, and his head drooped. He was submissive. Hannah watched and then slowly gave Paul a nod to allow him to enter the apartment. Marc took a few steps and closed the door behind him. He looked around and saw it was now also Paul's apartment.

"How long have you known about us?"

"Since your email. It was so obvious I wondered how you could've had a career as a lawyer. At least I know the real reason you stopped representing me."

"If you came here to be obnoxious, leave now, because I won't tolerate a word of it." Paul said curtly.

"You knew about us and didn't care! Am I supposed to be grateful you weren't jealous? Forget that I don't love you anymore, but the idea that this doesn't even bother you just makes me feel even more terrible about having *wasted* so much of my life with you." She spat.

"Is that how you really feel? None of it was good? And you find a way to hold my good will for your relationship against me?" He said contemptuously.

"Hannah?" Paul interjected, feeling threatened.

"No, I want an answer. How long, Marc? You should know something; I love Paul and I'm having his baby." She stepped into the light and pointed towards her stomach defiantly. "I want to know only because of what you've put me through." She turned to Paul. "This has nothing to do with you because there was no you and I at the time. This is for me! Marc, you let me believe you had another woman. I was your wife!"

Paul felt compelled to interrupt again. "It's not really appropriate that you are here. What do you want, Marc?" Paul didn't want to be an observer of an argument with his new fiancé and her ex-husband.

"Maybe you should leave." Hannah said to Paul's relief. "It was a mistake to let him in."

"I'm sorry. I really am. Like I said, I didn't come to fight." Mark reached into his pocket and pulled out the flask and took a large swig.

"Still an alcoholic, I see." Hannah jibed.

"It wouldn't matter if I told you no because you wouldn't believe it. I was never an alcoholic. I was drinking so much out of self-loathing. I've since been diagnosed with bipolar personality disorder, but that doesn't matter either, just like my past. Doesn't matter that I'm a little fucked up. I'm sorry I'm sick and that my life hasn't exactly been convenient."

"Oh stop feeling sorry for yourself. It still doesn't excuse what you did." Hanna asserted.

"I'm glad to know you feel this way. I suppose it also doesn't matter that I just cleaned up puddles of my mother's blood? She's in critical condition at Hackensack Memorial. Apparently, it matters even less that I came here just to apologize to you." He became more resentful.

"You were at your mother's?" Hannah asked.

Marc recounted the story of the accident and of his dead half-sister. "Forgive me, but I'm having a bad week and while I didn't expect a warm reception from you, I was hoping you could show me a little compassion. How many times do I have to say I'm sorry? Doesn't that matter? Paul, we were like brothers."

"Marc, of course we are sorry you're suffering but our so-called brotherly relationship ended a long time ago. I've always loved Hannah. When we all first met, I wanted her, but you had to get her first because you always had to win. When you got married, I buried my feelings because I actually hoped yours were genuine. But after what you pulled and then how you treated me in Italy, there was no reason to resist any longer. It's not about forgiveness and even if we could forgive you, it doesn't change the truth that there's no room for you in our lives. You are her ex-husband, and she will soon be my wife, and the mother of my child."

Marc's tone got more confrontational. "So, am I to understand this correctly, you fantasized about my ex-wife for years while we were married, and *you're* judging *me*? I should be furious about this, but I'm not. I wanted to make peace, but I guess that can't happen because I see it doesn't matter that I'm not the man I was. I came back from the dead. I found out my father married the wrong woman. He never loved my mother and I'm starting to think that was what happened with us, Hannah. That's why I'm not angry with you, Paul. Maybe this somehow sets things right?"

"Oh, you're telling me I was the wrong woman?" Now Hannah was aggressive. Her pride was wounded. "It's more like you were the wrong man. You should know that I tried so hard to find something redeemable about you in those last few weeks and I couldn't. Seeing you now just makes me angry."

"That's not how I meant it." Marc said.

Then the encounter escalated into a three-way battle of everyone talking over each other. Marc finally yelled "I have someone new also." It cut right through the room.

"You're in love too and now we're going to be all warm and fuzzy because it's convenient for you." Hannah grabbed Paul's hand. "Marc, I'm sorry you have suffered, but I'm not giving you this. I just can't. I want you to leave now!"

Marc looked at Paul. "Marc, we don't want you in our lives. There's too much pain and hurt."

"Paul, get him out of here now!"

"Don't ever come here unannounced again." Paul was cold and direct.

Marc listened calmly. He was almost emotionless. He opened the flask and drank the remainder and turned to Paul. "I know I don't have to tell you to take care of her because I know you will. I can tell you two love each other. No matter how you both feel about me, I want you to know I love both of you and I always will. I wish I could change what I've done, but I can't. I guess I have to live with that. Good luck with the baby."

Hannah clutched onto Paul's sleeve. She was shaking. Marc looked at him for some kind of an acknowledgement, but Paul glared coldly and gave him a short nod. Marc nodded back and left. He walked drunkenly away from the door. He got out of the elevator and said, "Take care of yourself, Hector." He made no eye contact and absently walked out the door.

The wind had picked up and the air was getting noticeably colder. He got in the car and just sat there replaying the incident in his head. It was clear Hannah still loved him. People don't get that angry otherwise. As for Paul, he was following Hannah's lead. The big picture revealed a now obvious truth: even if some things can be forgiven, they can't be forgotten. He contemplated how severely he had treated both of them, especially Hannah. He remembered what Giovanna said. He had no right to judge them or his parents. His father had sacrificed so much and what did Marc sacrifice? For his pride, he irreparably damaged a woman who loved him. His self-loathing had reached a fever pitch that was augmented by the alcohol. He pulled out of the driveway and made a left. He didn't know where he was going.

He was on Boulevard East, one of the most scenic roads along the southern Hudson river. It snaked along the edge of the palisade with a full view of Manhattan. He had run, walked and driven it innumerable times but this time, all he could think about was driving over the cliff. It was a 200-foot drop straight down. Luckily, the brick wall at its edge would render any attempt useless, but Marc was feeling manic and impulsive. He wanted to drive and the more he drove, the faster he went. He sped along the road screeching to a halt at traffic lights as he raced along the view of the New York skyline. The more he drove, the more his thoughts spiraled out of control.

Other cars beeped at him as he swerved into oncoming traffic to pass jitney buses and slow vehicles. He was amidst a silent tirade of self-deprecation. The encounter went as it should have, because he didn't deserve love. He felt like a fraud who was living a lie. Giovanna would eventually leave him. It was only a matter of time because he was really a monster. His brother was still a fool for not leaving him in the hospital. His father hadn't come to illuminate him, he was meant to be punished and he deserved it. That was the real truth and his thoughts raced faster and faster.

His eyes teared and his vision blurred as he wiped them. He continued along the road and veered towards the tunnel. He thought of dying alone, without Giovanna, Gabe, Sara, Giancarlo, Angelo and everyone who had come to matter so much to him. As he sped around a downhill curve, he lost control of the car. He crashed into the cars parked along the road and the front corner of the passenger side clipped the bumper of another car. It spun around and flipped over into a small outcropping of bedrock into which the road was carved. Glass shattered and metal crunched as Marc was thrown about the car. Every second was in slow motion. Now he was gripped by the sheer horror of leaving everyone he loved behind. The car groaned as it twisted and contorted, he screamed "No!" over and over. At that moment, he only cared about living but to his horror, he was in doubt. Then he felt a blunt impact on his head. It was like a bomb exploding. Soon his eyes blurred, he felt his body grow limp and everything faded to black.

7:6

The church of Saint Peter the Apostle in San Pietro al Tanagro was filled to capacity and a young priest named Father Matteo presided over the service.

"Dearly beloved. We are gathered here today to celebrate the life of Marc Diodato. There are not enough seats for the many who have come from far and wide to be here with us. That is evidence of a life that has touched so many. Marc was a son and father to this community. His philanthropy and leadership brought hope to this town and it is with great sadness that we mourn his passing."

Father Matteo said a prayer for Marc and paused for a moment of silence.

"At this time, I would like to welcome Sara Graziano to speak to you on his behalf."

Sara rose from the front pew and slowly walked across the marble floor of the church to the lectern.

"On behalf of my uncle and my family, I extend my gratitude to everyone who could be here today. Speaking for myself, I will miss him every day for the rest of my life. Some people don't have the fortune of having loving fathers. I had two, but two fathers means two heartbreaks. When my father Gabe left us three years ago, I was devastated and now I'm devastated again. My uncle has been as influential as any person could ever be in my life. Without him, I might not have my marriage or my son who also called him grandpa. A month before he died, my uncle sent this letter to me. He asked that I read it at today's service."

To my family and friends,
I might be the only man in this world who can say he died twice, on two different continents and in the same year. I realized I didn't want to die following my suicide attempt and in my car accident, I wondered if I deserved it. I was fortunate to be revived in both instances and throughout the remainder of my life, those events molded me as a husband, a father, an uncle, a friend, and a man. Nothing taught me more about life than death and I wanted to take the opportunity to share some of what I learned with all of you since I am more of an authority on the matter than most.

Some laughter echoed in the church, which drew a response from Sara. "My uncle would be happy that some of you find that funny and he would've been laughing the loudest." She continued to read.

My experiences with death were very different and also ironic considering the circumstances. In my first, I had hit rock bottom. I was torn apart by an MS diagnosis and succumbed to a hopelessness I hope none of you ever feel. I hated the world; I wanted to hate God and would have if I believed in him.

Gasps were heard throughout the church.

Against the advice of my therapist Dr. Rossellino, who is no longer with us, I came to Rome in some vain attempt to find purpose and it turned out I had to go halfway around the world to be led right back to where I should have looked in the first place: family and friends. I justified suicide, not necessarily because I was sick. It was because I was alone. I opened my veins on the banks of the Tiber and even felt satisfied with myself for a moment, but then something happened. I felt a fear like none other and it was not necessarily just a desire to live. I wasn't just thinking about myself as I bled trying to reach the police by Castle Sant'Angelo. I think my fear was leaving things as they were and that was an unbearable thought.

When I awoke from my coma, I learned that I had died and that was when I realized I had a near-death experience. I had a vision of my father Antonio who was baptized in this very church. The experience fundamentally changed me, but not how you might expect. I wasn't overcome by some grand revelation or inner peace. The idea that life did not end scared me even more than death itself. The idea that my father knew the man I had become left me feeling sick. Worst of all, I had to question everything I thought I knew. I was never at a lower point than the day my eyes opened in the hospital in Rome. Two days later, I awoke from sleep to see you, Sara. That is why I wanted you to read this. I thought it was a dream or that maybe I died again but soon, I realized that it was real, and you were actually there. That is what rescued me. You, your father, who I have missed every day since he died, and your husband Giancarlo, who thought more of me than I thought of myself. It was your love that saved me, but I didn't know that at first. I had what seemed like an insurmountable intellectual mountain to climb: figuring out what my experience meant. I labored and labored over it but one day, I found the answer by not finding it. I understood that it didn't need to be understood, simply because it couldn't be. There was no way to explain what happened or why. I had the choice to either accept it or not and I chose to accept it—not because I thought it was right, I chose what made me happy, and that made it right.

I learned that meaning is a decision, not a perception. My life before this experience was barren because I chose to be barren. My life after was full and profound because I made a decision to see fullness and profundity in life and its mysteries. When I realized I was both the problem and the solution to the problem, moving forward was easy. All I had to do was believe in life. It wasn't some esoteric and mystical riddle. It was simple and concrete. I chose faith and devotion, and it wasn't because of some moral imperative or religious edict, it was because these blessings make life beautiful. In the end, that is all that matters. It wasn't rational or logical, beyond the obvious that choosing a miserable life is stupid. All the results had to do was speak for themselves.

In the book of Matthew, there is the parable of the tree and its fruit. Jesus talks about good and bad trees and eloquently distinguishes one from the other by the quality of their fruit. When I chose meaninglessness, my fruit was rotten. When I chose life, my tree blossomed anew and the relationships that have been my essential joy have ripened into magnificence that few words could adequately express. To my wife Giovanna and my daughter Simona, you are the sweetest fruits on my tree, and I cannot thank you enough for every day of your love. I have lived ten lives of happiness in eighteen years. For that alone, I am fortunate.

As for my second near-death experience, it was different. In my typical fashion of doing everything in excess, dying once wasn't enough. I wanted round two.

Sara stopped reading and could not contain her laughter. Neither could the rest of the family. Giovanna especially laughed the loudest as she wiped tears from her eyes.

My second experience was quite different. I saw nothing. It was like being asleep and I have no recollection of any bright light or encounters with spirits. That could have been a life derailing event. It could have led me to lose faith in everything but instead, it just reinforced what I already believed after the first experience. I was not about to give up my peace and vision of my father. I was given an incredible gift of absolution. Countless sons and daughters lose parents, but I got to see mine again and I was not about to dismiss it.

I remember laying in the hospital and when I saw Giovanna come walking through the door, I knew I was where I was supposed to be. My love, your presence validated every single thing that happened. That day, you proposed to me and I want to state for the record that I was planning on asking you anyway, but I was on too much pain medication so you beat me to it.

The church filled with more laughter.

I can say that aside from the birth of our daughter Simona, that was the happiest moment of my life. Simona, I never thought I would be a father and there are no words to sufficiently describe what you have meant to me. You are the best of me, and I feel better about the world knowing you are in it and that you will make it a better place.

And if all this wasn't enough, I found out I didn't even have MS after my car accident. Because I had a head injury, they did scans of my skull and saw there were no lesions on my brain. They conducted more tests and figured out I had fibromyalgia.

When I got my cancer diagnosis last year, I shocked my doctor because I actually laughed. Needless to say, he thought I was nuts. Obviously, I wasn't laughing at having cancer; in fact I was terrified and not only because it would mean suffering and pain, I didn't want to leave my family. That was the worst part. As for my laughter, I thought it was funny that I almost killed myself over an illness I didn't even have. In hindsight, it was a whole lot of fuss over nothing. More than ever, I understood that you never know the long-term meaning of any given thing. Sometimes, the worst can lead to the best, and vice versa. A misdiagnosis sent me to hell, and I came back a saint. Who knew?

My parting advice to you is just to ride the wave of life and have courage. We don't know what we are capable of until we are tested. We also learn in the valley, not on the mountain. It is through loss that the best of our character can surface if we just have the courage to have faith. In conclusion, my experience with death didn't result in my knowing any more about it. Death didn't teach me about death, it taught me about life. That's why I have enjoyed every day of the 18 years I have spent with my wife and our daughter.

Above all, I advise you to appreciate each other. Nobody

is perfect, least of all me. We need to know that families will argue and disagree, but those conflicts don't have to be relationship-defining events. Suffering is so difficult, but in the end, the only thing that makes any of it bearable is that we go through it together. It is the medicine that remedies the sickness of loneliness. Some people call that God and maybe they are right and maybe they aren't. I'm not at liberty to say despite the experience I had with my father. I simply don't know because no one knows, that's why it is faith. If I can leave one last drop of wisdom in the world, stop arguing with your loved ones about truth. I have been dead twice and I can tell you with a reasonable degree of certitude that I don't know any more now than I did before. Humanity wages war, families break apart, and we ruin perfectly good lives with nonsense by asserting the unknowable. It is a huge waste of time.

If God exists, God is bigger and more profound than anything we can ever expect to comprehend. It cannot be understood. The closest we can come to it is to live it and we do that through our limitations. That is where we find wisdom and reach our greatest aspirations. As for mine, sadly, I will not be able to achieve them because I'm going to die. I would give anything for more time with my family. Love each other and savor every moment as if it were your last. I assure you, don't worry about dying because it's easy. Living is a lot harder. My final wish is that everyone could feel the love and joy I have been privy to in my life. I love you all. Goodbye.

Maybe I will see you on the other side?

Love
Marc

Sara left the lectern and sat with the family. Simona was at Sara's left with her mother at her right. They held each other's hands for the remainder of the service. Father Matteo said the final prayer and the family gathered in the rectory hall for a luncheon. By then, Angelo, Angela and Elaine had also long since passed away, but many others came from afar. The gathering was spirited because this was a vigil. His funeral was a small private event a month earlier. This was a celebration of life.

While everyone ate and chatted, Sara greeted three people who Marc would have been very happy to see. Hannah, Paul and their son David flew in for the service. Sara still called her Aunt Hannah and was soon joined by her son Antonio, Giovanna and Simona. As they reminisced and chatted, Simona and David found themselves deep in their own conversation. They got up from the table and wandered away, together.

The End

Acknowledgements

Thank you to my wife Simona for being the love of my life and for helping me realize this story. I never could have done this without you. Thank you to my parents Barbara and Frank and my grandparents Marie and Antonio who helped raise me. Grandpa, a special thanks to you for instilling the value of my heritage and for being the best part of my childhood. Thank you to my editor and friend Moriah Hamstad. Your contribution to this story is immeasurable. Thank you to my friends Adam Simms, Penny Donald, Giuseppe Satta, my cousins Patty Casale, Joyce Fleishner and Professor James Broderick of NJCU for taking the time to read earlier versions and giving me the encouragement to see this through. Lastly, thank you to all the friends with whom I have mused about the mysteries of the universe. Every conversation we've had over the years culminated in these pages. I am so grateful and fortunate to have had the companionship of curious and brilliant dreamers throughout my life. You not only made existence bearable, you made it wonderous.